Betrayed

Sharon C. Cooper

Disclaimer
This story is a work of fiction. Names, characters, organizations and incidents are either products of the author's imagination or are used fictitiously. Any resemblance to actual events, locales, organizations or persons, living or dead, is entirely coincidental.

Chapter One

"What part of *I'm done* don't you understand?" Angelo González yelled into his cell phone as he paced the length of his living room, his throat tightening as anger clawed through him.

"Come on, Lo. I know there's been some bad blood, but—"

"Bad blood?" Angelo pulled up short near the black leather sofa. "Dude, that's all you think this is? They tossed my ass in jail even when I told them I was innocent. This is way past bad blood. This is more like they can't ask me for shit. Ever!"

His chest heaved, and his breaths came in short spurts as he tried to rein in his temper. Memories of that horrific time in his life bombarded his mind all at once.

Scandal.

Death.

Betrayal.

No. The Drug Enforcement Administration couldn't ask him for a damn thing. Just the mention of them had him wanting to ram his fist through a wall. Why couldn't they just lose his number, and leave him alone?

"Lo, you know—"

"Jared, don't. There's nothing you can say that will

change my mind. And if you know what's good for you, you'd get out while you can. What they did to me, they'll eventually do to you, because they don't give a crap about their agents. All they care about is covering their own asses," Angelo warned his childhood friend, Jared Hudson. They'd grown up together and had joined the DEA around the same time. Now Angelo wanted to spare him the pain he had endured at their hands.

Silence filled the phone line. Five years had passed since Angelo had been arrested for obstruction of justice, a crime he was wrongfully accused of. He spent a couple of days behind bars until his arraignment. It took weeks for his legal team to get the charges dropped. What made the situation even worse was that the arrest happened right after a raid. A raid where several of his fellow DEA friends lost their lives. A time in his career that still sparked nightmares and anxiety. On top of that loss, Angelo was no closer to determining what exactly had gone wrong that rainy night.

Then another thought popped into his head. "Why would you guys want someone on the team who you don't trust?"

"You know damn well not to lump me into the same category as them. I stood by you from beginning to end," Jared snapped. "I'm the one who wants you back on the team."

Angelo ran his hand through his thick hair as frustration drummed through his veins. Strolling over to the wall-to-wall windows of his two-bedroom apartment, he looked out over Midtown's skyline in Atlanta. The corner unit on the twentieth floor gave him 180-degree views of the city, and though the place cost him a pretty penny, it was worth every cent.

But at the moment, the sight wasn't doing much to taper the disappointment he felt each time he recalled that last year with the DEA. Angelo wasn't the forgiving type, and the way the agency left him to be the fall guy for the clusterfuck op was unforgivable. But Jared was his boy.

"Yeah, you're right," Angelo finally said. His friend had supported him the best he could considering the circumstances. But back then, Angelo had lumped his whole team into the same category—people who betrayed him. Yeah, he could admit to having a problem forgiving folks when they did him wrong, but what they'd done to him was beyond anything he'd ever be able to forget.

"Just think about it, Lo," Jared continued, using a nickname that only a few of his friends called him. "This is your chance to nail Rock once and for all."

"Taking down Rock is no longer my life's mission," Angelo said of Monty Rockwell, a Miami drug lord who the DEA had been trying to get for years. Rock was slippier than a venomous king cobra snake, and no one could ever accuse him of being a fool. The man was always a step ahead of the agency. Like a cornered rodent, he was a master at getting out of tight spots.

"Just think about it, man. We could really use your expertise."

Angelo moved away from the windows and strolled into the all-white, state-of-the art kitchen, one of his favorite rooms in the house. He snatched his keys from the quartz countertop, then headed to the hall closet for his running cap.

"There's nothing to think about. I'm not interested."

Each time the DEA thought they had enough evidence against Rock, their case would fall apart. Angelo always wondered if there was someone on the inside feeding the drug trafficker information.

But now it didn't matter.

He was done.

Working at Supreme Security, an agency that provided personal security to a high-end clientele, gave him everything he needed. Good pay. Flexibility. And it was a job with a company he respected. More than all of that, he no longer had to work undercover, a role with the DEA he hated and never wanted to return to.

"Listen, I gotta bounce," he said, done with the thirty-minute verbal sparring. "I'm out."

Angelo disconnected the call right in the middle of whatever Jared was about to say. When his cell phone rang again, instead of answering, he shoved the device into the pocket of his jogging pants.

I need to get out of here.

He only had a few hours before the surprise birthday party that he and some of his co-workers were throwing for Egypt Durand, their executive assistant. She was the backbone of Supreme Security, and he didn't want to miss her celebration.

But right now, what he really needed to do was go for a run to ease some of the pent-up energy brought on by that phone call. Anytime anyone mentioned the DEA or Rock, it made his blood boil. Sure, he claimed he was done with both, but Angelo would be lying if he said he didn't want to be the one to put Rock behind bars for good.

"Man, just let it go," he mumbled to himself, pissed that he had let Jared get under his skin. He stepped out of his apartment and locked the door. Shaking off thoughts of the DEA, Rock, and the fury that usually consumed him whenever he thought about that chapter in his life, was no easy feat.

By the time Angelo arrived on the ground level, he was wound tighter than a coiled spring, ready to pop at any moment. Shake it off, he thought as he put only one of his earbuds in, a practice he had started whenever he ran outdoors. Though he used music to get into his workouts, he always made sure he was aware of his surroundings. That meant hearing anyone approaching from behind or getting too close. Paranoid? Maybe. Alert? Always.

Angelo started off at a slow pace. His gym shoes pounded rhythmically against the pavement as "Can't Stop, Won't Stop" by Young Gunz played in his ear. Within the first mile of his run, the tension that had settled around his shoulders started to ease. Nothing like a good run to wipe the fog of disappointment and betrayal from the forefront of his mind.

Picking up the pace, he turned down a treelined street and headed for Piedmont Park. Humming along to the music flowing through the earpiece, it was easy to get lost in the moment.

Up ahead, a woman whose long, even strides ate up the pavement jogged toward him. Either she was jamming to some music in her head or she had earbuds in that he couldn't see. The way her shoulders and arms were rocking, it was as if she was having her own private party while getting in a run.

Runner. Music lover. Tight-ass body.

A woman after my own heart.

If her face matched her slammin' figure, he might have to run alongside of her and get those digits. They were within thirty feet of each other, and the closer she got, the more interested Angelo became. But a dark sedan, barreling around the corner practically on two wheels, snagged his attention.

Where's the fire, he thought as the driver flew up the street in his direction. The guy turned his wheels sharply, barely missing two parked cars before screeching to a stop.

Angelo slowed, jogging in place as unease stirred inside of him. The next few seconds unfolded like something out of an action movie. Two burly guys rolled out of the four-door sedan and rushed toward the woman he'd just been ogling.

"What the…"

Shock blasted through Angelo's veins, thrusting him into action when the men snatched her up. Fear charged through his body, and he took off in a sprint. Her loud, panicked screams crackled through the air, but he stayed focused. He had to get to her.

The men wrestled with the woman, struggling to hold her as they zigzagged, staggering toward their vehicle. Her arms and legs moved like propellers on a plane as she clawed at their faces. Twisting. Kicking. Punching. Fighting for her life.

"Help! Help!" she shrieked, trying to pull out of their

grasp.

"Hey!" Angelo yelled when he reached them, catching them all off guard.

He lunged at the bigger of the two men. Yanking on the collar of the man's T-shirt, he managed to pull him away from her, but not without the guy swinging at Angelo.

He dodged the punch and returned one of his own, connecting with the bastard's nose, then landing one to his ribs. The man cried out in pain, holding his face and his side as he dropped to his knees.

The woman was no longer screaming, but yelling and still fighting the other thug who was still struggling to get her to the vehicle.

"Get off of her!"

Angelo shoved the man hard enough to knock him down. That freed the woman, but in her haste to get away, she stumbled and crashed into Angelo.

"Whoa," he said, grabbing her around the waist, trying to keep them both upright as he stumbled back. Her enticing scent of baby powder with a hint of lavender made him weak in the knees and he held her close. His traitorous body tightened as she clung to him, still trying to get her footing.

Angelo quickly righted them, but over the woman's shoulder, one of the men charged toward them. He gently spun her out of the way just as the man reached for her. Angelo turned slightly, lifted his leg in a side kick, and planted his foot in the center of the guy's chest. The impact sent the goon staggering back and bumping into the other thug.

When Angelo looked at the woman, she was standing on the sidewalk, her hand on her chest. Their gazes locked. Large hazel-brown eyes stared at him. It was as if the earth stopped spinning and nothing moved around them. Intense. Raw. A mind-numbing connection like nothing he had ever experienced seized him.

Her baseball cap had fallen off in the scuffle giving him an unobstructed view of her stunning face and heart-shaped mouth. She was the most beautiful woman he'd ever laid eyes on.

And then his heart slammed into his chest as realization dawned on him.

Sonofa…

"Get her," one of the guys growled behind him, snagging Angelo's attention just before strong hands gripped his shoulders.

Shit!

He glanced at the woman. "Run! Get out of here!" After a slight hesitation, she took off running.

Angelo twisted out of the man's hold, shoving him away in order to grab the other guy before he could run after her.

Oh, no, you don't. Angelo yanked him back and leveled the other one with a roundhouse kick. These guys might've been resilient, but they were definitely amateurs.

Who the hell would send amateurs after that woman?

Chest heaving as he gasped for air, Angelo glanced over his shoulder, glad to see that she was nowhere in sight. But when he turned back to the offenders, a beefy fist slammed into his jaw.

Damn!

Pain crashed through his skull, and his head snapped backward, throwing him off balance. But he was able to block the next punch. Lot of good it did, though. The second guy plowed into him, slamming his head into Angelo's gut, and sending him crashing to the ground with an *oomph*.

The back of Angelo's head whacked the concrete. A sharp pain ricocheted through his skull. Stars flitted in front of his eyes.

Ah, hell.

Laid out on the ground, he slammed his eyes closed as agony consumed him. Tires screeched away as voices and people talking at once seem to come out of nowhere.

Call 911.

Is he alive?

Did anyone see what happened?

No license plates.

Hey, buddy. Can you hear me?

Angelo was in too much pain, and didn't have the strength to open his eyes or respond to anything they asked. He clenched his teeth and willed himself to just breathe through the pain. All the while, in the back of his mind, he hoped Zenobia "Zen" Westfield was long gone.

Chapter Two

Don't stop.
Keep moving.
Two more blocks.
Just two more blocks.

Overwhelming fear coursed through Zenobia's veins as she pumped her arms and legs, running as fast as she could get her body to move. She cut across a parking lot, skirting around cars and kicking up gravel as she darted past men working on a driveway. Back on the sidewalk, she pushed herself harder. Her left eye throbbed and there was a dull ache in her side, but Zenobia couldn't stop. She couldn't ever remember running this fast.

Adrenaline. With enough adrenaline, a person could be dying and still do things they didn't think they could do. Her heart banged inside of her chest like a blacksmith's hammer against an anvil. What the heck had just happened back there? One minute she'd been jogging, enjoying her music and the comfortable morning temperature, and now she was literally running for her life. She could see her cousin's high-rise coming into view, but Zenobia wouldn't feel safe until she was behind closed doors.

Tears blurred her vision, but she blinked them away, refusing to fall apart as fear and panic warred inside of her.

Winded, she took a quick glance over her left shoulder again, glad those thugs hadn't followed her.

Just keep it together. You're almost there.

Telling herself that wasn't helping. Tears leaked from her eyes and she wiped them away as fast as they fell. She was within seconds from the main entrance of the complex. She couldn't let anyone see her fall apart.

Panting, Zenobia slowed and glanced back again to make sure the coast was clear. Then she frantically scrubbed her hands over her face. The luxury condominium complex rarely had people hanging out in the lobby, but the last thing she wanted was for anyone to know she'd been crying. Not only had one of her earbuds fallen out during the attack, but she had also lost her baseball cap, her meager disguise. Now there was a chance that someone might recognize her. The same way the other jogger, her hero, had done.

At first, when their eyes met, something so powerful and sensual passed between them. Something Zenobia couldn't put a name to, but she'd felt the intensity deep inside her soul. It was as if everything around them stopped. Like a captivating melody that only the two of them could hear started playing, binding them together in that perfect moment in time.

But then she noticed the moment he recognized her. His dark, penetrating eyes rounded, but even that hadn't broken the spell that connected them. She hadn't returned to reality until one of the kidnappers started for her again. She might've still been standing there in La-La land had her *hero* not yelled for her to run.

God bless him. Had it not been for him coming to her rescue, she didn't even want to think about what would've happened.

"Welcome back, Ms. Westfield," the doorman said, holding the glass door open for Zenobia while her heart pounded double time. He flashed her a warm smile, having no clue of the traumatic experience she'd just endured.

"Thanks," she murmured, and quickly rushed past him.

Hurrying to the elevator, she jabbed a shaky finger at the Up button several times, praying the doors would quickly open. The silver doors slid open and Zenobia dashed into the car, then pressed the button that read twenty-fifth floor.

Exhaustion mixed with fear had her slumping against the far corner of the elevator as a cold chill plagued her body. Her long-sleeved T-shirt did nothing to fight off the shivers as she ran her hands up and down her arms.

"I'm safe," Zenobia murmured to herself, realizing immediately that she really wasn't safe. She wouldn't be completely safe until she figured out who was behind the attempted kidnapping and other strange occurrences over the past couple of weeks.

When the elevator doors slid open, she bolted down the hallway to her cousin's condo as if she was still being chased. The building might be secure, but the tension swirling inside of her hadn't eased. Her anxiety inched up as she dug into the side pocket of her jogging pants for the keys. Her hands shook so badly, they slipped from her fingers and fell to the floor.

Come on. Keep it together.

This wasn't the first time she'd experienced a life-or-death situation. But it was the first time in over ten years that someone put their hands on her, intending to do her harm. She survived that, and she'd get through this, especially once she figured out what was going on.

After two tries, Zenobia finally slipped the key into the lock and opened the door. She hurried inside, slammed the door, and quickly twisted the lock before her knees gave out and she slid to the floor. No longer able to hold off the tears, they fell faster than she could wipe them away.

"You made it back, huh?" her cousin Kira said, strolling from the rear of the unit as she stared down at her phone.

Wiping her face with her forearm, Zenobia hurried into a standing position and tried to put on a brave front. She couldn't. The adrenaline high she'd been on for the last few minutes was crashing fast.

"How was your ru…" Kira's words trailed off as her gaze zoned in on Zenobia. After setting her cell phone on the glass dining room table, Kira marched across the room. "What happened? Are you hurt? Did you fall or something?"

Zenobia shook her head, biting her bottom lip to keep from bursting into tears. She wasn't a crier. In her world, you couldn't afford to be overly sensitive. Besides, she'd been taught years ago that crying was a sign of weakness, and she wasn't weak.

But right now, she struggled to form words. The full impact of what could've happened to her if those men had succeeded in their mission weighed heavily. They could've raped her or killed her.

At that thought, Zenobia slumped against her cousin. A few more tears leaked from her eyes just before she dissolved into wracking sobs.

"Zen, you're scaring me. What happened?" Kira asked, her voice frantic as she wrapped her arms around Zenobia's waist and walked with her to the sofa.

Tears continued spilling from her eyes, and frustration filled her. It had been a long time since she allowed anyone the power to make her feel weak and helpless. But this time she wasn't alone. She had her cousin. Kira had been a godsend since Zenobia had moved to Atlanta, and she couldn't imagine her life without her.

Still sniffling, but feeling a little more in control, Zenobia pulled out of her cousin's hold. She wiped her face with the sleeve of her shirt until Kira stuffed several tissues into Zenobia's hand.

"Thanks." She turned slightly and winced at the pain stabbing her side with every breath. One of the guys held her so tight, he might've bruised her ribs. Just thinking about those creeps made her tremble. Her mind kept replaying the last few minutes, still finding it hard to grasp what had just happened.

"Two guys…they tried to kidnap me."

Kira's mouth dropped open and her perfectly arched

brows shot skyward. "Kidnap!" she screeched. "What? Where? How? In broad daylight?" Horror clouded her pretty chestnut-brown face, and her mouth opened and closed as if she wanted to say more but didn't know what to say.

"Yeah." Zenobia sucked in a breath and released it slowly. "Scared me to death."

"Did you recognize them?"

"No. It all happened so fast, but I never saw them before."

"How did you get away? Oh, God. What if they followed you?" Kira leaped off the sofa and rushed to the living room windows as if she'd be able to see the would-be kidnappers. The only thing her garden view would give her was just that, a view of the gorgeous garden and a spectacular water fountain.

As a Fortune 500 company executive, her cousin had made a good life for herself. That included the beautiful three-bedroom, two-bathroom condominium in a much-desired complex near Piedmont Park.

On a sigh, Zenobia stood on legs that were still a little shaky. Running her hands through her shoulder-length hair, she realized that not only did she lose her hat, but also the scrunchy that had been holding her hair in a ponytail. "They didn't follow me," she assured her cousin.

"See, this is why you need a bodyguard."

Stylishly dressed in a red maxi dress flowing over her full-figured frame and an African head wrap covering her long braids, Kira paced around in a small circle.

"That reminds me. It's good you stayed here last night because the paparazzi are probably outside of your house. You're trending on Twitter." Kira hurried across the room to the dining room table and grabbed her phone, then unlocked it. "Someone snapped a photo of you and Stephen," she said of Zenobia's on-again, off-again boyfriend. Right now, they were off...again.

Kira found what she was looking for, then handed the device to Zenobia who stared down at the screen. She groaned at the picture of Stephen kissing her outside of Marlow's Tavern. She'd already been surprised to see him as she was leaving. He had walked outside with her, telling her how good it was to see her again. Before she could stop him, he had planted a kiss on her mouth.

She skimmed the comments. Of course, the photo didn't tell the whole story. "I wonder who took this picture and why it's just now coming out. This happened weeks ago."

"Yeah, I was wondering the same thing. People are starting to recognize you, Zen. I told you last year that after the success of your album and appearing on *Ellen* that your life was going to change. Granted, it's crazy that someone went so far as trying to snatch you, but that just proves that it's not safe for you to go anywhere by yourself."

The past year had been a dream come true and a nightmare rolled into one. Zenobia had always wanted to make it big in the music industry, and dreamed of having fans someday. But now she wasn't sure if this new reality was the life she wanted. She'd kept a low profile since moving to Atlanta. Now her personal business was trending on Twitter, and whoever started the tweet had it all wrong. The photo was misleading. She wasn't getting back with her ex. As a matter of fact, she'd told him that there was definitely no chance of a reconciliation. Especially after catching him backstage after his last concert hugged up with Li'l Tia, a supermodel-turned-rapper.

Zenobia returned the cell phone to Kira as dread settled around her. She'd had personal security escorting her to performances and other events until she cut them loose. Now, the last thing she wanted was a bodyguard shadowing her twenty-four-seven, but it looked like she had no choice.

After spending two weeks at Lake Lanier, she had arrived back in Atlanta the night before. She'd gone there for peace and quiet to finish writing a couple of songs, but after some unexplainable incidents at the house, her trip had been cut short.

Now this.

Kira leaned her hip against the table. "You don't think Stephen sent those flowers to the lake house or that he's behind the kidnapping attempt, do you? I know you told him you were dating someone else. Maybe he's jealous and this is an attempt to get back at you."

Off and on for the past few months, Stephen had been showing up out of the blue and calling, claiming he wanted another chance with her. *Why now?* she had asked herself. If she didn't know him better, she would think it was about money, but he didn't need her money. An award-winning R&B superstar, he didn't need anything from her. He was just another name on her short list of bad decisions.

Zenobia shook her head. An awful judge of character when it came to men, just once she wished she could choose better. Catching him kissing another woman after one of his shows had been the eye-opener she needed to realize he didn't give a crap about her. Just once she'd like to get with someone who was more concerned about her well-being than their own. Or who wasn't trying to use her for one reason or another.

Yes, she had lied to Stephen about having a new man, but it was only in hopes that he'd move on. Granted, he saw right through the fib, claiming if she'd been involved with someone new, it would've made entertainment news. Yet, she had made it clear to him that it didn't matter what he believed. She and him were done.

"I don't know. Kidnapping? That just doesn't seem like something Steph would be behind. And why? What would be the point? As for the flowers, he didn't know I was at the lake. Besides, he's not the flower-sending type," Zenobia explained, referring to the mysterious flowers she had received at the lake house. Throughout their time together, Stephen had only given her a gift on Valentine's Day and once on her birthday.

"Yeah, you're probably right. That idiot is too selfish and self-centered to think of anyone but himself. Either way, we gotta call the police."

"I'm not calling the cops, but I will call Ashton."

Ashton was a detective with Atlanta PD who used to live next door to Zenobia before her singing career took off. They'd become good friends and contacting him would be better than going to a police station.

Growing up, she wanted nothing to do with law enforcement. They made her uncomfortable for so many reasons, but in this case, they couldn't help her. She hadn't been kidnapped. She couldn't ID the perps, and more importantly, she didn't want the media to get wind of what almost happened. The fewer people who knew about the incident, the better.

Zenobia pulled out her cell phone, still feeling a little unsteady as she replayed the kidnapping attempt over in her head.

That's her, one of the men had said. There was no way they could've recognized her with her hat pulled low over her eyes. Besides that, she wasn't running in her own neighborhood. This was only her second time jogging in the area, ever.

Did that mean the men knew where she'd be? Had they been looking for her? There were only a handful of people who knew her plans had changed, but she trusted all of them. There was just no way any of them would be behind a kidnapping.

Instead of Ashton answering, his voicemail picked up, and she left a message.

"Hi, Ashton. This is Zenobia," she started, her voice cracking as her body shivered. She wasn't cold and could only attribute the chill coursing through her body as fear. "There was…I was…someone tried to kidnap me," she said, her voice catching on the last few words and she squeezed the phone tighter in her hand. Quickly leaving her contact information, she hurried and disconnected the call.

Kira stood directly in front of Zenobia and narrowed her eyes. "Did those buttholes hit you?" she ground out, anger suddenly replacing the concern exhibited only moments ago.

She reached out and gently pressed a finger on a spot just below Zenobia's eye.

Zenobia winced. "Ouch. That hurts." As a matter of fact, her thighs, her back, and her side throbbed. "One of them accidently hit me in the face when they were trying to shove me into their car."

"It's starting to swell." Her cousin continued surveying the area. "I didn't notice it at first, but it's getting darker. Come and sit in the dining room. I'll get some ice, but maybe you should go to emergency."

Zenobia eased down in one of the chairs and propped her elbow on the table. She rested her head in her hand as exhaustion settled in. With the open floorplan, she had a clear view into the contemporary kitchen. Kira was one of few people who preferred black cabinets instead of white ones. But they went well with the contemporary décor and her top-of-the-line stainless steel appliances.

Her cousin pulled an ice pack from the freezer and wrapped a towel around it before strolling back into the dining room.

"Here, put this on your eye." Kira sat in the chair across from her. "I don't know, Zen. I'm worried about you. I know you probably don't want to do this, but if you're not going to get the cops involved, maybe you should call Rock. He can—"

"Stop right there. You know I can't call him. We cut all ties." Zenobia didn't bother mentioning that he checked in periodically and left messages. Messages she refused to return. "He'd be the last person I call. No. I don't need his type of help. I'll wait to hear back from Ashton."

Kira sighed noisily. "Fine. I'll leave that alone, but if anything else happens—"

"I still won't call him. With my career taking off, I have too much to lose."

Kira nodded. "You're right. That would be a bad idea." She pointed at the ice pack that Zenobia had set on the table, gesturing for her to put it on her eye. "So, how'd you get away from the kidnappers?"

"This jogger… That reminds me." Zenobia set the ice pack on the table and pulled a wallet from the deepest pocket of her running pants.

Kira pounded her fist on the table. "Are you frickin' kidding me? You stole the guy's wallet? Damn, Zen. I thought you were cured from stealing! What's the point of seeing a therapist for years if they can't cure you?"

"I didn't need to be cured," Zenobia bit out. She could admit to having a problem as a kid, but back then, she had to steal in order to survive. "Besides, I saw a therapist for more than just the stealing."

Growing up in New York hadn't been easy, especially being raised by her single mom who had been diagnosed with schizophrenia and bipolar disorder when Zenobia was twelve. As her mother's health declined, and doctors couldn't seem to figure out the right medication combinations to help her, their lives fell apart. Zenobia had to do whatever was necessary to keep a roof over their heads. Sometimes that included stealing.

Kira gaped at her. "Unbelievable. A jogger helps you out of a jam and you steal his wallet? Who does that?" Disappointment dripped from each word. "And you took nothing from the kidnappers?"

"I didn't think to take anything from them while they were trying to stuff me into their car!" Zenobia grumbled, and started going through the leather billfold. When she slammed into her hero, it was like crashing into a wall of muscle. To say he was fit would be an understatement. She hadn't set out to steal from him, but had reached into his front pocket without much thought.

She wasn't proud of her actions and had no intention of falling back into bad habits, but she was glad she had taken the wallet. Now she knew who to thank and would make sure he received his property back before the day ended.

"All right, so what's the guy's name?"

There wasn't much in the wallet, but what he did have stored was organized. Pulling out his driver's license, Zenobia skimmed it.

"His name is Angelo González. There's a PO box, but no home address." Smart. It was years before she knew the state allowed PO Boxes on the driver's licenses.

Zenobia slid out a business card. *Supreme Security.* Below his name was *Security Specialist.* She wasn't exactly sure what that meant, but it might explain his fighting skills. With no help from her, he'd used some type of martial arts to fend off those two big guys.

"He works at Supreme Security." Zenobia glanced at her cousin. "Ever heard of them?"

"No, but hopefully they can help with personal security. After what happened today, you need to get serious about getting some protection."

Zenobia nodded. She still didn't want someone following her around, but conceded that it probably was time. If only she could just have a normal life for a change. Since her mother's death, shortly before Zenobia turned sixteen, her world had spun out of control. And for the first time in years, she thought that she was finally being allowed a normal life. Now this.

Returning the items to the wallet, she kept the business card, stuffing it into her pocket. "I doubt I have to tell you this, but I don't want anyone to know about the kidnapping attempt."

"Zen, you can't just act like it never happened. You have to tell someone."

"And I will. I'll tell Ashton." Trust had never come easy for her, except with Ashton. Unfortunately, it was becoming clear that someone in her inner circle couldn't be trusted. Going forward, Zenobia planned to stay tight-lipped about everything.

"Ashton will help me get—"

They both startled when the front door swung open. Zenobia bolted out of her chair, her heart practically pounding out of her chest. She didn't settle down until Kira's boyfriend, Elijah, came into view.

He was tossing his keys up and down but stopped when he saw them in the dining room. His brows dipped into a frown, and he looked from her to Kira.

"What's going on? You two are awfully jumpy. What? You talking about me or something?" Humor resonated in his tone as he walked further into the apartment and over to Kira. At over six feet tall and at least two-hundred-and-fifty pounds, Kira referred to him as her gentle giant. "You ready to go?" he asked.

Elijah had his own courier business that was steadily growing. He and Kira had been dating for almost six months. It was the first time in a long time that her cousin had been in a serious relationship.

A twinge of jealousy pierced Zenobia in the chest when he gave Kira a lingering kiss on the lips. She loved that her cousin had finally found a man who really seemed to care about her. Yet, watching them together brought home the sad state of Zenobia's love life.

Elijah strolled into the kitchen, grabbed a Coke from the refrigerator, and turned to them. Zenobia and Kira were still standing in the same spot.

"Okay, what's going on?" Elijah set the soda can down and leaned on the counter. "Because I have a feeling it wasn't me you were discussing. And Zen, what happened to your eye?"

"I fell."

"She ran into a door."

She and Kira said at the same time. Zenobia tried not to groan out loud. Though her eye was throbbing, she had temporarily forgotten that there was a bruise.

"She was getting ready to go into the gym downstairs and tripped just as someone was coming through the door. I was just telling her that she should probably go and get it checked out."

Still looking from one to the other, Elijah nodded, as if understanding, but he didn't look convinced.

Zenobia really didn't care. She was relieved her cousin

hadn't told him the truth. Now all Zenobia had to do was wait to hear back from Ashton.

First, she had a wallet to return.

Chapter Three

"Mama always said you had a hard head."

Angelo glared at his brother who was standing next to the hospital bed, a tablet in his hand. Of all the days to end up in the emergency room, it had to be while his brother, Dr. Mateo González, was on duty. He should probably be happy Mateo was on staff, but now Angelo had to convince him not to tell their parents about this visit. Having a close-knit family had its disadvantages.

"I assume we're keeping this visit between you and me, right?" Angelo asked in a whisper. "Doctor-patient privilege."

He was laying in one of the emergency rooms that had three curtained-off spaces and very little privacy. Though he was in the last bed near the farthest wall, he still wasn't trying to let everyone hear their conversation. And he was totally prepared to negotiate or even use a little blackmail to keep his brother from sharing his business with anyone.

"Not exactly," Mateo said, eying him critically. "According to the cops, witnesses say you blacked out, Lo."

The cops had just left the hospital after asking him a ton of questions about the incident. He gave them as much information as he could, except the identity of the woman. As far as he was concerned, she was just another jogger.

"And you have a mild concussion," his brother said.

"But I'll live. You don't have to say anything to Momma or Pops or anyone else for that matter." He might've been thirty-seven, but right now, Angelo was acting like he was ten, begging his brother to keep his mouth shut. His mother had put the fear of God in them years ago, daring them to keep important information from her.

"Too late, I already—"

Angelo bolted upright, but immediately regretted the move when the room started spinning. He grabbed his head with both hands and gently laid back down on the pillow.

"Why would you call them? You know how Mom is. I'm fine, and she'll be worried for nothing."

"If you'd let me finish, you'd know that I *didn't* call them. But I did call Kenton."

"Oh." Angelo relaxed, but winced when the bruise on the back of his head rubbed against the pillow. The banging in his skull was getting worse by the minute. He had refused any medication, but might have to break down and take something.

"You're going to need to be watched for a few hours, and since I can't leave, I called him. But now I'm thinking that I should've called a family member, and let one of them deal with you."

"Ken is family," he said, referring to one of his best friends and fellow security specialist. The Atlanta's Finest team, as many referred to them, was just as much of his family as Mateo and their brothers.

"When can I get out of here?" Angelo asked, rubbing his jaw where the would-be kidnapper had slugged him. Though he was hit hard enough, he was glad he didn't lose any teeth.

"I suggest you quit being a stubborn jerk and take the pain meds." Mateo nodded to the pill on the tray next to the cup of water. "I'll release you in an hour or so, but not until Kenton gets here."

As if saying his name conjured him up, Kenton Bailey appeared at the opening of the curtain, along with Myles Carrington, another one of Atlanta's Finest.

"Oh good, we were just talking about you," Mateo said to Kenton, shaking his hand before shaking Myles's hand. "He's being his usual pain in the you-know-what self, but you can take him out of here in a while."

Mateo said his goodbyes and closed the curtain behind him. Kenton flanked one side of the bed, and Myles the other.

Kenton, a former FBI agent and one of the biggest guys on Supreme's team, stood well over six feet tall and was built like a Mack truck. Myles might not be as big, but he was tall and had a lean, muscular body like an MMA fighter. He was the one who taught Angelo some of his fighting moves. A former CIA spy, the guy looked harmless enough, but moved like the wind and could kill a man with his bare hands.

"Concussion, huh?" Myles said.

"Mild concussion," Angelo corrected. His brother was right about one thing, he did have a hard head. He played football throughout most of their childhood. Getting banged up was second nature, and Angelo always bounced back. Once he got rid of the headache, he'd be as good as new.

"You missed Egypt's party and the big announcement. Your boy popped the question," Myles said, nodding toward Kenton.

"Get out of here. Does that mean congratulations are in order?"

"Yep, Egypt said yes, and she already requested that you sing at the wedding." Kenton grinned as if someone had just awarded him a million dollars. He and Egypt had been skirting around each other for years. Angelo wasn't surprised that Kenton had finally popped the question. Considering all that they'd been through the last few months, he and Egypt deserved some happiness.

"Whatever the queen wants. I'm there," Angelo said.

"She's also concerned about you. We all are. Wanna tell us what happened?"

"Not really," he said, but gave them the CliffsNotes version of what went down; a similar speech like the one he gave the cops with just a few more details.

"So, let me get this right." Kenton folded his arms across his massive chest. "Two guys tried to kidnap a woman while she was out jogging, and all of them got away, leaving you bleeding on the sidewalk?"

Angelo rolled his eyes, then slammed them shut and rubbed his forehead. He couldn't ever remember having a headache as bad as the one currently hammering inside his skull. Maybe he was being stubborn by not taking the pain medication.

He reopened his eyes to tiny slits. As if reading his thoughts, Myles handed him the small container holding the pill, as well as the cup of water.

Angelo took the items without comment, swallowed the medication, then laid his head back down.

"Would you recognize the woman if you saw her again?" Kenton asked.

Hell, yeah, he would recognize her, but instead of telling his friend that, he said, "Maybe, but right now, all I want to do is get out of here."

Angelo didn't know what was worse, having his friends know that he got his ass kicked. Or knowing that he could've been killed all because he'd let a woman distract him. Even now, he wondered if she'd gotten far enough away before those goons caught up to her.

Kenton's cell phone buzzed and he pulled it out of his pocket and glanced at the screen. "I'll be back." He left the tight space, pulling the curtain closed behind him.

"We spar together every week," Myles said the moment they were alone, looking at Angelo in that way that would make a weaker man shrink under his stare. He had a gift for making people squirm. "You should've been able to handle two untrained guys. So, what really happened?"

Angelo inhaled then exhaled slowly, suddenly feeling more tired than he had moments ago. "We had a moment," he finally said. He didn't add that the woman's hypnotic hazel-brown eyes had turned him stupid.

"What do you mean? You and the woman?"

"Yeah. I can't explain it, but something passed between us. Something I've never experienced before. I know it sounds crazy, but I got distracted."

"You're right. It does sound crazy," Myles said seriously, and Angelo chuckled. They both loved women, but neither of them was the settling-down type, especially Myles.

A former spy, Myles had once confided that he had too many enemies, known and unknown, to allow himself the luxury of getting into a serious relationship. He was already concerned that his family might someday be targets for people trying to get back at him. He didn't want to fall for a woman and then make her a target, too.

As for Angelo, his trust issues kept him single. It was his experience that most people, especially women, had ulterior motives for wanting to get close. Keeping them at a distance worked for him, and he never got involved with a woman unless she knew the deal.

"What else?" Myles questioned. Angelo opened his mouth to deny that there was anything else, but Myles lifted his hand and shook his head. "Don't shit me. You already know one of us," he said, referring to their teammates, "will find out the truth. So, spill it."

He was right. The guys he worked with came from every area of law enforcement and were the best in their individual fields. Supreme's owner had dubbed them Atlanta's Finest. They didn't only provide personal security. They were also good at digging for information.

"I recognized her," Angelo finally said. "It was Zen, the singer."

"Wait. The singer who opened for *Boyz to Men* a few months ago? The woman Parker said he needed to meet because he wanted her to be the mother of his future children?"

"That would be the one."

Parker, one of Atlanta's Finest younger teammates, had made the comment after seeing her in concert. The declaration hadn't bothered Angelo at the time, but now, for some reason, it bugged the hell out of him.

Myles blew out a long whistle and shoved his hands into the front pockets of his dress pants. Their usual uniform was a black suit, with a black button-down shirt and tie. Myles had been on the schedule earlier and must've shed his suit jacket and tie on the way to the hospital.

"She's a looker," he said. "It's no wonder you were distracted."

"It wasn't just her looks." Although that was part of it. "It was something else. Hell, I didn't even recognize her at first. She was wearing a baseball cap pulled low, barely revealing her eyes. It wasn't until those guys tried getting her into the car and the hat fell off that I recognized her."

"So, you gon' try and find her, see if she's all right?"

"Yeah, and I need to get my wallet back from her."

"Hold up." His friend leaned on the bed. "What do you mean? How the hell did she get your wallet?"

This was the part Angelo really didn't want to share, knowing he was never going to live this next bit of information down.

"Not only is she beautiful and sings like an angel, she's also a thief."

*

Zenobia yawned for the third time in minutes as she sat in the passenger seat of Ashton's Dodge Challenger, gazing out the tinted window at the city flying by in a blur. He had called her after midnight, telling her to stay put until he got off work. She ended up falling asleep and didn't hear back from him until morning, an hour ago, saying that he was getting her some protection.

For the most part, neither of them said much as the tunes of Sade flowed through the speakers. Zenobia had grown up listening to R&B artists like her, Anita Baker, Shirley Murdock, and a few others. Their voices and styles were so unique that it only took hearing a few notes of one of their songs to know it was them. They'd had a great influence on her tone and style.

She glanced at the clock on the dashboard. Nine o'clock. By nature, she wasn't one of those people who rolled out of bed bright and early and looked forward to getting their day started. No. She was a night owl, and after Ashton's call, it had been pure torture to get up and moving. Not even the strong cup of coffee she'd had a short while ago helped.

Staying the night at Kira's again instead of going home had been a good idea. Zenobia's 4,000-square-foot house in Buckhead had a top-of-the-line security system. Yet, she hadn't wanted to be there alone. Her housekeeper, Sofia, who was like a mother to Zenobia, was out of town for another week. Depending on what Ashton had planned, she might stay in a hotel until Sofia returned.

Pushing the large rimmed sunglasses up on her nose, she glanced at Ashton. "Where are we going?" A noisy yawn slipped through before she could stop it. "Sorry. I guess you're the one who should be yawning since you worked all night."

He gave her a crooked grin and split his attention between her and the road. "I'm sure I will be soon. I don't usually need much sleep, but I've been putting in long hours lately."

They'd been neighbors for years before she purchased a home and moved away. Their friendship had developed into one of brother and sister, but Zenobia didn't see or talk to him as often as she used to. Their individual lives kept them both busy.

Ashton turned off the main street. They were still in Midtown, but he drove through a neighborhood that Zenobia wasn't familiar with.

"While I look into your situation, I'm hooking you up with a group of people I would've recommended to you months ago had you told me what was going on."

Now she wished she had told him she was no longer using the other security firm. Between the occurrences at the lake house and the attempted kidnapping, Zenobia had to admit that she was a little scared. She didn't know who was behind the incidents, but knew she needed someone to watch her back.

Ashton made a right turn on a street that housed a huge warehouse. At least, it looked like a warehouse. When he parked in front of the building, Zenobia glanced at the signage.

Supreme Security.

Oh, no. What were the chances that he'd take her to the place where Angelo worked? She hadn't told Ashton about the wallet incident. As a matter of fact, she didn't plan on telling anyone. It hadn't been one of her proudest moments.

As for Supreme, Zenobia had done an internet search on the company. Though their reviews were stellar, she'd planned to look at a few other security firms for fear of running into Angelo again. It was safe to assume that he wouldn't be pleased to see her after she stole from him. Even if she had the wallet delivered by messenger only hours after she'd taken it, it was the principle of the matter.

Body wound tight, Zenobia wasn't sure if she wanted a face to face with him. What would he think of her? Besides that, what if he had bad-mouthed her to his coworkers? They would never take her on as a client.

"Ashton, I don't know if this is a good idea. Can't you recommend another company? Or better yet, can I hire you for my security detail?"

Ashton removed the key from the ignition and turned to her. He was such a good-looking man with smooth honey-brown skin, kind eyes, and a smile that would put anyone at ease. He might've been one of the nicest men she knew, but there was still a hardness about him that peeked out from time to time. As a police detective, he saw a lot of craziness on the job, but for the most part, his work hadn't made him bitter.

"If I had the time, I might would take you up on your offer, and you already know Atlanta PD can't provide the type of protection you need," he explained, his right arm resting on the back of her seat. "I do a little moonlighting for Supreme from time to time when I'm off duty. They're good people, and I would trust any of them with my life."

She had only met one of their employees, but if the rest of them leaped into action the way he had, she believed she'd be in good hands. She thought about Damon Cannon, the owner of the last security firm she'd used. He put on a nice front, but he'd ended up being a total asshole.

"Come on. At least meet the managing partners. I already made an appointment for you. They'll be able to answer any questions you have and address any concerns. If you're still not convinced after meeting them, then I'll come up with another plan."

Zenobia nodded. "Okay, and thanks for your help with this. I know you must be tired. If you need to leave, I'll understand."

"I'll stick around until you meet with them, but I'm pretty sure you'll be satisfied with what they have to offer."

Yeah, that's what she was afraid of. She had a feeling Angelo had the ability to satisfy any woman. At least a woman who wasn't a thief.

Chapter Four

Angelo González.

Seeing him again was like a fantasy come to life. He was even more breathtakingly handsome than he'd been the day before. She and Ashton had just stepped into the spacious receptionist area, and to her surprise, another man and Angelo were standing there.

Zenobia's gaze slid over him. Warmth spread through her body like a wave crashing against a seashore. He was even bigger and more intimidating-looking than she'd remembered. There was also an air of mysteriousness about him that aroused all her girlie parts. Especially the ones that hadn't been touched in God knows when.

. She couldn't stop looking at him. When she was growing up, her friends would've referred to him as a pretty boy. His coal-black hair looked so thick Zenobia itched to run her fingers through it. Yesterday when she saw him, she thought he was white with a nice tan. After learning his name, she realized he was Latino. But now seeing him up close and personal, he looked to be mixed-race. With what, she wasn't sure.

Goodness.

Mr. Tall, Gorgeous and *Downright Sexy* was dressed completely in black. James Bond and Idris Elba in a tuxedo

31

had nothing on this man. His tailored suit enhanced his ultra-fit body to perfection, showing off a wide chest and broad shoulders that tapered down to a narrow waist. The shirt and tie, a glorious shade of onyx, only added to the sophisticated ensemble.

Zenobia glanced at the other man, almost as handsome, standing nearby and dressed exactly the same. Good Lord. Was this how they sat around the office? Looking like sex on a stick waiting to be chosen by a client?

But it was Angelo who kept snagging her attention. Those eyes. Dark as the night sky, his sharp, assessing gaze took her in as though seeing straight to her soul. Ashton said that he'd called ahead, but Angelo stared at her like he couldn't believe she was standing in his presence. It was safe to assume that he was just as surprised to see her as she was to see him.

Ashton cleared his throat loudly. "Have you two met?" He looked from her to Angelo, then back to her again.

Neither responded. Silence stretched for what seemed like eternity before Angelo finally said, "We haven't been formally introduced." He slowly moved toward her, watching Zenobia with the intensity of a lion zoning in on its prey and planning an attack.

She tried not to fidget under his perusal, but those eyes… His mesmerizing gaze rooted her in place, stole her breath, and practically had her panting. Which was a first. Definitely a first.

He stopped within inches of her, close enough to entice her with the scent of his cologne, a mixture of bergamot and a hint of citrus. *Damn.* He smelled as good as he looked, and her entire body heated at his nearness.

His eyes narrowed and he now studied her with a slight tilt of his head as if trying to figure out something. He reached up to remove her sunglasses and Zenobia stiffened, then stepped back on reflex. Her heart was already pounding erratically, and every nerve in her body went on high alert.

"Relax, sweetheart," he said gently. His hypnotic voice,

smooth as butter, sent a shiver scurrying up her spine. "I'm not going to hurt you."

Zenobia's breathing evened out and her shoulders relaxed almost instantly as if being under some spell. She had never responded to any man this way before. Instead of feeling embarrassed, knowing he probably could see her bruised skin just below her sunglasses, an unexplainable comfort settled around her. A peace she hadn't felt in, like, forever.

After a slight hesitation and with a controlled slowness, Angelo removed the glasses. His eyes widened. "Who did this to you?" The growl of his voice was mixed with disbelief and anger as his jaw clenched and unclenched.

There was no doubt that he was a protector by nature, but Zenobia was a little surprised by his reaction. He didn't know her. She had stolen from him. And it looked like he, too, had gotten a little roughed up the day before if the slight bruise on his cheek was any indication. Part of her wanted to reach out and touch his jaw, and hope that it didn't hurt as much as her eye had hurt the day before. She also wanted to wipe away the frown marring his beautiful face. She would never be able to properly express how much she appreciated his help the day before. His concern about her bruise was sweet.

When she had awakened that morning, her eye looked worse than it had the day before, but not as painful. Since she hadn't been diligent about keeping an ice pack on it, she was definitely going to start today. Going to the hospital for a black eye was out of the question, though.

If Angelo had noticed the darkness and swelling around the eye even behind her glasses, clearly the little makeup job she'd done earlier hadn't been enough.

"It happened yesterday," she finally said. "When you saved me."

*

Anger gnawed inside of Angelo's gut at the sight of Zenobia's black eye. He'd had no idea that she'd been injured. He knew nothing about this woman, except for what was portrayed through the media. But a protectiveness he couldn't explain charged through his body. If he ever got his hands on those bastards again, he would make them sorry they'd ever laid hands on her.

Slowly reining in his anger and still holding her shades, Angelo took in her appearance. Her hair, black with light brown highlights, was thick and a little unruly and hung loosely just past her shoulders. She looked as if she had just rolled out of bed, ran her fingers through the strands, and then slipped into a shirt and the first pair of worn jeans she found. Even with her carefree appearance, black eye and all, Zenobia Westfield was still the most beautiful woman he had ever laid eyes on.

"If you two are done ogling each other, will one of you care to tell me what I've missed?" Ashton asked, then turned to Zenobia. "You told me a jogger stopped and helped you get away. You never said it was Angelo."

She gave a slight shrug. "I—I had no idea you two knew each other."

"How do the two of you know each other?" Angelo asked, hoping they weren't a couple. Then again, why would it matter? He might be crazy-attracted to the woman and wanted to get to know her better, but that wasn't going to happen.

Ashton's right brow lifted and he looked at Angelo pointedly. "We're *friends*. She's like a sister to me."

Angelo nodded, understanding the warning behind the words and the tone, but glad to hear they weren't more than friends. Right now, it didn't matter. If she was there to seek personal security, then she was off limits. The company didn't have any specific rules about fraternizing or getting involved with clients, but Angelo had his own rules. Besides, he wasn't the commitment type of guy, and she probably wasn't into flings, which was all he'd ever be interested in.

"Besides running into each other yesterday, have you guys met before? You seem awfully...familiar with each other," Parker said from behind him.

Angelo glanced over his shoulder at the security specialist. He had temporarily forgotten that he was nearby. Parker, a former SWAT officer, had moved from Chicago to Atlanta a little more than a year ago. His question reminded Angelo of the conversation with Myles about how Parker wanted to get with *Zen*.

"This is our first time meeting. Officially, I mean," Angelo explained. He and Zenobia might've just been introduced, but he was pretty sure Parker and Ashton picked up on the sexual vibe between them. They had a connection. It didn't make sense, especially since they'd just met, but whatever was transpiring between them was too strong to go unnoticed.

The desk phone beeped, signaling a call from one of the managers upstairs. Parker walked back around the long counter to answer the call.

Angelo handed Zenobia her shades. "You need to get that eye checked out." The makeup covered the bruising some, but as a person who'd had his share of black eyes, hers looked pretty bad.

Zenobia lifted her chin defiantly. "Like I told Ashton, I'm not going to a hospital." She met Angelo's gaze as if daring him to try and make her.

Beautiful and stubborn. My type of woman.

Angelo's lips quirked, but he fought the smile threatening to break through.

"Mason will be down shortly to meet with you, Ms. Westfield," Parker said. "He asked that I show you to conference room A."

She and Ashton followed behind Parker.

"While you're in your meeting," Angelo called out, and Zenobia stopped and turned to him. "I'll contact a doctor who makes house calls." Angelo pulled his phone from the front pocket of his pants, hoping his brother had time to stop by Supreme.

Zenobia backtracked and stopped in front of him. "By the way, I'm sorry about the wallet situation," she said, only loud enough for him to hear. "I hope it didn't cause you too much of an inconvenience."

"No harm done, but I do have questions about your, um, unique skill," he said and gave a slight smile. If he was honest, he was a little impressed that she'd been able to lift his wallet without him realizing it immediately.

She batted her long eyelashes and glanced away, a shy smile lifting the right corner of her luscious lips. When she looked at him again, she asked, "Would you mind sitting in on the meeting?"

Angelo searched her eyes, wondering why she'd want him to be a part of the meeting. Normally, those meetings were run by one or two of the managers. However, if Angelo accepted her request, it would give him a chance to find out what was up with the kidnapping attempt.

"Sure. I'll be right there."

Chapter Five

"So, you think the kidnapping and the incidents at the lake house are connected?" Mason Bennett, the owner of Supreme Security-Atlanta, asked.

Zenobia was slow to respond, noting how the other man, Hamilton Crosby, a managing partner, was watching her. Yet, it was Mason who unnerved her. A big guy with a bald head, dark skin, plus a little scruff on his face, and intense eyes that had him looking handsome and dangerous at the same time. It wasn't his large presence that gave her pause, though. No, it was the way he studied her, as if trying to determine if she was being completely honest with them. His unwavering stare was a bit unsettling. It had been that way from the moment he'd walked into the large conference room.

Before leaving a short while ago, Ashton assured her that she was in good hands. Zenobia didn't doubt him, especially after Mason told her more about the company. She wished that she'd hired them months ago—the first time she shopped for personal security. Their professionalism was evident in the way they spoke, how they presented themselves, and even in the way they dressed. Their team looked like they meant business. She was even impressed to learn that their security team was made up of individuals from various branches of law enforcement and many had military backgrounds, like Mason.

And then there was Angelo. He had eased into the room twenty minutes ago, and her gaze kept drifting to where he stood leaning against a nearby wall with his arms folded across his chest. If he was trying to stay in the background and not be a distraction, he was failing miserably. There was something so magnetic, a sensual pull between them that even if he was in another part of the building, she'd be able to feel his presence.

"Zenobia?" Mason prompted, and her eyes snapped to him.

"Oh, sorry. I—I honestly don't know if there's a connection between the incidences. It's the timing that has me thinking that could be a possibility. I returned to Atlanta less than twenty-four hours before the attempted kidnapping. Only a few people knew I had cut my trip short."

"People in your inner circle," Hamilton said, his deep voice as powerful as his presence.

Another notable thing about Supreme was that they had some of the finest-looking men she'd ever met. Which said a lot since she was in the entertainment industry and encountered plenty of nice-looking men. Mason had referred to his team as Atlanta's Finest, and she had to agree that the name fit them in more ways than one.

"Yes, the people who are the closest to me are the only ones who knew my itinerary."

Disappointment clawed through her body and settled in her chest at the thought that one of them might be out to hurt her. As a newbie in the music industry, the circle of people she associated with had grown, but there were only a select few that she let get close. She didn't have much family, nor did she have many friends. There had been a few people she'd cut loose after leaving Miami, but that had been years ago. Why would someone suddenly target her?

Mason tapped his pen against the yellow legal pad in front of him. "You mentioned that your cousin, your housekeeper, and your manager Octavia Hilton, as well as an assistant, were the only people who knew you were at the lake house."

"That's correct."

"But it's possible that one of them told someone, intentionally or unintentionally," Hamilton said.

"Yes, I guess that's possible."

"Or maybe someone in town recognized you," he continued.

"I doubt anyone in Lake Lanier recognized me. I barely left the house. Even if someone had recognized me, I can't see them sending flowers. The person used my real name Zenobia, instead of my stage name Zen," she explained.

Staying at Lake Lanier to work on a couple of songs had been the plan. Then she started getting hang-up calls, but didn't think much of them. It wasn't until flowers were delivered that she started to think something was going on. Zenobia couldn't remember the last time she'd received flowers. Those who knew she was there insisted they hadn't sent them. What really disturbed her was the fact that she was staying at the house under an alias—yet the flowers were addressed to *her*.

"I can't wrap my brain around who or why someone is targeting me," Zenobia said, frustration punctuating her words. She was physically and mentally tired, but she needed to figure out what was going on. Soon she'd be dropping her next album and then going on a short tour to promote it. But she didn't want to do that with some unknown enemy lurking out there.

"What did the cops say regarding the break-in at the lake house?" Hamilton asked.

Zenobia shuddered at the thought, remembering how she had returned to the house after a long run and found the back door ajar.

"They claimed that since there wasn't forced entry and that nothing had been taken, there was nothing they could do. Dusting for fingerprints was out of the question. There would've been too many, considering it's a rental."

"And you're sure you set the alarm and locked the doors before going for your run?" Hamilton asked.

Zenobia was trying not to take offense to their questions, but they were acting as if they didn't believe her.

"I'm positive. Someone had been in that house. While the cops were there, I called the leasing office and they assured me that they changed the door code after every guest." Zenobia took a breath, realizing she was getting worked up, remembering how scared she'd been. "Before the cops left, I packed my bags and I left when they did. Then I drove back to Atlanta."

Hamilton nodded, looking as if he wanted to say more, but Angelo spoke.

"I don't think the lake house issues are connected to the kidnapping," he said. He hadn't spoken since easing into the conference room. "Why wait until she was back in Atlanta to snatch her up when they could've tried to get her at the house?"

Okay, that was a good point, Zenobia thought, but that still didn't answer the questions: Who was trying to get to her and why?

"You're probably right," Hamilton said to Angelo, then turned to Zenobia. "We're asking these types of questions because we do more than just provide personal security. In situations like yours, not only would we offer protection, but we'd also do some investigating. Keeping you safe would be our top priority while we try to determine the who and the why regarding these instances."

He might be trying to set her mind at ease, but knowing that they would be digging into her life had her on edge. Some things were better left buried, especially her past life. A life that she had walked away from and tried not to look back on. If Atlanta's Finest were as good as Ashton claimed, how much of her past would come to light?

Zenobia swallowed hard at the disturbing thought. She might need their protection, but what she didn't need was anyone poking at the hornet's nest of her past.

"Tell us about this photo and your relationship with Stephen Landry." Mason handed over his iPad and Zenobia groaned. "Is it possible that he's behind any of this?"

Zenobia explained their history. Discussing Stephen and their ridiculous past was enough to remind her what a horrible judge of character she was when it came to men. Which was why she'd been taking a break from dating. That, and she needed to stay focused on her career.

"He's never done anything to physically hurt me, and I can't see him trying to have me kidnapped. I'll admit that he caught me off guard with that kiss, but that happened weeks ago. What the photo doesn't show is me shoving him away. I have no idea why the picture has suddenly surfaced, and I have no idea who might've taken it."

"What about Octavia Hilton?" Mason asked of her manager. "You said that she's always trying to keep you in the public's eye. Could she have leaked the photo? Or maybe someone from Stephen's camp?"

"It's possible that Octavia is behind the picture. I don't know that for sure since I haven't spoken to her. Right now, she's out of the country, but I wouldn't put anything past her."

Octavia was great at managing Zenobia's music career and keeping her in the spotlight, but some of her unsavory methods made her uncomfortable. Like the time Zenobia ended up in the emergency room with a sprained ankle. She had called Octavia, informing her that she'd be late for their meeting. Paparazzi were camped out in front of the hospital by the time Zenobia was ready to leave. Octavia had admitted being the one to contact them, saying all publicity is good publicity.

"She insists that I need to stay relevant and in the spotlight for my fans, and she doesn't care about the circumstances."

"Why'd you tell your ex that you were seeing someone?" That question came from Angelo.

Zenobia stared down at her lap where her hands were folded. What must he think of her? She'd stolen from him, and now she had admitted to lying to her ex-boyfriend.

"Despite me telling Stephen that I wasn't interested in us reconnecting, he's been calling and showing up at my house. So, the last time I saw him, I told him I was involved with someone and that he needed to back off."

Angelo's narrowed gaze bore into her. "Yet, you don't believe he's behind the attempted kidnapping or the incidents at the lake house." What was it with the men at Supreme? Did they all go through some type of training that taught them how to stare people down?

"I honestly don't know who is out to get me," Zenobia bit out. "All I know is that someone is trying to make me think that I'm going crazy, and trying to cause me harm."

"Yet," Angelo continued, "you were out running alone yesterday in an unfamiliar neighborhood where anyone could have snatched you."

"Okay, let's dial it down some," Hamilton said, eyeing Angelo as if carrying on some secret conversation.

Angelo pushed away from the wall and ran his fingers through his hair. "My apologies," he said, his gaze pinning her in place.

All she could do was nod. In hindsight, maybe jogging alone hadn't been the best idea in light of the incidences that had happened days earlier. When she'd gotten up that morning, after a long drive the day before, she needed air. The thought of not being safe hadn't crossed her mind.

"I always run by myself," she attempted to explain. "I usually wear some form of a disguise, either a cap, sunglasses, or something. I've never had any problems."

Those in the room nodded, but were slow to speak until Hamilton said, "You used to use DLC Security firm. Why didn't you go back to them?"

Zenobia cringed inside. The meeting was slowly going downhill. The last thing she wanted to discuss was Damon "Lughead" Cannon, the owner of DLC.

"I used their services mainly when I had to perform somewhere or when I was requested to show my face at an event. I didn't use them on a day-to-day basis. Except, the last time I hired them, it was for a month while I did the East Coast leg of Anthony Tate's R&B tour with him. But I had to release the security team before the tour was over."

"Why?" Angelo asked, a hint of impatience in his voice.

What the heck is his deal? Zenobia couldn't tell if he was pissed at her for some reason, or if he was like the others and just trying to determine who could be after her.

"When I hired them in the past, I was assigned some pretty nice guys who I got along with great. This last time, Damon, the owner, oversaw my detail. Everything was fine the first couple of weeks, but a week before the tour ended, he made a pass at me."

"An unwanted pass?" Angelo asked.

"Yes, an unwanted pass despite his version of the story."

Zenobia's cheeks heated. She assumed they'd heard the lie that he'd shared about how things had gone down. Damon turned out to be a misogynistic ass, thinking he could force himself on her and get away with it. Even though she hadn't gone to the police and filed harassment charges against him, TMZ had gotten wind of the story. Of course, Damon's version of what happened was different, claiming they'd been flirting, and he had misread her.

She could admit that he was attractive, and in another life, she might've been interested in more than a professional relationship. But as she got to know him, there'd been an underlying creepiness about him that grew the longer he traveled with her. So far, she wasn't picking up anything like that with any of the men of Supreme.

"There's a chance Damon might retaliate," Hamilton said, watching her carefully.

"It's possible, but that happened months ago. I haven't seen or heard from Damon since. I didn't file any charges against him, but I told him I would if he ever came near me again. So far, he hasn't."

"Is there anyone else you can think of who might want to cause you harm? Old friends you cut loose? Former assistants? Family? Anyone who might be trying to get back at you for something?" Mason asked. "And has anything else strange happened recently?"

Zenobia didn't trust easily, and the more questions they asked, the less she wanted to share. In her world, at least the world she had left behind in Miami, you kept your business to yourself. Otherwise, anyone could come along and use it against you.

"No. That's it."

*

"She's lying," Angelo ground out as he followed Hamilton into his office. "Or at least she's not telling us everything. Either way, she's hiding something."

Despite the serious electric current crackling between him and Zenobia, he couldn't stand liars. He'd been deceived one too many times and had no tolerance for people who willingly withheld the truth.

"Yeah, I picked up on that." Hamilton set his tablet on the desk before claiming his office chair. "But Zenobia wouldn't be the first client to leave out a few details. We just have to determine if those details are anything that could put any of our people in danger. It could be that something has her spooked, and she's slow to trust us. Which is understandable. She doesn't know us, but she'll soon learn that we can be trusted."

Angelo unbuttoned his suit jacket and settled in one of the upholstered chairs in front of Hamilton's desk. He couldn't argue with his boss's rationale. People came to them because they were afraid and unsure of next steps when it came to their safety. Right now, since Zenobia confirmed that she wanted to hire their services, they were all taking a short break. Mateo had arrived and was checking out her eye, while Hamilton and Mason determined the best plan of action for her case.

"Whatever her reasons for not being straight with us," Hamilton continued, "I would think you'd be curious about what's going on with her. Especially after saving her life."

"Yeah, I might be a little curious." Hamilton's brows shot up and Angelo conceded. "Okay, I'm more than a little curious, but I hate the idea of us going into anything blind."

Hamilton chuckled. "We practically go into all of our cases blind. This one is no different."

Actually, this one was very different. Considering their impressive clientele, this was the first time Angelo was enamored with one of their clients; to the point of requesting that he not be placed on her detail. She'd been a distraction from the moment he laid eyes on her. Now that he'd been in her presence for a period of time, he was even more intrigued, despite the fact that she was lying about something.

"I sense there's more going on with you and Zenobia than you're letting on."

Angelo shook his head. "Not really. It's just her…this case, something's not sitting right with me, and I can't put my finger on it." He learned a long time ago never to ignore his gut. It had saved his life on more than one occasion. The problem now, though, he couldn't get a good read on Zenobia. The inkling that whatever she was holding back was huge and his fierce attraction to her were at odds.

"You like her," Hamilton said, a sly grin tilting the right side of his mouth. "I recognize the look and the tension that resonated between you two. Hell, I can relate to it."

Angelo grinned, recalling a couple of years ago when the tornado that was Dakota Sherrod crashed into Hamilton's perfectly put-together world. At the time, his boss hadn't known what to do with the fabulous stunt woman. They were opposites in every way, but had managed to find some common ground. Now that they were married with a daughter together and were also raising Hamilton's son Dominic, Hamilton had never been happier.

"I'm not sure if this will put you at ease, but when

Ashton called, filling us in on what little he knew about Zenobia's situation, Egypt did a little digging. So far, there are no red flags, but you know we'll keep digging. In the meantime, we're moving forward and taking her case. I want you on her detail."

Before Angelo could decline the assignment, something he never did, a knock sounded on the door. Mason and Myles strolled into the office, closing the door behind them.

"Good, I'm glad you're in here," Mason said to Angelo, as he perched a hip on the edge of the large desk and faced him. "I've already filled Myles in on Zenobia's case, but I wanted to run an idea about how we'll proceed by the three of you at the same time."

"Hopefully your idea includes Angelo, since Zenobia seems to be most comfortable around him," Hamilton said.

Angelo sat up straighter. "About that. I don't—"

"Actually, it does," Mason said as he unwrapped one of those gourmet lollipops that he was addicted to. His wife didn't allow them in the house, not wanting their kids to pick up the same habit. "Since we need to get close to those who are closest to Zenobia, and see who's hiding what, what better way than to find Zenobia a fake boyfriend."

"Whoa. Wait. What?" Angelo pitched forward in his seat. "If you're saying what I think you're saying, my answer is no." He wanted to say *hell* no, but had to remember that these guys were his bosses.

Myles grunted, his mouth twitching trying to fight back a smile.

Angelo jerked out of his seat, shaking his head and trying to figure out where the hell this idea came from. "I don't see how that's going to help any—"

"Actually, Mase, I think you might be on to something." Hamilton rocked in his chair, studying Angelo. "We have no idea who is after her. Could be the ex, her manager, cousin, or even that prick Damon Cannon."

Angelo hadn't met the guy in person, but had heard about Damon and his company. It was a wonder the guy had any clients considering he was a world-class jerk. Just the thought of him pawing Zenobia made him want to pay the miscreant a visit.

Whoa. Slow your roll, man, Angelo chastised himself. He had no claims on the woman, and he needed to remember that.

"There's no way someone's going to suddenly think we're dating seriously enough for me to spend 24/7 with her."

"I'm sure you'll be able to make the relationship look real enough, and maybe she'll open up to you. We all agree that she's holding something back," Mason said.

"Yeah, and with his charming ass, he'll have her and the people in her inner circle eating out of his hands in no time," Myles added.

"Man, shut up," Angelo grumbled. Myles was the only one who knew that Angelo was feeling her, like, *really* feeling her. Which was why he should know this hairbrained idea wasn't a good idea.

Zenobia Westfield was a distraction. A sweet, sexy, gorgeous distraction. Because of that, those two thugs from the day before had been able to sucker-punch him. Angelo couldn't ever let something like that happen again, and it probably would if he had to spend any type of time with the woman.

"Find someone else," he said. "Get Parker. He'd be a good fit for the assignment." Besides, he already had a thing for her, but Angelo kept the thought to himself.

"Parker could work, but he doesn't have your undercover experience," Myles explained, his tone back to being serious.

"Pretending to be her man won't be a stretch since you two have chemistry," Hamilton added. "According to Ashton, she already has that hero-worship thing going for the man who saved her. Granted, she didn't know who you were at the time, but she'll feel safe with you."

"And once she learns that you two have something in

common, she probably won't have any problem getting into the role," Myles added.

Angelo frowned. "What do we have in common?"

"You both can sing. Who knows, maybe she can hook you up with a record deal."

The guys always ragged him about trying out for *The Voice* or *American Idol*. He loved singing and knew he was good, but he didn't want that type of life. Based on some of her comments early on in the meeting, he could already tell that Zenobia didn't like being in the spotlight. He would probably like it even less.

Angelo shook his head. "Again, I'm tellin' y'all, this is a bad idea." The sexual tension between him and Zenobia was too strong. He couldn't fake what he was feeling for her.

"Besides, she'll never go along with this."

Chapter Six

"No. No way. I'm a singer, not an actress. I can't pretend he's my man. It'll never work," Zenobia insisted, shaking her head as disbelief showed on her face.

Angelo wanted to say *I told you so* to his coworkers who were at the table. He and Myles sat to her left, and Hamilton and Egypt were to her right. After they'd laid out a preliminary plan for the assignment, Mason had left for another appointment.

Zenobia glanced around the table as four sets of eyes watched her. "Why is it necessary for me to have a boyfriend?"

Angelo was glad he wasn't the only one who couldn't get with this plan. Part of him had hoped that she would shoot down the idea. If the bewildered expression on her face was any indication, she was no more interested than he was. Although he had to admit, it might've been fun to spend some time getting to know her.

When he and the guys returned to the conference room, she and Egypt were already there, chatting and laughing like old friends. Mateo had come and gone, saying that Zenobia's eye was no worse than any other black eye, but if she wanted it to heal quicker, she'd have to keep ice on it. As it was right now, her ice pack was sitting on the table wrapped in a towel.

"While we're protecting you, we need to start ruling out

potential suspects," Hamilton explained. "Once you're seen with Angelo, word will get out that there's a new man in your life. Whoever sent the flowers will definitely be interested in this development. Whether it was your ex, or Damon, or someone else, they're going to show their hand and we'll be right there to reel them in."

"As for the attempted kidnapping, we're going to have to go at that from a different angle," Myles added. "But having Angelo close to you, and one of us as your driver, it'll be a lot harder for anyone to attempt to grab you again. In the meantime, Ashton and our team will do some digging into that incident."

Angelo might hate the idea and was still trying to convince himself to go along with this charade, but he wanted her safe. Not only because she'd hired them to do a job, but also because he was really attracted to her.

He also had to admit that Mason's plan of a fake relationship had merit. They'd used this technique in the past, and it worked. It was just that Angelo hadn't been at the center of the plans in the past. The thought of doing any covert work no longer appealed to him. After his last assignment with the DEA, he never planned to do undercover work again, even something as simple as this one. Inserting himself into a target's life was easy, for the most part. This situation might be different, but the same skills were needed. Play a role and blend in to the target's world. Zenobia wasn't his target, but those around her were.

She shook her head and released a humorless laugh. "This is crazy. No one is ever going to believe that I'm suddenly in a serious relationship."

"Outside of that picture of you and Stephen, you haven't been in the media for a couple of months. You've also been at Lake Lanier for a while. We'll be able to use your absence from both to our advantage," Hamilton said. "We'll come up with a story to use when someone close to you asks how long you've been together, so don't worry. Having at least one of our people inserted into your everyday life will work, and

Angelo's the perfect person for the job."

"It won't take much acting. You two already have a connection, and anyone who sees you together will feel it," Egypt said.

As the executive assistant, Egypt played a valuable role in most assignments. Everything from making sure the teams had everything they needed for an assignment to digging for information about potential clients.

"You mentioned that you didn't want bodyguards following you around, but if you were dating one..." Egypt let the idea hang out there.

"No one would be the wiser," Myles added. "However, with that said, we will be pulling in some of our other guys on this assignment, but mainly it'll be Angelo."

Zenobia frowned and fingered the ice pack that should've been covering her eye. "What do you think of all of this?" she asked Angelo. "Do you think this is necessary? Do you actually think pretending we're a couple will work?"

He studied her for a moment. All types of thoughts of why he and her pretending to be a couple wasn't a good idea flowed through his mind. But if he was going to agree to this charade, there was something he had to do first. Something that would help him get into character.

Angelo pushed his seat back and stood. Ignoring the stares from those in the room, he extended his hand to Zenobia. Her gaze bounced from his eyes to his hand and back again as she looked at him warily.

"Come with me," he said. What happened next was between him and her. From the moment he laid eyes on this woman, the protectiveness he felt for her was unsettling. So was the undeniable pull between them.

Yes, she was extremely attractive, but it was more than just her looks. There was a fearlessness about her mixed with a deep-seated vulnerability that he couldn't quite make peace with. Normally he'd run the other way when it came to complex women, but this beauty intrigued him—which could lead to a bit of recklessness if he wasn't careful.

Zenobia searched his eyes, then her gaze dropped to his hand. Seconds ticked by before she grabbed hold and allowed him to pull her up from the chair. Hand in hand, they headed to the door. No one said anything, but he could feel Myles's gaze burning a hole in his back.

Angelo led Zenobia down the long hallway, planning to take her to one of the crash rooms on the premises.

Years ago, upon opening Supreme Security-Atlanta, Mason had the old warehouse converted to a state-of-the-arts facility. In addition to offices, conference rooms, and even a war room, the place included a large kitchen, phenomenal gym, and several crash rooms. Some of the guys, especially those who lived outside of Atlanta, used those spaces to grab a nap in between assignments, or to just unwind.

"Where are you taking me?" Zenobia finally spoke as Angelo led her to the elevator. He was actually a little surprised that she hadn't said something sooner. What he was about to do was unconventional, but Angelo decided to take a chance.

"I'm taking you to a place where you and I can...talk. If we're going to pull off this dating thing and make it look believable, there are some things we need to discuss."

"Have you pretended to be a client's boyfriend before?"

Angelo shook his head. "No. Never, but I did do undercover work in a past life." They took the elevator up two floors, then exited. He unlocked the room he used on occasion and ushered her in before closing the door behind him. Now that he had her in there, he was having second thoughts about his intentions. He rarely had second thoughts about any of his actions.

He stood near the door and watched as she roamed around the generously-size bedroom with an attached bathroom. Egypt had recently updated the decor in the space, adding blackout blinds, a leather recliner chair, and a new black and gray comforter. The space was like home away from home.

Angelo's gaze zoned in on his assignment, who was now

staring out the window. Tall, at least 5'7" and shapely, she was fit, but not skinny. Curvy, but not fat. Actually, she was exquisite, no matter what part of her enticing body he was looking at.

She turned around, and he slowly moved toward her.

"Why'd you bring me up here?" she asked, her voice quiet as she looked at him shyly. She was like a puzzle that he so wanted to piece together. How could a woman who sang with such emotion and power seem so timid and unsure of herself? Then again, the way she fought those guys off the other day proved that she was also a fighter.

Yep, definitely a puzzle.

"If you don't want to be a part of my detail, I understand. I don't blame you. Why would you want to protect someone who stole from you? Someone who ran off and didn't look back?"

"You ran off because I told you to." Angelo kept his voice as low as hers. "With us taking your case, you'll be expected to do whatever we tell you to do."

She leaned back and frowned, looking as if she was about to argue. Angelo didn't give her a chance.

"Whatever we tell you to do is always for your own good. Everyone who'll be assigned to you will put your safety first. You're not going to like everything we'll insist on, but—

"So, does this mean you're going to pretend to be my boyfriend?"

Angelo inched closer, close enough to see her take a hard swallow. "Under one condition."

She worried her bottom lip, that shyness that he'd seen earlier returning. "What condition?"

He moved in even closer, close enough to feel her shudder. "I need to see if you can handle being close to me, because when I go undercover, I'm all in." Without giving her a chance to speak, or even process what he was saying, he cupped her face between his hands and kissed her.

At first the kiss was sweet, gentle, and cautious, but when she moaned into his mouth, he couldn't help but deepen the lip-lock. His tongue slid between her juicy lips and he explored the inner recesses of her enchanting mouth. Testing. Savoring. He'd only planned to get a little taste of her, see if there was any way to pull off this boyfriend/girlfriend idea, but he was getting more than expected. So much more.

His hands slid down the sides of her body, grazing over every dip and curve until they landed on her hips. When she whimpered and looped her arms around his neck, it spurred him on. He pulled her flush against him, loving the feel of her body against his.

Oh yeah. This was going to be one hell of an assignment. Angelo would make sure he kept her safe, and he planned to enjoy every minute of being *her man.*

*

Oh my.

Zenobia rocked against his hard body and her nipples pebbled against the lace of her bra. She was enjoying this test a little too much. His experienced lips didn't let up and she felt the power of the kiss down to the soles of her feet. When was the last time she'd been kissed like this? Hell, she couldn't remember a time, which was a shame. Now she knew what she'd been missing out on.

The heat from his large hands as they grazed over her curves warmed her from the inside out. How was it possible that a man she didn't know could have this type of effect on her?

From the moment their gazes had connected after Angelo had saved her life, everything within her had responded. This connection between them wasn't normal. Hell, the whole situation wasn't normal. Yet, this *test* stirred something so potent within her. The kiss, the feel of his hands on her body, the desire blossoming inside of her were way more than she could've imagined.

His hands moved back up her body. Before she knew it, his fingers were in her hair, sending a whole new wave of desire pulsing through her veins. If a kiss had this type of effect on her, what would she do if his mouth made contact with other parts of her body?

Before she could fully embrace that thought, Angelo slowly ended the kiss and dropped his hands to his sides. He stared at her for a long minute before putting a little space between them.

Zenobia stared right back at him. The man was one of the most gorgeous human beings she'd ever seen. Add that to the air of danger that shadowed him, and she had a man who could easily make her forget her name. Especially after being kissed the way he'd just kissed her.

"Did I pass?" she asked with more sass than she felt, and discreetly blew out a calming breath as she tried to slow the pounding of her heart that was still beating double-time. Being so close to this man had fried every nerve in her body. And her girlie parts screamed for a sampling of what else he could do with that mouth and that talented tongue.

Oh, no. Don't go there. This is just pretend.

They weren't really dating, she reminded herself, and that was assuming he'd even go along with the crazy idea.

"Yeah. Yeah, you passed." Angelo's voice was thick and several octaves deeper than before. He studied her for what seemed like several long minutes, but were mere seconds. His gaze volleyed from her eyes to her mouth and back to her eyes again. He turned and moved a few feet away before he stabbed his fingers through his coal-black hair. Thick hair that she wanted to run her own fingers through.

Apparently, she wasn't the only person effected by their tongue aerobics. Good. Why should she be the only person vying for more of what they'd just shared?

Question was: how much more would they share?

By the time Angelo escorted her back to the conference room, Zenobia felt like a new woman. The hell she'd endured twenty-four hours ago hadn't left her mind, but suddenly she had a feeling that Atlanta's Finest were going to take good care of her.

When they walked into the conference room,

conversations stopped and everyone's attention turned to them. Zenobia wasn't sure what they saw, but it was as if they could tell what she and Angelo had done. But how?

"Okay, I'm in," Angelo said, and pulled out the chair she had vacated, and waited for her to sit before reclaiming his seat.

Myles gaped at him. "Damn, man. What the hell? You couldn't wait until after the meeting?"

Oh. My. God. Heat rose to her cheeks and Zenobia was pretty sure those around her could see her blush. Her skin wasn't as fair as Angelo, but she knew her cheeks had tinted. All Angelo had done was kiss her. How could they possibly know?

Zenobia made the mistake and glanced at Egypt, then Hamilton. Yep. The gentle smile on Egypt's face and their boss's raised brows said it all.

Oh, this is just great.

"If we move forward with this charade, you won't be able to tell anyone the truth," Angelo said. "So, tell us, are you in?"

Was she in? Could she really pull this off?

"On one condition."

Angelo drummed his fingers on the tabletop as he looked at her. "Which is?"

"I want my cousin and Sofia to know the truth about you and—"

"No," he said without letting her finish.

She gritted her teeth and glared at him. "Why not? Those are the only two people in this world I trust." Besides that, her cousin already knew Angelo existed. Kira would never believe that they were suddenly an item. And if he was going to be spending any time around her house, Sofia would know something was up. "Either they're in on this or no deal."

Angelo released a frustrated sigh that bordered on a growl. "Zenobia, it's better if no one knows that we're not really dating, especially since we don't know who in your camp you can trust. Remember, we're trying to ferret out whoever is trying to hurt you. We can't rule out—"

"That's non-negotiable, Angelo." She held her head high, and leveled him with her most intimidating gaze. She'd agree to follow their lead on most things, but not this. "At least we have to let my cousin in on it. I trust Kira. She would never do anything to hurt me."

Zenobia would just have to make sure her cousin didn't tell anyone, not even her boyfriend. Elijah was a nice guy, but Zenobia agreed with Angelo; the idea might actually work, especially if only one or two people knew the deal.

"Sofia has been in Mexico for the past four weeks. So, we might not have to share the truth with her."

The guys at the table looked at one another in what appeared to be some silent communication before Angelo spoke.

"Fine. Tell your housekeeper that we've been dating for a few weeks."

Angelo laid out the plan as if he'd been planning this for weeks instead of the past hour. He even referred to her as his woman.

Zenobia's body heated all over again amazed he was already getting into his role. What was he thinking? Was he remembering how good they felt in each other's arms? Or how perfectly their lips meshed together?

If he continued looking at her the way he was doing now, how in the world was she going to be his girlfriend without actually falling for him?

Her problems were just beginning. Having a boyfriend/bodyguard might keep her physically safe, but who would protect her heart?

Chapter Seven

With her hands wrapped around a hot steaming cup of tea, Zenobia leaned a hip against the large center island in her kitchen. She wasn't sure what to do with herself as Angelo and some of the other security specialist searched her home. They were checking the house for listening devices.

When they first mentioned doing a sweep of the house, she'd thought they were kidding. There was no way someone could've planted a bug, cameras, or anything and she would not know it. At least she hoped. The thought of someone listening in on her conversations, no matter how vanilla they were, was unsettling at best. Even worse than that, if listening devices were found, her assumptions were correct. Someone close to her was plotting against her.

The home—including a guest house which she planned to turn into a studio—had been a gift to herself after she'd signed her first record deal. She glanced around the eat-in kitchen that overlooked the dining room and family room. She might not be much of a cook, but she'd wanted Sofia to have the kitchen of her dreams.

Zenobia sipped her tea thinking about how Sofia would be returning from her annual trip to Mexico next week. What would she think of all of this? Angelo still wasn't feeling the idea of telling her, even though Zenobia had already informed

Kira and swore her to secrecy.

Zenobia's cell phone vibrated in her back pocket and she pulled it out. "Hello."

"Darling, I'm so glad you answered," Octavia said, her tone overzealous as usual. She was one of the most well-known entertainment managers in the business, representing singers as well as actors. Considering how dramatic she could be at times, it was a wonder she hadn't been cast in a few movies herself.

"Hey, Octavia. How is Paris?"

"As lovely as ever, but I'm sitting on a plane waiting to head back to the States."

"Oh? I thought you weren't expected back for at least another week."

"I did everything I needed to do here and had planned to spend a couple of days touring, but something came up. I'm heading back to Atlanta."

A chill followed by goosebumps raced up Zenobia's arms. She hated having to question everything someone close to her said or did. What if Octavia was the person behind the attempted kidnapping? Just the idea of that seemed ludicrous, but until they determined who was after her, she would stay vigilant and wouldn't rule anyone out. Not even her manager.

As Octavia chatted to someone on the other end of the phone, Zenobia's gaze went to the back stairs that led to the second floor. Supreme's team was so quiet, it was easy to forget that she wasn't home alone.

On the way to the house, Angelo had explained what would take place once they arrived. He had instructed her to act as normal as possible, and to do whatever she usually did. More importantly, she couldn't say anything about having security, or anything that would allude to their relationship not being real. At least not until they made sure the house was free of any listening devices. Even after that was done, he suggested that going forward, there would be no mention of their fake relationship.

"Sorry about that, dear," Octavia said. "I wanted to put

in my dinner order. Gotta love first class service. So, did Brett call you?"

Her assistant had called the day before and again a couple of hours ago. Things had been a little hectic that Zenobia hadn't taken the time to listen to the voicemail or return his call.

"You need to get back into the studio as soon as possible. I know you said you're struggling with that last song, but time's up. You need to get it done."

Zenobia rubbed her forehead, knowing her manager was right. For some reason, the song wasn't coming together. Which was why she'd gotten away for a little while, hoping to finally finish it. Instead, there was another song playing around in her head. She wrote her own music and had plenty of material started. However, the producer wanted her to finish the song they had agreed on, thinking it would be a great fit with the other songs on the album.

"Brett was also supposed to remind you about Tremaine Dempsi's album release party coming up."

Zenobia groaned internally. She hated celebrity parties. Too many people. Too much drinking. Too much everything.

"Before you try to come up with an excuse of why you can't attend, you're already on program to do one song. Also, let me remind you that you need this exposure, especially with new music dropping soon."

Octavia started into her usual speech that Zenobia could probably recite by heart, but she remained quiet, letting her manager reiterate the importance of staying in the public's eye. She claimed that everybody who's anybody would be in attendance. Which also meant the paparazzi and fans would be out in full force.

"I'll be there," Zenobia said. At least she wouldn't be there alone. She had already invited Kira—who hadn't stopped talking about the event—and Elijah.

"I'll be there, too, but we really should find you a date," Octavia continued. "You walking in with some delicious arm candy would garner even more attention. I have a couple of men in…"

Angelo strolled into the kitchen, and that weird tingling sensation that gripped Zenobia's body whenever he was near started up again. Why'd he have to look so sexy in the gray T-shirt and dark jeans that he had changed into? The shirt hugged his muscular chest and flat abs, and clung to his thick biceps, while the jeans made his impossible long legs look even longer.

His head was down as he looked at something on his cell phone. "I was thinking tonight we can have…" his voice trailed off when he realized she was on the phone.

Instead of turning around and walking out, like Zenobia expected him to, he shoved his phone into his pocket and moved to the refrigerator. Pulling out a pitcher of sweet tea, he set it on the counter. He seemed so comfortable in her space as he opened one of the top cabinets, and then another before finding the glasses.

"I saw the photo of you and Stephen." Octavia's comment snagged Zenobia's attention. "You two looked awfully intimate in that picture. Is there anything you'd like to tell me?"

"Actually, I was going to ask if you had anything to do with that photo being conveniently leaked," Zenobia said, a little pissed that the picture was still trending on Twitter. It was hard keeping a low profile. She valued her privacy too much to have personal photos of her floating around.

Angelo had been just about to take a sip of his drink when his glass stopped only inches from his mouth. He watched her carefully.

"Darling, I know how much you hate the attention," Octavia said. "Even though I had nothing to do with the photo, I would've leaked it had I known you and Stephen were back together."

"Octavia, Stephen and I aren't back together and we never will be." Zenobia couldn't hide the bite behind her words. She was tired of being linked to him, a constant reminder of her bad decision in getting involved with him in the first place.

Her manager's noisy sigh barely registered since Zenobia's attention was suddenly on Angelo. He had set the glass on the counter and slowly strolled toward her, a sensual gleam in his eyes that sent a shiver through her body.

"Oh well, I'm sorry to hear that," Octavia said, but it was hard for Zenobia to think straight with the way Angelo was watching her. "I guess that means we need to find you a date."

"Wait. No…" Zenobia hurried to say. "I already have a date."

She gasped when Angelo's arm snaked around her waist and he pulled her flush against his hard body. He lowered his head and started nibbling on her neck, making her squirm.

"Angelo," she said in a hushed tone that sounded breathier than intended, but she couldn't help it. He'd made contact with that spot behind her ear, the ticklish spot that had her giggling as she tried wiggling out of his strong hold.

"Come on, baby. How much longer you gon' be on the phone?" he asked, his deep voice loud enough for Octavia to hear. "*Regresa a la cama.*"

"Oh my." Octavia gasped, as if knowing he'd said *come back to bed*. The excitement in her voice emitted through the phone line. "Who is that?"

Zenobia giggled again, unable to help herself as Angelo continued the sweet torture that he was inflicting with his lips and tongue.

"Zen?" Octavia called out.

"Yeah…um, I'm still here. Oh, and that was my date. You'll meet him at the par—" Angelo took the phone from her hand and disconnected the call.

Zenobia stared at him, her mouth hanging open. "Really? You did not just hang up on my manager!"

The right corner of his lush mouth quirked into a roguish grin, and he gave a half-hearted shrug. "I didn't like the idea of her trying to fix you up with anyone. Besides, if I wouldn't have taken the phone, she probably would've kept talking, and I wanted you all to myself."

Okaaay. "I can't believe you distracted me by talking like that."

"You looked so tempting, I couldn't help myself."

Damn, he was good. Clearly, he had done this pretend nonsense before, because for a moment there, she almost believed him. Or maybe it was the fact that she hadn't been that turned on in so long, her mind and body wanted to believe him.

Her gaze followed him as he strolled back to the other side of the center island where he had left his drink. The way he gulped down the iced tea, one would think that it was his body that was on fire, not hers.

This wasn't good. His mouth on her body, the fresh scent of his cologne, and the way he had her believing his words, was a sure sign that she was in way over her head. She'd have to be careful with him.

"So, shall we get back in bed?" she asked, and smiled when one of his brows inched up. Clearly, he was surprised she understood what he'd said in Spanish. Considering she'd spent time in Mexico and Spain, and had a Spanish-speaking housekeeper, Zenobia didn't speak the language fluently, but knew enough to get by. "Are you going to speak more Spanish to me?"

He chuckled and started to say something, but stopped, probably thinking about the potential of listening devices being in the house.

"You're just going to have to wait and see," he said, then lifted the pitcher of iced tea. "Want some?"

"Uh, no. I'm good."

He turned and opened the refrigerator. The way his shirt stretched across his broad back and how his muscles rippled with each move held her attention. When he turned back to her, Zenobia couldn't look away. Who would want to? Sexy. Dangerous. Manly. More importantly, he was hers if only for a little while.

Mine.

The word rattled through her mind. She could either play it safe and miss out on a little fun. Or she could do like he was doing—get into character.

Why not enjoy her new man, take what he offered, and give as good as she got?

*

If only he could act on the *going back to bed* idea. It had been hard as hell to go for her neck instead of her sweet lips with the little stunt he'd just pulled, but it was for the best. The kiss they'd shared earlier had already shaken him. It had him imagining what it would be like to do more than kiss her. He needed to tread lightly in this farce because this woman had the ability to bring him to his knees, literally.

"So, what do you need a date for?" he asked, watching as she tugged on the collar of her T-shirt, giving it a little shake as if needing air.

Angelo couldn't stop the smile that spread across his mouth. He was glad to witness that he affected her as much as she affected him. Problem was, one of them was going to have to keep their head in this situation. Unfortunately, he wasn't sure he could be that person.

"I need to make an appearance at Tremaine Dempsi's release party in a couple of weeks. I hope you don't have plans."

He grabbed the cloth-covered ice pack that he'd put in the freezer earlier and strolled around the counter toward Zenobia. Her eye was looking a little better than it had that morning, but the bruise was still noticeable.

"Here." Angelo handed the cold pack to her. When she didn't put the ice on her eye, he grabbed hold of her wrist and guided her hand upward. He ignored her grumbling and held the ice pack in place until he was sure she wouldn't lower her arm. "My plan is to spend as much time with you as possible. I'm glad we don't have to sneak around anymore."

He hoped she was right and that there were no listening devices in her home. But just in case there were, he wanted whoever might be listening in to know that he was there and had no intention of going anywhere.

"I want the world to know that you're mine," Angelo said, and almost burst out laughing at the suspicious look she gave him. Then, as if a shade had been lifted and sunlight burst in, her eyes widened and a grin tugged up the corners of her lips. His heart did a somersault inside his chest.

This woman. She probably had no idea how much she turned him on. But when she slid her free hand up his chest and her arm went around his neck, Angelo had a feeling she knew exactly what she was doing to him. Torture. No doubt she was going to torture him for what he'd done while she was on the phone. Maybe he should just say to hell with faking, because at this very moment, he wanted this woman more than he'd wanted anything or anyone in a long time.

"Yeah, I want the world to know that you're mine, too. I hope you're ready for the type of public attention that I usually cringe at."

She gave a little laugh, but he knew she was serious. What he didn't know yet was why she got into the music industry if she didn't like all of the attention. She had to know that with her looks and her angelic voice that she would be a star.

The thought of the paparazzi being in his face didn't appeal to Angelo, either. There was always a slim chance his past would come back to haunt him, meaning he'd have to stay alert and not look directly into anyone's camera.

He slid his arm around her narrow waist. "I'll cook us some dinner soon, but is there anything else you wanted to do tonight?"

Her smile grew wicked. "You know that's a loaded question, don't you?"

"I do, and it's a question I'm waiting for you to answer." Before she could respond, movement behind him snatched Angelo's attention.

Without removing his arm from around Zenobia, he turned to the stairs to find Lazarus Dimas, a fellow security specialist, easing down the stairs. Laz had been a detective with Atlanta PD for years. He had also been Ashton's partner before signing on to Supreme full-time. That was how he knew Zenobia. They'd met a couple of times over the years.

Laz pointed to both of them, then nodded his head toward the front of the house. A bad feeling seeped into Angelo's bones, especially when his friend led them outside to the driveway where two of their SUVs were parked.

"So far we found three listening devices."

Zenobia gasped. The ice pack dangled from her fingers as shock marred her beautiful face. "How is that possible? How could someone have planted them without me knowing?"

Angelo wrapped his arm around her shoulder and had her to put the ice back over her eye. If only she knew how easy it was to plant bugs without being detected. Now they just had to figure out who'd done it and why.

Laz leaned against one of the vehicles, and told them that they'd found a device in her office. She was using it as a temporary studio until renovations started on the guest house out back. They had also found one in her bedroom and one in the family room.

"While the other guys are still checking the guest house, Myles is going to check the kitchen. I'd bet my paycheck that he finds at least one in there," Laz said.

A short while later, Myles exited the house and walked over to where they were standing in the driveway. "Found another one. Now we just have to decide whether to leave them or remove them."

"What?" Zenobia's gaze bounced to each one of them, looking at them as if they'd lost their minds. "You're not seriously thinking about leaving them in there."

"It would be one way of catching whoever planted them," Angelo said, explaining to her that it would be a good way to set someone up. They could pretend they were going to be somewhere and see who showed up.

Zenobia pulled away from him shaking her head. "I can't live in this house knowing someone is listening in on me. I'm sorry. I just…I just can't. It's too creepy. It's bad enough knowing that someone has been spying on me, and I don't know who. I don't even know how long this has been going on."

"It's not a problem to remove them. When the person realizes they no longer have access to you and your conversations, they'll come out of hiding," Myles said.

"Yeah, we just have to be ready because we're still not sure who or what we're up against," Laz explained. "This could be your ex trying to scare you back into his arms."

"Or it could be someone who wants to hurt her," Angelo added, hoping it wasn't the latter.

Zenobia stared up at him and the worry in her eyes gutted him. He had no doubt they could protect her and eventually find the person behind this, but he wasn't sure how to erase her fear. She folded her arms around her waist.

"How could someone do this without me knowing?"

"They are actually easy to install and only take seconds," Laz explained. "It could've been anybody. Considering where they were located, they could've installed them while standing there talking to you, and you wouldn't have been the wiser."

The weariness Angelo saw in her eyes moments ago was replaced with sadness. "That means I was right. Someone close to me has it in for me." She shook her head. "I can't stay here."

"Come here, *Cariño*." Angelo pulled her into his arms and placed a kiss on top of her head.

This might've been a job, but she felt right in his arms. He was behaving so out of character with her, it was almost scary. He didn't do relationships. Outside of his family and his close friends, he didn't let people get close. Yet, there was something about Zenobia that called to him.

Not caring that his friends were watching, he held her tight for a few minutes. At first, she was stiff in his arms, but only for a second before relaxing. With her forehead on his chest, she didn't say anything. It didn't sound like she was crying, and he was glad for that. He hated to see women cry.

After a few minutes, he eased her back, keeping his hands on her upper arms.

"Listen to me. We don't know who we're dealing with or why, but I promise we will find them. In the meantime, are you saying that you're going to let some asshole run you out of your home?"

He saw the moment some of the stubbornness he'd witnessed earlier seep back into her. She lifted her chin and pulled her shoulders back, fisting the ice pack in her hand and shaking it at him.

"You're right. I'm not letting someone scare me away from my own home. I've worked my butt off to finally have a place where Sofia and I feel safe. There is no way I'm letting someone take that from us!"

Angelo stiffened at her words. What the hell? That sounded as if she'd had other times when she was in danger. Times that she hadn't told them about.

A quick glance at his friends and he knew right away that they were thinking the same thing. Myles's left brow was cocked, and Laz's hazel-eyed gaze connected with Angelo's.

Instead of trying to get it out of her now, he'd wait. As they dug into her life more, the truth would eventually come out. He just hoped her secrets didn't get anyone of them killed.

"Take out the listening devices," Angelo instructed. "Whoever is behind this shit will reveal themselves soon enough, and we'll be ready for them."

Chapter Eight

Holding the phone between his shoulder and ear, Monty 'Rock' Rockwell reached for the pack of cigarettes on his desk and shook one out. He listened as his lawyer explained why it wasn't a good idea to move forward with the strip mall Rock wanted to purchase.

"I highlighted a few areas of concern on the paperwork that I'll send back to you. I know you want property in that area, but that mall has been in a decline for years, losing stores and in turn, losing customers. Rock, I think you should pass on this one. It's too deep in a hole."

Since he was twenty, Rock had worked his ass off and built a multimillion-dollar drug empire in Miami, pushing the purest cocaine and heroin money could buy. Fifteen years in the drug game, he had never planned to go straight until a few years ago when he almost lost everything. He had gotten sloppy. He had trusted the wrong people. The DEA's sting operation nearly cost him his life and the life he had built for himself. In the end, he'd come out on top. In the process, he had taken out DEA roaches who meant him no good.

After blowing their plans to hell at the last minute, Rock had decided it was time to go legit. Time and time again, the government had tried building a case against him. Each time they failed, but their last attempt had come too close. Never again. Never would he risk them getting close enough to rip his organization apart. He'd seen them do it too many times with some of his competitors, and do it successfully.

For the last few years, Rock had been putting his life in order and buying up businesses around the country like beauty salons, strip joints, and had recently purchased another liquor store. He was finally getting out of the drug game, despite it making him millions. Now he had enough legal businesses to set him up for life.

He rocked back in his leather desk chair and took a long drag from his cigarette. "You don't have to send the paperwork back to me," he finally said to his lawyer. "You haven't steered me wrong yet, and I trust your judgment. Do whatever necessary to take the deal off the table."

They talked for a few minutes longer before Rock disconnected the call. His LLC already owned a few strip malls in Miami Beach and Coral Gables, but he wanted one in Coconut Grove. This particular property was a foreclosure, but Rock was confident that he could bring it back to life. However, if his real estate attorney suggested passing, that's exactly what he planned to do.

Hearing a lawn mower, Rock swiveled his office chair around and faced the patio door that led out to a side yard of his massive Miami estate. He had a view of his pool as well as his own private beach just beyond it. He had fallen in love with the property after touring it once and put in an offer that would ensure he got the house. He had also wanted the properties on each side of him, not wanting any nearby neighbors. The owners hadn't been planning to sell, but he'd made an offer they couldn't resist.

After a quick knock, the door to his office burst open and Rock didn't have to turn around to see that it was his second-in-command. Gavin was the only person brave enough to walk in without being invited. They'd been best friends since they used to skip classes in high school, and were tighter than brothers. They would kill for each other and they had.

Rock turned toward the door and snuffed out the cigarette butt in the ashtray on the corner of his desk. He tossed the remaining pack of smokes into the top desk drawer.

"You might want to pull those back out. We have a situation."

At six-four and tipping the scale at two-hundred-and-fifty pounds, most people assumed Rock played professional football. Unlike him, though, Gavin—barely six feet tall and maybe a hundred and eighty pounds—looked like a harmless businessman. As one of Rock's top enforcers, those who hadn't heard of Gavin underestimated him at first sight, but they soon learned. He could take down a man twice his size with a perfectly placed punch in the throat or a bullet to the head without flinching. What Gavin lacked in bulk, he made up for in ruthlessness.

"Don't bring me any bad news," Rock said, as he pulled the dreadlocks that hung down his back away from his face and bound them with a thick rubber band. "You or someone else should be able to handle whatever has come up. Hell, that's why I pay yo' ass the big bucks."

"Someone shot up the beauty shop in Liberty City."

Rock slowly sat forward in his seat as unease settled around him like a thunderous cloud. In that neighborhood, the craziest shit happened, but who would dare shoot up a place he owned? No one who wanted to live. Rock might be taking his empire straight, but he wouldn't hesitate to snuff out anyone who destroyed what belonged to him.

"Anyone hurt?" he asked, standing to his full height and bracing himself as dread seeped into his veins. He already knew there was more. Otherwise, Gavin would've handled this and brought him up to speed after everything was cleaned up.

"Nah, Cassandra hadn't opened yet," he said, referring to the head stylist and manager of that location. "She was in the back office working on the books. When she heard the explosion of gunfire, she took cover under her desk and called the cops. Then she called me."

Rock nodded, a little of the anxiety easing from him. "All right. Get the place cleaned up ASAP so that they don't lose—"

"That property is the least of your problems."

"Why? What else has happened?"

"The Cameeso Cartel is coming for you. They're out for revenge and I'm pretty sure they're the ones behind this."

Almost a decade ago, Rock had destroyed their organization from the drug lord down to most of their street soldiers. He heard they were rebuilding, but he wasn't worried. They didn't have the manpower or the balls to come after him.

"Don't underestimate them," Gavin said, reading Rock's mind. "Word on the street is that they've reorganized and they're coming hard. Meaning they will go after everything you have and *anyone* who's important to you."

Rock's nostrils flared as he stared at his long-time friend, already knowing who he was referring to. Rock had made a promise years ago that he'd stay out of Zenobia's life and forget she ever existed. He rarely broke a promise and went to great lengths to keep his word. But if what Gavin proclaimed was true and Rock found out Zen might be in danger, all bets were off. He wouldn't let harm come to her again, and he would kill anyone who got in his way.

Chapter Nine

Enamored by her sweet and sultry voice, Angelo stood against the back wall of the recording studio, unable to take his gaze off of Zenobia. Hearing her music countless times on the radio was one thing, but watching her now, experiencing her perfectionism as she worked with the producer and an engineer, was a unique experience.

They had arrived a couple of hours ago. After going over Zenobia's schedule, Angelo had insisted on mixing up her routine in hopes of drawing out her enemy. Not only was she at the studio on a different day than planned, but they were at a new location. The first couple of hours were spent laying down tracks for two songs. Now Zenobia was singing a piece that she had finished writing the night before.

So talented. She wrote all but one of the songs on the new album, and no doubt the compilation would be a hit. Her tone, passionate and soulful with a slight rasp, seeped into Angelo's soul and left him in awe. Just when he thought she'd gone as far as she could go with a high note, she'd belt out another that sent chills down his spine. Except for maybe Mariah Carey, there weren't any other artists who could hit those notes so powerfully.

Zenobia suddenly stopped singing. Angelo stood straighter, not missing the frustration marring her lovely face.

She was in a small sound booth on the other side of the glass, standing in front of a microphone with headphones over her ears. This was the third time in a matter of minutes that she'd stopped. Each time was at the same spot in the song. It wasn't that she was forgetting the words. Her notebook was on a stand in front of her. Something else was going on.

She lifted her arm and twirled her index finger for the producer, Kevin, to start again. His engineer adjusted the various gauges and knobs on the mixing board. There seemed to be a hundred of them. A few minutes later, they had her start at the top.

Zenobia began again. This time her eyes were closed, unlike earlier when she glanced everywhere but at him. Was it his presence that threw her off? He hadn't considered that possibility, especially when she'd given the okay for him to listen in.

The singing and the music stopped again. This time, instead of having the producer and engineer start over, Zenobia didn't say anything. She didn't give any signals. Instead, she removed the headphones and stepped away from the mic. When she turned her back to him and the producer, Angelo wondered how often this happened. Maybe it was part of her process.

The producer huffed out a frustrated sigh and dropped his head back to stare at the black ceiling.

"Maybe we should call it a day," the engineer said.

Angelo didn't think that was a good idea. Especially since Zenobia had told him that her deadline for completing the album was quickly approaching.

"Let me talk to her." Angelo left the room before giving either of the men a chance to respond.

He stepped into the dimly lit hallway. As for studio buildings, the modern design and square footage was more impressive than he'd ever seen. The few that he'd been to were usually under a thousand square feet. Not this one. This space was at least twice the size. It had an inviting reception area, a small kitchen area, and several studios with sound booths. By request, Zenobia was the only client in the building, which meant she needed to make this time count. They only had another hour left.

Angelo walked the short distance down the hall and tapped on the door leading to the sound booth she was using. Not waiting for her to answer, he pushed the door open.

Zenobia turned, her troubled gaze meeting his before she glanced down at the floor. Her shoulders slumped and she sighed.

"Come here," Angelo said gently. She glanced at him again, and he gestured with a nod of his head for her to step into the hallway. He wasn't sure if the producer still had ears in the sound booth, but Angelo didn't take any chances. Not sure where the conversation would end up, he wanted a little privacy.

Zenobia didn't speak when she joined him, and suddenly Angelo wasn't sure what to say. So, he didn't say anything. He pulled her into his arms and loved the way she relaxed into him. It didn't matter how many women he'd been with, his connection to Zenobia was like nothing he had ever experienced. He wasn't sure what to do with what he was feeling for her.

"What's on your mind?" he asked, still holding her close.

She shook her head and the ponytail on top of her head brushed against his chin. "Nothing... No, everything. I can't focus."

"Is it me? I can wait out here while you finish up."

"It's not you. It's all me," she mumbled, her head still down and her voice filled with emotion.

Angelo leaned back and lifted her chin with his finger, forcing her to look at him. "Then talk to me. Tell me what's wrong."

"I have so many thoughts about everything floating around in my head. It's hard for me to feel..."

A long silence fell between them. "Feel what?" he prompted. "What aren't you feeling."

"Passion...joy. My life is a mess right now. Someone is

after me and I don't know who or why. You guys found listening devices in my house," she screeched, her eyes wide before she glanced around to see if anyone was in earshot. "I'm a little freaked out right now. I'm not in the mood to sing, but I have to finish this album."

Staring into her eyes, Angelo cupped her face. He wanted so bad to kiss her, but he couldn't. He needed to maintain some type of professionalism. Instead, he brushed the pad of his thumbs over her cheeks. Her baby-soft skin stirred something intense inside of him.

"I'm not a motivational speaker. So, I'm not sure what to tell you." He lowered his voice. "I know we have this fake relationship going and I'm your boyfriend, but maybe pretend for a moment...or at least another hour...that what we have is real. Sing to me. Pour your heart out in that song and make it about you and me."

She didn't respond, but some of the weariness in her eyes slipped away.

"So...no pretending for an hour?" Her hands slid up his chest and a shiver shot through Angelo. Maybe talking to her alone in the semi-dark hallway, a hallway that set the mood for making out, wasn't a good idea. "You're saying that you're mine and I'm yours?"

Instead of responding, Angelo tried throttling the dizzying desire suddenly racing through his veins. His intention was to give a pep talk, not give a green light to do what they both clearly wanted to do. Make out. He didn't want to recall all the sexual things he'd done to her in his dreams the night before, but damned if they weren't at the forefront of his mind.

No. He had to be strong for both their sakes. Yet, when he opened his mouth, he said, "The outside world can't touch you in here. It's just you and me. No one else."

"It's not just us. Kevin and his engineer are here. Besides, that kiss you planted on me the other day at Supreme has me wanting a repeat."

That kiss was hot and almost led to a point of no return,

Angelo thought, deciding not to voice the thought out loud. "Tell me what I can do to help?"

Zenobia lifted her gaze to his, mischief sparkling in her pretty eyes. "I might need a little motivation." Her words were spoken quietly, but Angelo heard them loud and clear. When her tongue slipped out, gliding lazily across her bottom lip, a low growl bubbled inside his chest. For a man known for his strong willpower, he had none when it came to her.

He shook his head. He shouldn't give in on what they both wanted, but when Zenobia's eyes darkened with hunger, Angelo couldn't help himself. He lowered his head and nibbled on her lower lip. Then her top one. He only intended to have a little taste, but her sweetness and how good her soft body felt against his chest made him yearn for so much more.

He crushed her to him, and Zenobia slid her arms around his neck, deepening the kiss. The last couple of days of trying to keep his hands and mouth to himself had been pure torture. He'd been doing well in keeping things between them professional, except for his vivid dreams at night of them together. The daytime was filled with his craving for her. Now this.

Longing spiraled through his body as they both moaned, the sound echoing in the hallway. No doubt she felt the bulge behind his zipper pressing against her stomach as his desire for her continued rising. His and Zenobia's relationship might've been fake, but what he felt each time she was in his arms was real. Very real. He had to be careful not to mistake the attraction and comfort they had with each other for anything other than it was—an assignment.

But why couldn't he get his body to adhere to what his brain knew? Each kiss was getting more intense, and right now, he wanted to be buried deep inside of her.

Whoa!

Angelo suddenly broke off the kiss. Chest heaving, he braced his hands on her shoulders and put some distance between them.

"You gotta stop kissing me like that," he half-joked. "I

can't take it."

Her laughter rippled through the hallway, and he was glad that he had been able to break some of her tension.

"Now go in there and sing for me."

She fisted the front of his shirt and pulled him close. Then she placed another lingering kiss on his lips before releasing him.

"In case I haven't mentioned it, you're an amazing boyfriend." She winked and returned to the sound booth, leaving him standing there still panting.

He ran his fingers through his hair and huffed out a breath. "I am so screwed."

*

"Let's start from the top, Zen. I'll count you down." Kevin's voice boomed into the sound booth minutes later.

Zenobia slipped the headphones back on as her gaze connected with Angelo. He winked and heat flooded her body. The man was too sexy for his own good. Pretending they were dating was turning out to be the easiest thing she'd had to do in a long time.

She released a slow, calming breath and waited for Kevin. When he lifted his hand, Zenobia readied herself and watched as he started the countdown with his fingers.

Three.

Two.

One.

Music started playing. A beautiful melody that she had worked on with them weeks ago, that went great with her lyrics. The music pierced something deep inside her soul as the words flowed from her mouth.

As the high and low pitches played through the headset, Zenobia's body swayed, arms and hands moved, punctuating every note and hitting them flawlessly. Her heart was full as she imagined her and Angelo making love under the moonlight. The next words of the song were a mixture of her past and her present. The good and the bad.

Betrayed and tossed to the side,

All I wanted to do was hide.
But you wouldn't let me,
You wouldn't let me be.
You came out of nowhere and promised me,
You promised me love.
When you found me, I found love.
When you found me, I found love.
You brought so much joy and wiped so many tears,
You even stood guard to block my many, many fears.
You've planted the seed and watered it with love and laughter,
And then promised that we would live happily ever after.
When you found me, I found love.
When you found me, I found love.

Angelo's unblinking gaze stayed on her as if taking in every word, melody, and heartfelt emotion of the song. When she wrote the lyrics, Zenobia imagined what it would be like to finally find that one person who could wipe away the hurts and fears of the past. Angelo might not be that man, but his presence in her life was right on time.

When Zenobia finished singing, the producer pumped his fist. "Yes! Daayum, girl. That was lit!"

Zenobia joined them in the studio, and Angelo pulled her into his arms, placing a kiss against her temple. "That was amazing, baby," he whispered. "You can sing for me anytime."

Kevin approached and shook Angelo's hand. "I don't know what you said or did to get all of that out of her, but I might need you to come back in a couple of days. We have another song to get through."

A lazy smile spread across Angelo's lips. "I'll be here," he said, staring down at her. With the respect radiating in his eyes, Zenobia could easily forget that they weren't a real couple. Now she understood why he was chosen to play the role of her love interest. He was good. He was damn good.

For the next half hour, Zenobia couldn't stop grinning as Kevin played her song back for her to listen to it. Even though there were some areas that needed tweaking, she was proud of the piece.

Angelo's phone buzzed and he glanced at the screen. "Myles is out back when we're ready."

Zenobia nodded. Since parking was practically non-existent, Angelo had arranged for Myles to drop them off at the studio and then pick them up. The day before, Angelo had drove her anywhere she wanted to go and Zenobia wished for some alone time with him. Then again, maybe it was good they wouldn't be alone because she was sure she'd want another sample of his sexy lips against hers.

After setting up another session with Kevin, she and Angelo headed down the hall that led to the back entrance. When they walked out, Myles was standing at the back door of the SUV.

Zenobia pulled up short. "Crap. I left my bag. I'll be right back."

She went back into the building and jogged down the hall, wondering how she'd managed to forget her oversized bag. "Angelo," she mumbled to herself. The man was such a distraction, and a good kisser. A real good kisser.

Smiling at the possibility of going another round with him, Zenobia rushed into the women's lounge. Retracing her steps to one of the stalls, she found the large Coach bag hanging from the hook on the back of the stall door. A quick search inside confirmed nothing was missing. Good thing they'd had the building to themselves.

Zenobia headed to the door, pulled it open and a scream ripped from her throat.

"Oh, good. You're still here. Why haven't you returned my calls?"

"Damn it, Stephen, you scared me!" With a hand on her chest, her heart pounded against her palm. "What are you doing here?"

"Looking for you. We need to—" His words were cut off when Myles wrapped his arm around Stephen's neck and roughly pulled him into the women's lounge.

Angelo was right behind him and reached for Zenobia.

"You all right?"

Heart beating a mile a minute, she nodded, unable to speak after witnessing how fast everything played out.

"Get off me!" Stephen choked out, pulling on Myle's forearm and trying to free himself. With one arm keeping Stephen in a choke hold, Myles used his free hand to quickly pat him down before shoving him into the vanity.

"What the heck's going on in here?" Kevin roared from the doorway. "Stephen? What are you doing? How'd you get in the building?"

"That's what I want to know," Angelo said, his arm sliding around Zenobia's waist.

Coughing and holding his throat, Stephen looked around the room with wide-eyed shock. "Dude, who the hell are you?" Then he glared at Zenobia. "Who is this chump?"

"My security," Zenobia said as Myles moved to the door, letting Kevin know that he and Angelo could take it from there.

"How'd you know she was here?" Angelo asked.

"Man, I ain't gotta tell you shit. If I want to talk to my girl, then—"

"See, that's where you're wrong," Angelo said. His deep voice was filled with venom as he moved closer, towering over Stephen by at least five inches. "She's mine now. So, I'll ask again. How'd you know she was here?"

Stephen's gaze bounced from Zenobia to Angelo, back to her again. He was always trying to act all hard, when in reality he was a cream puff, especially standing next to Angelo. Suddenly, she wondered what she ever saw in him. Then again, he was another example of her poor judgment.

Stephen might've had an amazing voice, but he came off as childish and silly. A year younger than her, at twenty-nine he looked more like twenty. His style probably didn't help. Tall and lanky, baggy clothes similar to what other rappers were wearing was his thing. He wore his hair in short twists with blond tips and tattoos covered much of his body, something Zenobia hated.

Angelo folded his arms across his chest. "Start talking."

Stephen looked at her. "So, it's like that, huh?"

"I told you I was seeing someone, but that's beside the point. How'd you know I was here?" His stony glare suddenly turned guilty, but he didn't respond. Zenobia got in his face. "How'd you know I was here?"

"Answer her!" Angelo bellowed when Stephen was slow to speak.

"I tracked her."

"Wh—what?" Someone could've knocked Zenobia over with a feather. "How are you tracking me? More importantly, why?"

Angelo stepped around her. "Hand over the phone."

Stephen chuckled. "Man, you got balls, but you better reconi—"

Angelo slammed him against the hand dryer and without a word, took the phone out of Stephen's back pocket. "Now unlock it." Stephen didn't move, only glowered at him before Angelo shoved the phone in his face. "Look at it."

"Steph, just do it and quit screwing around."

Once the phone was unlocked, Zenobia watched as Angelo opened an app on the home screen. It was as if he'd done it a hundred times, knowing exactly where to go and what he was looking for.

Zenobia glowered at Stephen. "I can't believe you've been tracking me. When did this start?"

"When we were dating."

"Why?" Angelo asked.

"Cause I wanted to know where she was. Why do you think?" he shouted, then turned his attention to Zenobia. "How you think I knew you was at Lake Lanier?"

"Wait. You were there?"

"Nah, I wasn't there, but who you think sent the flowers?" Then he glanced at Angelo and narrowed his eyes. "You took credit for my flowers, didn't you?"

Angelo shook his head in disgust and started rattling off one question after another. It became clear pretty quick that

Stephen knew nothing. He hadn't planted listening devices in her home, and he had nothing to do with the kidnapping.

But the question remained. Who was after her and why?

Chapter Ten

Zenobia laid in bed in her semi-dark bedroom, staring up at the tan and brown tray ceiling as the ceiling fan rotated around and around.

Four hours.

It had been four hours since she had retired to her little slice of heaven on the second floor, hoping to forget about the events of the last couple of days.

No such luck. Each time she closed her eyes, images of the attempted kidnapping played on loop inside her mind. Then there was the meeting at Supreme where she hired a security firm and, in the process, snagged a boyfriend. If that wasn't enough, she came home, to her sanctuary, the one place where she felt safe, only to find out that some lowlife had been monitoring her conversations. And she didn't even want to think about the encounter with Stephen.

Zenobia closed her eyes and shook her head, her hair brushing back and forth against the satin pillowcase. What the heck was her life coming to? She couldn't even find tranquility in her own home. Her ex and some unknown enemy was messing with her peace of mind. And the gorgeous hunk sleeping across the hall had her body tied up in knots. She was horny and tempted to march across the hall and slide into bed beside Angelo and have her way with him.

Sighing, Zenobia turned onto her stomach and punched the pillow before burying her face into it and growling. "Who am I kidding?" Her inner bad-girl had walked out on her years ago, leaving behind *Zen, the singing sensation*, as the media referred to her.

"I want my life back." Her muffled words sounded like gibberish even to her own ears, but they were true. She wanted the life that she'd had right after signing her first record deal, but before she became a household name. That time had been exciting, yet simple.

Now everything was different. She had money, a beautiful home, and her songs were being played on the radio day and night all over the world. Basically, she had everything she'd always wanted. Yet, she felt like a prisoner in her own house.

Zenobia lifted her head. "No. I'm not a prisoner. This is my home and I refuse to let anyone scare me to the point of cowering in my bedroom or behind double-locked doors."

She leaped up, adjusted the white tank top and shorts that she'd been lounging in, and padded to the door. With her ear against it, she listened to see if she heard Angelo. After they ate and cleaned the kitchen, he had double-checked the doors, set the alarm, and then they retired to their rooms. Since then, Zenobia hadn't heard a sound out of him.

She eased the door open and quietly crept down the stairs. Two o'clock in the morning was as good as any time for a snack. Salty, sweet, she didn't care. She just needed something to help take her mind off of her current situation.

She flipped on the light, illuminating the large space as she trekked across the cold tiled floor to the pantry. "What do I have a taste for?" Not seeing anything she wanted, she went to the cabinet for a glass.

"Kind of late to be eating isn't it?"

Zenobia screamed. The stemware slipped from her hand and chards of glass scattered across the floor.

"Aw hell," the deep voice murmured.

With a hand on her chest, Zenobia's frantic gaze went to

the stairs where Angelo stood, and her heart skidded to a halt. It should've been against the law for anyone to look that sexy in the middle of the night. She'd already been fantasizing about straddling him and then riding him like a cowgirl. Now here he stood, hair mussed, as if he had been running his fingers through it and bare chested with worn jeans hanging low on his hips. She itched to turn her earlier fantasy into reality, and in the process quench the sexual need throbbing between her thighs.

Slipping a black T-shirt, one that seemed to appear out of thin air, over his head, Angelo covered his glorious chest, then hurried the rest of the way down the stairs. He skirted around the center island and stopped short.

"Damn, you don't have on any shoes. Don't move."

Like she could actually move. She was still willing her heart rate back to normal after getting the crap scared out of her.

"I can take…" Zenobia gasped when he suddenly lifted her onto the center island as if she weighed nothing. Even the coldness of the quartz countertop against the back of her legs wasn't cold enough to cool the heat consuming her body. Her gorgeous bodyguard boyfriend had just revealed another skill in his arsenal. Not only was he smart, fearless, and could make a woman hot and bothered with just a smile, he was also ridiculously strong.

"Sit tight," he said, and bent down and picked up the larger pieces of glass. That's when Zenobia noticed the handle of the gun in the back waistband of his jeans. Even trained to be a good marksman, Zen hated guns. She'd been forced to learn how to use one, but hadn't seen or touched one in years.

"Do you always walk around the house with a gun?" she asked when he returned from the mudroom with the broom and made quick work of sweeping up the glass.

"No, but I do have it on me almost always when I hear someone creeping around the house in the middle of the night."

Her cheeks burned. So much for her stealth abilities. "Sorry I woke you. I tried to be quiet." She wasn't sure how he'd heard her considering the stairs were carpeted and the floors didn't squeak.

"I'm a light sleeper, and there's no need to apologize. This is your home. I just wanted to make sure everything was all right."

"By sneaking up on me?"

Angelo chuckled. "Scaring you wasn't my intent."

He finished sweeping, and Zenobia started to jump down from the counter, but he stopped her with a hand on her thigh.

"Hold up."

She should be used to the zing that coursed through her body whenever he touched her, but apparently, she wasn't. A stupefying tremor of lust rocked her body and had her toes curling. Pretending they were a couple wasn't going to be the hard part over the next couple of weeks. Keeping her body in check and her heart protected were going to be nearly impossible.

"I'll be right back."

He disappeared to the mudroom, and returned seconds later with a pair of her flip-flops. She usually kept a few in a small basket near the door that led to the swimming pool. Instead of handing her the shoes, he blew her mind when he gently gripped her ankle and slid them onto her feet. It might've been a simple act, but the gesture was one of the most sensual things he could've done for her.

Once he helped her down, Angelo rinsed his hands in the kitchen sink. "It's two o'clock in the morning. What are you doing up?"

"Couldn't sleep. I figured I'd come down for some water and a snack."

"What type of snack?"

"Um, I'm thinking an ice cream sundae. I can make us both one if you want." She started grabbing items from the walk-in pantry. When she stepped back into the kitchen, her arms were filled with chopped pecans, M&Ms, sprinkles and gummy bears. Then she pulled out a container of vanilla ice cream, as well as butter pecan and rocky road ice cream. From the refrigerator she grabbed whipped cream, chocolate sauce, a small container of pineapples, and cherries.

Once she was sure she had everything, she glanced at Angelo. "What do you want on yours?"

"Seriously?" His eyes were wide as he looked over everything that covered the oversize countertop. "You're going to eat all of this?"

She *tsk*ed and slammed her hands on her hips. "Well, not all at the same time. I like to have options. Oh my God, please don't tell me you're a vanilla kind of guy."

He flashed that wicked grin that had peeked out earlier, and again sent heat rushing through her body. "Sweetheart, there is nothing vanilla about me." He winked at her, and his sexual magnetism had her fighting the need to be up close and personal with him. Before all was said and done, Zenobia had a feeling that her inner bad-girl would make an appearance. She was going to have this man, and there wouldn't be anything fake about all that she planned to do with him.

Her lascivious gaze followed Angelo as he moved around the kitchen. He set a couple of tall glasses on the counter. "What were you planning on drinking?"

"Water."

He removed the water pitcher from the refrigerator, poured two glasses and handed her one. After returning the pitcher to the refrigerator, he grabbed some bowls from a cabinet and placed them on the counter.

"It's been a while since I've had ice cream." He went for the butter pecan, and she added rocky road to her bowl.

"Really? What's your snack of choice?"

"I'm not a big snacker."

No kidding. With a body like that, showing no fat anywhere, it was obvious he rarely indulged in junk food.

"On occasion, though, I'll go a little crazy and eat some

chips or popcorn."

Zenobia strolled to the pantry. "Well, if you prefer, I have both."

"Nah, this is cool." He carried his bowl to the other side of the counter and claimed one of the barstools.

Zenobia added extra nuts, M&Ms, and pineapple to her ice cream, but hesitated before adding anything else. The last thing she wanted to do was make a pig of herself in front of him, but she wanted chocolate sauce and a couple of cherries. She risked a peek at Angelo, not surprised to see him watching her.

"Do you, baby. I won't judge."

Now that the house was free of listening devices, she was surprised that he used terms of endearment. Before they were playing up their fake relationship for anyone listening, but now they didn't have to pretend. At least when they were at the house.

"As you've probably guessed, I have a sweet tooth and enjoy midnight snacks."

"Oh, so eating at two o'clock in the morning is a norm for you?" He stuffed a spoonful of ice cream into his mouth and slowly pulled the spoon back out. Zenobia's knees went weak as his dark, spellbinding gaze nailed her in place as he licked the utensil.

Who knew watching someone eat ice cream could be such an erotic experience? Was he intentionally trying to turn her on? He had to know how suggestive the move looked, making her mind wonder at what else he could do with his tongue.

Don't even go there.

This is a fake relationship.

We're just pretending.

It didn't matter how many times she tried reminding herself of that fact, a part of her didn't want to pretend. The man stirred something so salacious inside of her that she wanted to explore the foreign feeling and see where it led.

"No, I wouldn't say eating this late is a norm, but I am a

snacker," she finally said. "That's why I have to work out so much. I'm trying to keep all the crap I eat from landing on my hips."

His gaze did a slow crawl down her body, lingering on her hips, before working its way back up. "Whatever you're doing is definitely working."

Heat crept into her cheeks, and Zenobia looked away. She grabbed the remote control from the counter and pointed it at the Bluetooth speaker sitting on a shelf across the room. Within seconds, Kenny Lattimore's smooth baritone filled the quietness of the kitchen as "Stay On Your Mind" flowed through the speaker. She turned the volume down a little, then took the seat next to Angelo.

They ate their ice cream while listening to music, and Zenobia had to admit, she liked his company. It wasn't often that she was immediately comfortable with someone, especially with a man, but Angelo wasn't just any man. He was a man who she felt an intense connection with, a connection she hadn't experienced in a very long time. It didn't hurt that he was the total package, at least from what she knew of him. That realization sparked a thought.

"Are you, um…in a relationship?" she asked.

He turned his head slightly to look at her. "Sweetheart, if I was in a relationship, I wouldn't be pretending to be your man. I wouldn't have taken the assignment."

"You can choose which assignments you want?"

"For the most part, but I rarely turn down assignments unless there's some type of conflict of interest, or scheduling issues."

"Sooo, there's no special woman in your life?"

He chuckled. "No one but my mother and my sisters. Why? Are you interested?"

"Yes. No. I mean…" Her pulse quickened, and she wished the floor would just open up and swallow her whole. "I—I was just wondering."

He studied her for a few minutes longer, then flashed a sexy grin. Her pulse amped up. She loved when he smiled. It transformed the hard lines of his chiseled features and had her belly doing funny things.

He returned his attention back to his ice cream. "I'm not really the relationship type. Don't get me wrong. I love women, but I don't do long-term commitments."

"Let me guess. You had a horrible childhood. Your parents fought all the time and their relationship ended in divorce. Since then, you're afraid to get involved with anyone for fear the same will happen to you."

Angelo chuckled and shook his head. "That's some imagination you have there, but no."

"Oh, so some woman hurt you and you're not willing to give your heart to another."

His expression turned serious. "There used to be someone special, but things didn't work out. I can't be with someone I can't trust, and let's just say, she wasn't the most trustworthy person."

A stab of guilt bloomed inside Zenobia's chest. She might not have really come out and lied to him, but during the questioning earlier, she hadn't been completely honest. But it was for the best. Some things were left better unsaid.

"As for my parents," he continued, "They're the opposite of what you just described."

Zenobia listened as he told her about how his parents had fallen in love at first sight. She didn't believe that was possible, but considering they'd been married for almost forty years, maybe there was something to it. He spoke fondly of his three brothers and two sisters and talked about how close they all were.

Hearing Angelo speak so highly of his tight-knit family only reminded Zenobia of the dysfunction she'd grown up with. Heck, at thirty, her life was still dysfunctional in some ways. What would it be like to have parents who loved each other and adored their children? How would it feel to hang out and confide in siblings who you could call on anytime for anything?

She would never know, but if she was lucky, maybe one

day she would get married. Then she'd have a bunch of children and create the life she always wanted. A normal life filled with love and laughter.

"Besides music, what else do you enjoy?" Angelo asked.

Music was her life. Considering how her career had suddenly taken off, she didn't really have time for much of anything else. "I enjoy running. Well, I used to before someone tried snatching me off the street," she said it jokingly, but deep down, the incident still freaked her out.

"Yeah, I could see where that would take the fun out of jogging outside. I think for now on, even after we catch the perps, you shouldn't run alone."

Zenobia sighed as she continued eating. "You're probably right. For now, I'll just run on my treadmill, unless you're willing to go for a run with me sometime. At least while you're still around."

Angelo nodded. "That could be arranged. What else do you enjoy doing?"

"Reading, but nothing too heavy, and I like to swim."

"I noticed the Olympic-sized pool out back."

"Oh, please, it's not that big, but I've always enjoyed swimming. I had hoped to make it to the Olympics one day."

"Really? You're that good?"

"Not really." She gave a little laugh. "It was just something I dreamed of accomplishing."

"But instead you got into music, huh?" She nodded. "How long have you been singing?"

"Since I was a kid. My mother loved music and had an amazing voice. Whenever she cooked or clean, she would sing. Everything from R&B to country. After a while, I sang along with her. I didn't realize how good I was until my freshman year. My high school did a production of *Fame,* and I got the lead role."

"Damn, that's cool."

It had been cool. Something she would never in her life forget, for more reasons than one. Singing and performing gave her the outlet she needed to be herself, especially as her mother's mental health declined. As long as she was at school, Zenobia didn't have to worry about stealing so that she could eat. She also didn't have to be at home where she had to watch her mother battle with the voices inside her head. All Zenobia had wanted was for her mother to be healthy so that they could go back to the way things used to be.

A sudden bout of sadness pierced her heart and it took everything within her not to succumb to the emotion. She would never forget opening night of the play. All of her friends had family in the audience, but she had no one. She had never known her father, and at that time, her mother rarely left the house.

Angelo touched her hand and Zenobia startled.

"Where's your mother now?"

After a slight hesitation she said, "She committed suicide months before I turned sixteen."

Chapter Eleven

"Aww, baby. I'm sorry."

As Angelo listened to her tell him about one of the darkest times in her life, all he wanted to do was gather her into his arms to comfort her. That wouldn't be a good idea. For one, he couldn't promise that he could stop at just a hug. Seeing her in the tank top with no bra on and the tiny shorts already had him in an uncomfortable state of arousal. Secondly, he needed to keep her talking. Needed to make her feel comfortable with him in order to learn as much about her and her past as possible.

But hearing Zenobia discuss her mother's death, and how she'd been bounced around in foster care, was hard to hear. So often, he took his big loving family for granted, forgetting that there were so many who didn't have the great life he'd had growing up.

"Once I aged out, I bummed around the country, doing a little of this and that." She shrugged. "My big break came when there was open mic night at a club I hung out at. Octavia happened to be there, and like they say, the rest is history."

"At what point did you start stealing?" He hadn't planned to bring up the talent, but curiosity got the best of him.

Her flushed cheeks deepened to crimson. "I—I...I started when I was in high-school. Sometimes that was the only way my mom and I ate. She'd gotten to the point to where it was hard for her to keep a job, and though I worked a few hours a week at a record store, I wasn't making enough money." Zenobia shrugged. "I did what I had to do to survive."

"And now?"

"Now..." She shook her head. "I'm not sure what made me take your wallet. I'm so sorry. I haven't done anything like that in years, and I promise I'll never steal from you again."

He noticed she hadn't agreed to never steal again, just not steal from him.

Angelo nodded, sensing she was still holding something back. Something critical. He wanted to question her more about where she'd been and what she did while floating around the country.

Instead he said, "Tell me more about Octavia."

As Angelo stood and walked around to the other side of the counter to rinse his bowl, Zenobia started talking about her manager. Octavia might be a drama queen and a bit high strung, but it seemed as if she was serious about business. Sounded like she played the role of both agent and manager in Zenobia's career. She negotiated contracts and taught her everything from what to expect with music producers to how to dress to impress. The woman was even responsible for some of Zenobia's onstage choreography.

"Octavia might be a pain in the ass, but she propelled my career forward faster than I could've done on my own."

"Sounds like she's played an important role in your success. Like a mentor of sorts," Angelo said as he leaned on the counter facing Zenobia. He was trying like hell to listen to everything she had to say, but standing in front of her was a bad idea. His gaze kept dropping to her breasts, where her nipples pushed against the ribbed material of her tank top. Beautiful and sexy, she had a body he would love to...

Focus, man. Focus.

His thoughts were going into dangerous territory. A territory that could have him doing something stupid, like kissing her again. Or worse, throwing her over his shoulder and carrying her back upstairs where he could thoroughly worship that luscious body.

"Yeah, she has, but I just…" Zenobia's words trailed off, but Angelo had a feeling he knew what she was going to say. During one of their private conversations earlier, she had mentioned not being satisfied with her life. Not sure if what she was building was what she really wanted. She loved her fans, and the lifestyle her career provided, but felt something was missing.

Angelo reached over and placed his hand on top of hers. He loved touching her. Probably a little too much. "You just what?" he prompted.

"I just don't know if I want to do this any longer."

He removed his hand and frowned. "Do what? Sing?"

She nodded. "I want to sing. Singing stirs something so passionately deep down in my soul, but I don't know if I'm cut out for all that goes with having a music career. Performing, spending hours in the studio, and constantly being in the spotlight is starting to take its toll. I like my privacy too much. Which is impossible to have these days. I can barely go anywhere just for fun without showing up in entertainment news."

Angelo leaned on the counter. "I get it, but didn't you think about that before you signed with a label?"

"I did, but… Even though I've dreamed of being rich and famous, I didn't really think about what came with this type of fame. Besides, most people dream of making it big, but there's a small part of us that doesn't think it will actually happen."

"But it did happen."

"Yeah, and everything happened so fast. It's been a whirlwind and more than I ever imagined. I just…I just want a normal life."

"What would *normal* look like to you?"

"Good question. I've never had a normal life," she said quietly, glancing down in her bowl where the ice cream was starting to melt.

That one statement spoke volumes, confirming to Angelo that there was something she wasn't sharing. He felt it in his gut, and his gut rarely steered him wrong.

"I have no idea what a normal life would look like."

"Well, maybe you should think about what you want. In the meantime, come here." He strolled to the edge of the counter and reached for her hand. "Dance with me."

"What?" Zenobia gave a little laugh. "Here? In the kitchen?"

"Yeah, why not? We have Luther Vandross playing in the background. We have plenty of space to get our groove on, and you want to feel normal. So, let's dance."

This was such a bad idea, but she looked as if she carried the weight of the world on her shoulders. Angelo wanted to believe that he was asking her to dance for her own good, but if he was honest, he longed to have her in his arms again.

Even though she was shaking her head, she let him guide her to the side of the center island. He set his gun on the counter.

"I can't believe we're going to dance in the kitchen. Who does that?" she mumbled as he pulled her close. Holding one of her hand, he brought it to his chest while his free arm slid around her narrow waist. "I don't think this is normal."

"It can be," he said quietly near her ear. "Now relax."

Relax? Ha! His body was wound so tight, he sounded like a hypocrite telling her to relax. His pulse pounded in his ear as he struggled to keep the lower part of his body in check as they started moving to the music. It wasn't working. Her clean fresh fragrance permeated his senses, and Angelo bent slightly, his cheek brushing the side of her head. Inhaling deeply, her scent filled him, reminding him of springtime and a fresh ocean breeze. She smelled like heaven and moved with a gracefulness that had his body vibrating with need.

Zenobia slowly slid her arms around his neck and

molded against him as she hummed along with the song. It was so easy to get lost in the moment. They moved as one, totally in sync as if they danced together all the time.

Yeah, getting her to dance with him might've been a bad idea, but damn if he wasn't loving having her in his arms. The more time he spent with Zenobia, the more she was getting under his skin like no other woman had ever done, especially not as quickly.

"I take it you dance often," she said.

"Actually, not as much as I used to, but whenever there's a family gathering at my parents' home, there's always singing and dancing. Most of us love R&B. My father, not so much." Angelo chuckled, recalling the number of times his father grumbled about them playing songs over and over. "He's more into Latin rock."

"He's Latino?" Zenobia asked.

"Yeah, and my mother is African-American. Their taste in music might be their only differences, except for maybe some foods. But for the most part, my pops likes anything she cooks, except for collard greens. He still can't get with those."

They both laughed.

"Your parents sound wonderful."

They were, but what Angelo didn't want to do was regale her with stories that might have her sinking back into her feelings regarding her mother. He couldn't imagine losing either of his parents the way her mother had died.

The song changed to Luther's "A House Is Not A Home," and Zenobia released a soft sigh. "This is one of my favorites by him," she said.

"*Really?* Mine too." Angelo held her tighter, and placed a kiss on the side of her head without thinking. That shit was going to get him into trouble. He had to keep reminding himself that he was on assignment. They were in a fake relationship, but pretending with her felt a little too real. Telling himself that he was only playing the role to get close enough for her to feel comfortable opening up to him was bullshit. He was feeling this woman. Feeling her way more than he should. And the sweet torture of her firm breasts pressed against his chest wasn't helping.

Focus, man, he told himself again. Maybe he should walk around with a recording of those words, something that could remind him whenever his thoughts veered in the wrong direction.

To distract himself, Angelo started singing along with Luther Vandross. Like Zenobia, lyrics and melodies aroused something inside him and he couldn't help but sing along. Most of the time, he'd start singing without being conscious of what he was doing.

"Wait a minute." Zenobia stopped moving and Angelo loosened his hold on her, wondering what he'd missed. She leaned her head back to look at him. "You sing too?" she said with awe and shock in her voice. "You cook, clean, protect, *and* sing? *Dude.* You're almost too good to be true."

Angelo threw his head back and laughed. "Baby, I'm the total package."

"Yeah, I'm starting to see that."

He pulled her back into his arms and started singing again as they moved to the rhythm of the beat.

"Your voice is so smooth and rich, almost hypnotic." She looked at him. "Have you ever sung professionally?"

"No."

"Why not? Angelo, I'm serious. You can *sang.* Everybody can't sing like Luther, and you're killing it. Sing something else."

Shaking his head, he couldn't keep his smile at bay. "So what? You want me to protect you *and* perform for you?"

"We have to get you into the studio. Let's do a duet together. Your voice is too incredible not to be shared."

"Not going to happen."

"Why not?"

"For the same reason you're second-guessing your career. If by chance I get discovered, my life might change the way yours did. No more privacy. No more singing just for the love of it." He shook his head. "Nah, I'm not interested."

She nodded. "I hear you."

They were still dancing as the song ended and another one started. Johnny Gill's melodious voice filled the space as he sung about the soul of a woman. It was another one of Angelo's favorite songs.

"Sing," Zenobia demanded, and Angelo loosened his hold on her and burst out laughing again.

"Damn, woman. Bossy much?"

"You know, I don't want to pull the you-work-for-me-card, but I will because that's just how much I want to hear you sing."

He shook his head and pulled her back into his arms, and snug against his body. Without further prompting, Angelo started singing again. He was glad he did, especially when Zenobia moaned and snuggled into him more, but then his heart jolted. Desire pulsed through his veins when she ran her fingers through the back of his hair. His shaft leaped to attention. Unbeknownst to her, his scalp was one of his erogenous zones, and she was killing him. No doubt she felt his erection against her stomach, but she didn't say anything. Instead, she ground against him, her hands still in his hair.

He growled, the low sound rumbling in his chest. "If you keep that up…" he murmured against her ear. When she didn't stop, his hands slid down to her curvaceous ass which fit perfectly in his palms. He cupped her cheeks, then squeezed, pulling her firmly against him. "Zenobia," he warned gruffly, his body tight with need.

She looked up at him, her eyes like molten lava and her parted lips begged to be kissed. Angelo couldn't stop himself. He dipped his head and covered her mouth with his. A hunger like what he experienced the last time he kissed her burned through his body.

Before when they kissed, it had been a test to see how she'd respond to him, but this… This kiss was so much more. More potent. More passionate. More mind-blowingly intense. The velvety softness of her lips made his need to taste more of her grow like an out-of-control windstorm. He couldn't get enough.

Music all but forgotten, Angelo backed her to a nearby wall. As he deepened their lip-lock, he slid his hand under her shirt, marveling at the softness of her skin as he cupped her breast. Heat blasted through his body. The little control he had when they first started—gone. He wanted her. Wanted her more than he'd wanted any woman in a long time.

His mind screamed for him to stop, but the stiff bulge inside of his pants pressed firmly against his zipper wanted him to keep going. He brushed the pad of his thumb over her taut nipple, and Zenobia gasped. She trembled against him, whimpering as he tweaked, teased, and tugged the hardened peak.

Zenobia ripped her mouth from his and groaned, the sensual sound turning him on more. Her hands were back in his hair. "Don't stop. Please, don't stop."

That was all the encouragement Angelo needed. He trailed a path of feathery kisses along her jaw and worked his way down the scented column of her neck. He didn't stop until his lips reached her breast. She was more than a handful and he cupped her mound, lowered his head and swiped his tongue across her nipple.

Zenobia whimpered, gripping his hair tighter as she bucked against him. Her erotic moans only made Angelo want to experiment more with her delectable body.

Three loud consecutive beeps from Angelo's phone, and it was like ice water being poured over his head. He pulled back slightly and Zenobia's nipple plopped out of his mouth.

Shit. What the hell was wrong with him?

He staggered upright, struggling to catch his breath and pissed that he'd lost sight of what he was supposed to be doing. Simultaneously, he reached for the gun on the counter, and pulled his phone from the back pocket of his jeans.

"What?" Zenobia asked next to him, her chest heaving as she pulled her tank top into place. "What is it?"

"An alarm. Someone's on the property."

Angelo opened the security app and pulled up the cameras that would give him a view of outside. Earlier that day, Supreme had sent several teams out to update Zenobia's security system. They had installed cameras outside of the home and had placed sensors strategically around the perimeter of the huge yard and along the sides of the driveway. No one could get close to the house without them being alerted.

A vehicle drove up the long driveway toward the house.

"Do you know someone with a dark SUV, maybe a Jeep?" Angelo asked. He started to call Myles, who was on watch outside, but received a text from him.

Three people. Man driving. A woman in front and back.

"Kira's boyfriend has a black jeep," Zenobia said, walking toward the front of the house before Angelo gently tugged on the back of her tank top.

"Hold up." He opened the door of the hall closet and quickly perused the items inside. Seeing a lightweight running jacket, he pulled out the garment. "Here put this on and zip it up."

A possessiveness Angelo hadn't experienced in a long while engulfed him. Protecting her was a given, but he sure as hell didn't want another man gawking at her enticing body.

With one arm loosely around her waist, Angelo guided her toward the front door. He motioned for her to stop a few feet away near the entrance of a sitting room and brought his index finger to his mouth, signaling for her to be quiet.

As he inched toward the door, someone fiddled with the lock and doorknob. Zenobia had already told them that her housekeeper and cousin were the only two who'd had keys to her home. While updating the security system, they had changed all the locks.

Angelo glanced through the peephole, recognizing Kira from the photos Zenobia had shown him. He shot off a quick text to Myles, letting him know who the visitor was.

"It's Kira," he whispered, just as the woman got more insistent with ringing the bell, before she started pounding on the door.

Zenobia frowned. "What the heck is she doing here in the middle of the night?"

Angelo went to the alarm control panel that was in the front foyer near the door and disarmed it before walking back to where Zenobia stood. "Myles said that there are two other people. In a minute, let them in. I'll be right beside you."

As they moved forward, Angelo secured his pistol into the back of his waistband. Once he pulled his shirttail over it, he nodded for Zenobia to open the door.

Chapter Twelve

Open the door?

Heck, that was the last thing Zenobia wanted to do. Angelo's hands and mouth had rocked her to the core, and her body was still pulsating. The rousing heat between her thighs needed tending to. Instead of inviting in company, what they should be doing was heading upstairs to finish what he started.

"Zenobia." Angelo's deep voice put a halt to the battle going on in her mind. His hand on her lower back wasn't helping her situation. It only reminded her of how he made her skin tingle only moments ago.

It scared her to think that had the alarm not sounded, she would've let him have his way with her. And no doubt she would've enjoyed every tantalizing moment.

Who does that?

Zenobia didn't even know the guy, not really, but she wanted him bad enough to leave Kira and whoever else outside on the front stoop.

"Go ahead and open the door," Angelo urged.

Without a word, Zenobia unlocked the door and pulled it open. "Do you have any idea what time it is?" she bit out, glaring at her cousin who looked fresh and awake, as if it was nine o'clock in the morning instead of the middle of the night.

"I know exactly what time it is, but what's up with the lock? My key didn't work," Kira said as she stepped across the threshold. "I was about to..." Her words trailed off when Angelo moved to stand next to Zenobia. Her cousin's gaze did a slow, appreciative sweep down his body. She started at his tousled hair and worked her way to his untied Timberland boots. "Oh...my. No wonder it took you so long to come to the door."

Zenobia wasn't a violent person, but right now it took every ounce of control not to scratch her cousin's eyes out for checking out Angelo. Who could blame her, though? The man was too gorgeous to miss. Powerfully built. Sexy as hell. No, she couldn't blame Kira for noticing.

"It's almost three o'clock. Why are you here?" Zenobia asked as she closed the door.

"Wait." Kira stopped her. "I have a surprise for you."

At that moment, someone nudged the door open and Sofia walked in, Elijah following behind with two suitcases. Shock, followed by a burst of joy, slammed into Zenobia.

"Oh my God, *Mamita!* What are you doing here?" Zenobia lunged forward and wrapped her arms around the woman who she loved like a mother. The last three and a half weeks with her gone had been tough. Not just because of the crazy occurrences, but because Sofia was not just a housekeeper, or mother-like figure, she was Zenobia's heart. The one constant in her life for over twelve years, and she hated when they were apart.

"God, I've missed you," Zenobia murmured into the older woman's neck, holding onto her like a lifeline. She understood Sofia's need to return to where she'd grown up in Mexico, but Zenobia hated the separation.

At 5'4" with salt-and-pepper hair and lightly tanned skin, Sofia didn't look a day over fifty, though she was in her early sixties. She might've been petite, but she had a huge heart filled with so much compassion and love.

"You're not supposed to be back for another few days,"

Zenobia said, her arms still around her dear friend.

"I've missed you, *mija*." Sofia lowered her voice. "And I had a feeling."

She didn't have to elaborate. Zenobia already knew what that meant. In the past, when Zenobia was having a bad day or was having trouble, her *mamita* got a sixth sense about it. It didn't matter if they were nowhere near each other, Sofia got that *feeling* that she once described as a light tickle on the back of her neck. They weren't biologically related, but since meeting in Miami years ago, they had an unexplainable connection.

Sofia pulled back and held Zenobia at arm's length. "*Que le paso a tu ojo?*"

Her English was fairly good, and she only spoke Spanish when it was just the two of them, or when she didn't want others to understand.

"I fell," Zenobia said regarding her eye, but Sofia wasn't buying it. She narrowed her eyes and twisted her mouth in that way that let Zenobia know that she knew she was lying.

"We'll talk, but first I want you to meet someone. *Mamita*, this is Angelo, and Angelo, this is Sofia," Zenobia said proudly, and then introduced Kira, as well as Elijah who had just returned from taking Sofia's bags down the hall to her bedroom,

"*Es un placer conocerla, señora,*" Angelo said, as he reached for her left hand and brought the back of it to his lips.

Zenobia smiled and shook her head when the older woman batted her long eyelashes and giggled like a schoolgirl.

"Pleasure to meet you, too," Sofia said. Normally, her accent was heavier when she returned from Mexico. Not this time. Not with that statement.

She stood in front of Angelo, eyeing him thoughtfully. Though there hadn't been many, Zenobia always introduced Sofia to the men in her life. She trusted the woman's judgment. Never one to withhold her opinion, Sofia would occasionally mention that Zenobia's discernment regarding men was off.

Granted, Angelo was just playing a role, but still, Zenobia wondered what Sofia would think of him. He'd told her earlier in the day that mothers loved him. He might've said it jokingly, but he was so charming, she bet there was truth to the comment.

A smile lifted the corners of Sofia's lips and she lovingly patted Angelo on the cheek like one would do to their child. Leaning in, she spoke quietly, only loud enough for him to hear.

"Gracias," he said, flashing that damn grin again. The grin that always ignited an intense sensation to scurry through Zenobia's body.

"It's been a long day. I go to bed now." Sofia embraced Zenobia again and gave her that customary squeeze before releasing her. She thanked Kira and Elijah for the ride, and then bid them all a good night.

"It's nice to finally meet you," Kira said to Angelo.

Angelo gave a slight nod and slid his arm possessively around Zenobia. "Same here. I've heard a lot about you."

Kira beamed. "Really? All good, I hope."

"Absolutely."

"Why was Sofia on such a late flight?" Zenobia asked her cousin. "I talked to her last night. She didn't say anything about returning today. Otherwise, I would've picked her up or at least sent a car for her."

Kira yawned, reminding Zenobia just how late it was. "She was expected in hours ago, but because of the weather in Houston, her layover got extended. I think she wanted to surprise you. She called me early this morning with her itinerary."

Zenobia nodded. There was probably more to this little surprise. She'd talk to Sofia in the morning to find out what was really going on. Or maybe it was that *feeling* Sofia had that brought her home earlier.

"So, you two are dating?" Elijah asked, his dark brows slanted into a frown.

"And who are you?" Angelo asked smoothly, even

though Zenobia had showed him pictures of everyone close to her. He seemed unfazed by Elijah's skepticism.

"This is Kira's boyfriend," Zenobia explained.

"Zen, exactly what do you know about this guy? Kira hasn't said anything about him." Elijah's gaze bored into Angelo. "How'd you meet?"

"What's wrong with you?" Kira asked, looping her arm through his. "Since when did me or Zen have to tell you about who she's dating?"

"I just don't want some chump trying to take advantage of her. He shows up out of nowhere, and she's got him spending the night here. Nah, somethin' ain't right."

Zenobia fought to control the sudden annoyance bubbling inside of her. "Elijah, not that it's any of your business, but Angelo and I have been together for a while. I met him one morning when I was out jogging, and we hit it off."

"Sweetheart, you don't have to explain anything to him." Angelo's cool, calm demeanor was on full display and Zenobia forced herself to relax. Elijah had always been kind to her, even treating her like a sister at times when the three of them hung out, but this suspicious attitude spilling from him was new.

"Speaking of hitting." Elijah nodded his head toward Zenobia. "She starts dating you and all of sudden she's walking around with a black eye."

"He didn't hit me!" she snapped, bristling at the accusation.

Kira tugged on Elijah's arm. "Why would you assume he's done anything to Zen? She already told you the other day that she fell."

"I'm not buying that shit. Nobody falls and gets a black eye."

"Hold up," Zenobia started, but Angelo silenced her when he tightened his arm around her waist.

"I appreciate your concern for my woman, but you have nothing to worry about. I would never do anything to hurt her. As a matter of fact, I'm taking very good care of her." The innuendo in his words and tone sent heat rushing through Zenobia as her mind went back to their passionate moment in the kitchen.

Zenobia turned slightly in his arms and placed her hand on his chest as she gazed up at him. Yes, this little charade was only temporary, but she couldn't help the way her heart beat double-time when he said stuff like that.

Angelo stared into her eyes and didn't miss a beat when he leaned down and kissed her sweetly. Zenobia knew she should, but at the moment, it was too darn hard to remember that what they were sharing wasn't real.

"You guys are too cute together," Kira said wistfully, as if not knowing they were pretending.

"Thanks. We're happy," Zenobia said, zeroing in on Elijah.

"Is that right?" Elijah stepped out of Kira's hold and moved closer to Angelo. They were similar in height, but Elijah had at least twenty pounds on Angelo. "Because if he's mistreating you, he's going to have to deal with me."

"You know what? You seem awfully angry about our relationship. What's that about? Shouldn't your concern be on your woman?"

"It is. When Zen is hurt or upset, that means Kira is, too. So, I'm not going to sit back and let some pretty-boy punk like you hurt her."

Though Angelo kept his expression cool and calm, his breathing changed. "Well, I can tell you now that you'll never have to worry about Zenobia. *Ever.* She's in very good hands."

"That remains to be seen. If she ends up with another black eye or any harm comes to her, I'm coming for you."

"Man, be careful," Angelo warned in a low, threatening growl. He dropped his arm from around Zenobia's waist. "You don't know me. So, don't be making…"

Elijah charged at Angelo. A soft gasp slipped through Zenobia's lips, and her hands flew to her mouth. As if expecting the move, Angelo jabbed him in the ribs with the quickness of a ninja. Then he slammed Elijah into the closet door and jerked his right arm back, keeping him pinned against the door.

Zenobia curled her hand around Angelo's bicep, his taut muscles contracting under her touch. "Don't," she said quietly. She had no clue what Elijah was capable of, but she knew the damage Angelo could do. One wrong move and he could easily break his limb. Elijah might've been out of line, but she didn't want him hurt.

"I'll let him go, right after I make something clear," Angelo said with the same calm as moments ago. He leaned his head closer to Elijah. "If you ever come at me like that again, I'm going to lay your big ass out."

"Uh, we should go," Kira said, and looked at Zenobia, worry in her eyes. "I'm sorry."

Angelo loosened his grip, and Elijah pushed back and shook roughly out of his hold. If the look in his eyes was a weapon, Angelo would be dead. Elijah rubbed his right arm as he moved to the door.

"I'll talk to you later," Kira said to Zenobia in a rush before hurrying after her man, but she stopped abruptly. She glanced at Angelo, her expression unreadable, then she exited, closing the door behind her.

Angelo locked up and reset the alarm. When he turned to Zenobia, his expression was more serious than she'd seen since meeting him.

"What do you know about Elijah?"

Chapter Thirteen

From the moment the guy walked in with Sofia's bags, Angelo had a bad feeling about him. It could've just been his protective instincts being off-kilter, but he didn't think so. His senses had gone on high alert immediately, and Angelo had learned a long time ago to trust those feelings.

He followed Zenobia to the refrigerator as she explained how Elijah and Kira had been dating for months. They'd met at a party and hit it off immediately.

She poured herself a glass of water and took a healthy gulp. "He's never acted like a jerk before, but maybe he was just trying to shield me. The last time he saw me was right after the kidnapping attempt. I'm sure I wasn't acting like myself. That was also when he'd noticed my eye. Even then, he hadn't looked as if he'd bought the falling excuse."

"I'm going to need his last name, place of employment, and anything else you can think of. His ass said that somethin' wasn't right, and that's exactly how I felt about him."

Zenobia shook her head. "Two extremely protective guys thinking something's up with the other. Sounds about right."

"Maybe, but remember, I'm here to keep you safe. I'm not sure what his deal is, but I intend to find out."

"Okay, but for Kira's sake, I hope you don't find anything incriminating. She's crazy about him."

Angelo hoped he *did* find something incriminating. He didn't like the guy, but he also didn't want to cause her cousin any heartbreak, unless her life was in danger. Then he'd do whatever necessary to keep him away from Zenobia and her cousin.

"What did Sofia say to you before she went to bed?"

Angelo smiled. He liked the older woman. "She said I had kind eyes."

Zenobia nodded. She finished off her water and placed the glass in the dishwasher, looking everywhere but at him.

"About what happened in here earlier," he started, but Zenobia lifted a hand.

"Don't say it. Don't say it was a mistake." She watched him warily as he moved across the room and approached her.

"I definitely wasn't going to say that, and I ain't gonna lie. I wanted to kiss you. Taste you. Love on you. I could keep going on and on, but I won't. I actually owe you an apology."

"For what? You didn't do anything that I didn't want you to do."

"Maybe, but I was way out of line." He moved closer until he was directly in front of her and brushed the back of his fingers down her cheek. Touching her soft skin ignited that desire again. The desire to pull her into his arms and kiss her until she couldn't think straight. "It's hard as hell being around you and not touch you, but I—"

"I like it when you touch me and when you kiss me," Zenobia interrupted, placing her hands on his torso. The fiery heat from her touch scorched him through his shirt as she moved her hands slowly up to his chest. "I know this is just a job for you, but why deny what we're both feeling?"

His heart pounded wildly against her palm, and he resisted the urge to strip her bare and take her right there on the counter.

He couldn't.

They couldn't.

Not only because Sofia was right down the hall and might walk in on them at any moment. No, it had everything to do with his lack of control. This was the first time in a long time that Angelo questioned whether he could control himself around a woman. Not just any woman, but a woman who made him want to say to hell with his own rules and throw caution out the window.

Her small hand still rested on his chest, and he covered it with his hand. "You already know how attracted I am to you," he said, realizing he had moved even closer. Their faces were inches apart as he stared into her soulful eyes. "Nothing can happen between us. My job is to keep you safe. I can't do that if I'm distracted, and you, love, are a serious distraction. A tempting, hot, sexy-ass distraction."

She searched his eyes as if looking for some sign that he would change his mind. Then she slid her hand from beneath his. "That's right, this is a job for you. This is not real."

Angelo's arm shot out when she started to move away, and he blocked her path. "Wait." He got back in her face, needing her to hear and understand him. "The magnetic sensation that keeps pulling us back to each other is *very* real. So, don't get it twisted. My need to put a little distance between us has nothing to do with my attraction to you, but everything to do with keeping you safe."

She nodded, her gaze lingering on his mouth before returning to his eyes. "Okay, I'll try to do this your way. But for the record, I can't make any promises about not kissing you again." She stepped around him and headed for the stairs. "Have a good night…what's left of it."

Angelo watched as she proceeded up the stairs, her hips swaying left, right, left. He shook his head and ran his hands through his hair as a low growl bubbled inside his chest.

How the heck was he going to keep his libido in check when just thinking about the woman turned him on? And he had to spend 24/7 with her and not go beyond their little charade. If he didn't have his own personal rules about getting involved with a client, he'd be following her to her bedroom.

Damn principles. They were going to be the death of him.

*

Days later, Zenobia was awakened by the smell of bacon wafting up the stairs to her bedroom. She loved breakfast foods and no one laid out a spread the way Sofia did.

After freshening up in the bathroom, Zenobia walked out of her bedroom. Sofia and Angelo's voices drifted up the stairs. She listened for a moment and smiled when Sofia laughed at something he said. The two of them had become quite fond of each other. Angelo had mentioned that she reminded him of his *abuela*, his father's mother. As for Sofia, she loved having him around because he was a big eater and she loved feeding people.

Zenobia proceeded down the back stairs, still feeling as if she could use a few more hours of sleep. Before she reached the last four steps, Angelo glanced her way. It didn't matter how quiet she was, he sensed her presence. He knew whenever she entered a room

His smoldering gaze slid slowly down the length of her body, and butterflies took flight inside her belly as heat flared within her. With just a look, he had her frozen in place and somehow managed to arouse that sexual need that she'd been able to restrain the last couple of days. His eyes took in the messy bun on top of her head, her nipples that pebbled against her pink fitted T-shirt, and moved down to her hips and legs wrapped in yoga pants.

When his attention returned to her face, a smile played around his kissable lips. He stood, leaving his stack of pancakes, and strolled across the kitchen to her.

"Hey, gorgeous. I'm surprised you're up considering how late you went to bed."

He placed a sweet kiss on her lips, but when he tried to pull away, Zenobia fisted the front of his shirt and deepened the lip-lock. It might've seemed desperate, but she planned to take every opportunity to take what she wanted from him.

When the kiss ended, Angelo's brows raised inquiringly. What could she say? She couldn't help herself when it came to him.

With a firm grip on her hand, he guided her to the stool next to where he'd been sitting. They'd stayed in character, especially around Sofia, but if Zenobia was honest, she wasn't pretending with Angelo. She liked everything about the man, especially the way he cherished her.

Without asking, he poured her a cup of coffee and added one sugar the way she liked, then set the mug in front of her. Man, she could get used to this. She inhaled the strong brew before taking a tentative sip. Zenobia had never been with a man who was as thoughtful and attentive as Angelo. After the night that he'd told her that nothing sexual could happen between them, she thought things would be awkward. They weren't. If anything, they were quickly developing a solid friendship.

"Morning, *Mamita*. Looks like you've been busy." Zenobia eyed the platter of pancakes, hash browns, sausage, and bacon. Sofia was an amazing cook, but often complained about not having more people to cook for.

"Yes," she said. "Let me heat up your food and make you some eggs."

"You don't have to do that. What's here is more than enough."

"No, you like eggs. You get eggs," she said, turning to the stove.

Zenobia rolled her eyes and shook her head, knowing there was no sense in arguing with the woman. She glanced at Angelo, who grinned and winked at her before shoving a forkful of hash browns into his mouth.

"How long have you been up?" she asked him, a yawn bursting free before she could stop it. She quickly covered her mouth. "Sorry. Why didn't you wake me?"

"Because you needed the sleep." Angelo reclaimed his seat "How do you feel?"

She'd been waking up early and going to bed late, trying

to finish a song before needing to be in the studio in a couple of days.

"I feel all right. Still a little frustrated that this song is not coming together. I can't say that it's writer's block because words are coming, but they don't feel right."

"Well, let me know if I can help."

Her mug stopped inches from her mouth and she turned and looked at him. "Don't tell me you sing *and* write music."

"Okay, I won't tell you."

"Seriously? You write, too?"

He chuckled. "Nah, I'm just messing with you, but feel free to bounce some ideas or lyrics off of me. I'll help if I can."

"You're a singer?" Sofia asked him, setting piping hot blueberry pancakes, eggs and three strips of bacon in front of Zenobia. She also placed a glass of orange juice next to the plate.

"I sing for fun, but I'm not a real singer," Angelo explained. "Not like Zen."

That was the first time she'd heard him refer to her as *Zen*. He was one of few people who actually called her Zenobia.

"You should get him to sing something for you, *Mamita*," Zenobia said between bites. "He sounds better than some of the entertainers out there who have record deals."

For the next few minutes, the three of them chatted over breakfast as if they'd done it for years. It was going to be hard to go back to normal when Angelo's assignment ended. Zenobia loved having him around. He filled a void in her life that had been dormant for far too long. She wasn't looking forward to going back to life as usual once they went their separate ways.

"Are you done eating?" Angelo asked her as he stood with his plates.

"I think so, but you don't have to help clean up. I can—"

"Neither of you will help. Cooking and cleaning give me something to do." Sofia took the plates from Angelo and shooed him back to his seat.

He settled back on the bar stool and placed his hand on Zenobia's back. She wasn't sure what his intent was, but the small circles he was making with his hand stirred her woman parts awake. A touchy-feely kind of guy, she loved having his hands on her. If only she could persuade him to touch a few of her more intimate areas.

"What's on the agenda today?" he asked her.

"I need to for us to run a few errands, and then this evening Octavia wants me to—"

"Who are you...really?" Sofia interrupted, her unflinching gaze drilling into Angelo. "My *mija* has never let a man stay overnight in the house. Yet, you have been here for days. You do everything together, but you don't sleep in her room. I know this." She waved around the wooden spoon that she'd been washing. Droplets of water flew across the counter, one landing on Zenobia's forehead. "Your room is above my room. I only hear you."

Unease crept through Zenobia as she and Angelo shared a look. She didn't want to lie to Sofia. Not because Angelo and his team wanted to keep the charade going. No, she didn't want to lie to the most important person in her life because she trusted Sofia. Zenobia also didn't want her worrying. For days, Sofia seemed to buy their story about dating. Especially since she hadn't said anything to the contrary.

Apparently not.

"*Mamita*, we—"

"No more lying, *mija*."

Zenobia almost laughed when Sofia pointed the spoon at her, daring her to speak anything but the truth. Memories of when she was younger, and Sofia used to ream her out for lying, surged through Zenobia's mind.

God, she loved this woman. During some of the most trying times in her life, Sofia was always there. Teaching her. Loving her. Good or bad, she never left Zenobia's side. She was the one constant in her life.

"I see how you look at her…with such passion." Sofia's voice softened as she spoke to Angelo, and she no longer waved her wooden spoon. "You take very good care of her. Your mother raised you right. You're a good man, but there's something happening. Something you both are keeping from me. *Mija's* eye. New locks on door. New alarm. You care very much, but you no sleep together. What has happened?"

Angelo chuckled and ran his hand over his mouth and down his chin. He looked at Zenobia. "Your *mamita* is very perceptive."

"Tell me now," Sofia demanded, back to waving her spoon.

"I do care about Zenobia," Angelo said, reaching over and curling his hand around hers. At the heartrending tenderness of his touch, something too intense to identify flared inside of her. There was no doubt their attraction to each other was real, but it was moments like this that she also wanted their relationship to be real.

Together they told Sofia about what was going on and the role Angelo was playing. He also told her that she would soon be meeting other members of his team, and that they had every intention of finding the person involved. In the meantime, she couldn't tell anyone that their relationship wasn't real. Angelo also assured her that they'd keep both her and Zenobia safe.

Sofia moved around the center island and wrapped her arms around Zenobia's shoulders. "You should have told me. I would've come home sooner, *mija*. You can't keep secrets like that from me. Remember before…"

An icy chill scurried down Zenobia's spine, afraid Sofia would say more. When she didn't, Zenobia made eye contact with Angelo. Of course, he was alert and watching them both. Since that meeting at Supreme, she'd had a feeling that he somehow knew that she was holding something back. She hadn't shared everything. Sofia's words just confirmed his suspicions.

Would he question them? Or would he continue the way

they'd been going, where she fed him information about herself a little at a time?

"Secrets destroy," Sofia continued. "No more. No more secrets, *mija*."

"I know, *Mamita*. I know."

Chapter Fourteen

Lounging on the leather sofa in Octavia Hilton's home office, Angelo observed Zenobia with her manager. They were across the room at a round conference table discussing the details of an endorsement contract. He didn't know the dollar amount attached to it, but Octavia seemed pleased with what she'd negotiated. Zenobia, not so much.

She smiled at the right time and nodded as they went over the contract's details. Even the mention of other entertainers who would be included in the project—some of her idols—didn't get much of a rise out of her.

Angelo wondered if her subdued behavior had anything to do with the conversation between her and Sofia during breakfast. *"Secrets destroy,"* Sofia had said. *"No more. No more secrets, mija."*

The ghostly expression that Angelo had witnessed on Zenobia's face after that comment had all of his protective instincts rising to attention. She was afraid of something or someone. Ever since that conversation, she'd been lost in her thoughts and answering questions with one-word responses. Whatever was on her mind was definitely bothering her. If only she would confide in him.

Angelo readjusted his position, crossing one of his legs over the other and spreading his right arm along the back of the sofa. In their short time together, he'd become sensitive to her moods, needs, and some of her quirks. Like the way she nibbled on her thumbnail when she was nervous or uncomfortable, the way she was doing now.

Zenobia was also starting to chip away at the armor around his heart. Something he never thought would happen. It had been a long time since he'd allowed a woman to get as close as she was getting. There was just something about her. Even with her secrets, he was falling for her, and that wasn't a good thing.

So far, out of the people on their short list of suspects, they'd only been able to rule out Damon, the owner of DLC Security. For the last three months, he'd been out of the country on assignment, providing protection for an A-list actor.

As for Zenobia, Supreme hadn't found anything incriminating in her past or the lives of those in her inner circle. Yet, that feeling that she was keeping something important from them, whether she knew it or not, bugged the hell out of Angelo. Hopefully, she gave him something soon that would shed light into her situation. Until then, he'd bide his time and stay alert.

"Thanks for all the work you put into this deal," Zenobia said to Octavia and stood, slinging the strap of her Louis Vuitton purse over her shoulder. "I'm glad it'll be a few months before filming starts. That'll give me time to wrap up this next album."

"Speaking of the album. When are you getting back in the studio?" Octavia asked.

Looking to be in her early fifties with a fair complexion and shoulder-length red hair, she was stylishly dressed. The low-cut white dress with sheer sleeves stopped just below her knees. Instead of dressing for a meeting at home, she looked as if she was dressed for a hot date.

"Later this week," Zenobia explained.

"I trust that the last song is almost done, because you're really pushing the deadline." Octavia smoothed her hands down the sides of her hips, and glanced at Angelo with a slight smile. She'd been flirting all evening. At first, he thought she was just kidding around, but as the night went on, he quickly realized she wasn't. Some of her comments to him were inappropriate, but he blew them off. From what he'd heard about the manager, she was just being herself.

"Everything will be done on time," Zenobia said, an edge to her tone. Angelo met her gaze as she sauntered across the room, then slid her hand into his.

"Angelo, if things don't work out between you and Zenobia, give me a call." Octavia winked at him. He hadn't liked the woman upon first meeting her, and he liked her even less now.

"That's never going to happen," Zenobia said, a bite in her tone as her grip on his hand increased.

"No?" Octavia's left brow lifted.

"No. I'm going to treat him so good he's never going to want to leave my side." Zenobia looked at him, a gleam in her eyes.

Angelo leaned down and kissed her sexy lips, making sure to keep it short. He had to be strong. He knew from experience that one kiss from her always sparked a desire in him to go further.

"Have a good night, Octavia," he said as they left the office. She followed them down the short hall where dark hardwood covered the floor and abstract paintings graced the walls.

Walking out of her home, Angelo took in their surroundings. Octavia lived in Johns Creek, a suburb of Atlanta, in a neighborhood graced with one large house after another. Like Zenobia's, her home was positioned deep on the lot away from the street. It was late, and the limited lighting along the driveway and in the front yard had him extra vigilant.

With one hand at the small of her back and his other arm free where he could easily reach for one of his guns, Angelo guided her to his Dodge Charger. He helped her into the vehicle, then hurried around to the driver's side.

"You didn't seem all that excited about the commercial deal," he said as he drove down the long driveway and onto the street. "Why'd you sign the contract if you really weren't that interested?"

"I'm interested in the project, it's just that I'm leery of trusting anyone right now, especially Octavia. She can be an insensitive businesswoman, and I don't always know if she has my best interest at heart."

Angelo understood being skeptical of people. After leaving the DEA, he didn't trust anyone. When he joined Supreme Security, the Atlanta's Finest team almost seemed too perfect. But after a few assignments, Angelo soon learned that they were great at what they did and more importantly, they had his back.

"At the end of the year, I think I'm going to cut ties with my manager."

Angelo glanced at Zenobia, splitting his attention between her and the highway. "Why? And don't tell me it has anything to do with her flirting with me?"

"That's part of it. It's apparent she doesn't respect me. The way she was flirting with you all evening proved it. I wanted to snatch out her hair."

Angelo's mouth twitched as he fought back a laugh. She sounded serious, but there was a sweetness about her that made it hard to imagine her causing harm to any human being.

"It's more than the flirting with you, though. I don't really like her. I've seen her mistreat too many people for the sake of getting what she wants. It's only a matter of time before she does the same to me."

"Like mess with your mind or have you kidnapped?"

Zenobia shook her head. "No, I honestly don't think she's behind those incidents. I wouldn't put planting listening devices in my home past her, though, but not the other stuff."

Angelo wasn't as convinced. He hadn't ruled anyone out.

It was only a matter of time before the culprits identified themselves.

"I think it's time I start looking for new representation. Maybe I'll wait until after I know for sure what I want next out of my career."

"Well, let me know when you're ready. I know a guy."

She snorted a laugh, but quickly covered her mouth.

"Why is that funny? I do know someone. Have you ever heard of Wesley Bradford?"

Her eyes widened. "Of course. He's one of the most sought-after agents in the entertainment business. It's impossible to even get an appointment with him, let alone get him to take you on as a client. So, you really know him?"

"I do. He's Hamilton's father-in-law."

Despite almost getting Dakota killed a couple of years ago, Wesley had made a complete one-eighty, and seemed like a different, new and improved person. Hamilton and Dakota had found a way to forgive him. Angelo might not be the forgiving type, but had mad respect for anyone who had that ability.

"Would you be willing to introduce me one day? Not yet, but one day?"

"Yeah." Angelo changed lanes, went around a slow-moving car, and then hopped back into the right lane.

"What's wrong?" Zenobia asked.

"Nothing," Angelo responded absently, and checked his rearview mirror again, his attention on the large Ford truck three cars back.

"Then why do you keep looking in your mirrors?"

He chuckled, a little surprised that she was paying attention. "I'm looking because that's what drivers are supposed to do."

No need worrying her when he wasn't sure they were being followed. Though the streets were dark, with intermittent light illuminating from the limited number of streetlights, he had noticed the vehicle earlier. The first few miles, it had been directly behind him. It wasn't until traffic thinned and the driver had several opportunities to go around him, and didn't take them, that Angelo started to get concerned.

For the past week, he'd been with Zenobia around the clock, going where she went and taking the time to get to know her. A fascinating woman, she didn't hang out much. When she'd mentioned early on that she was a loner, his time with her was proving that. The more time they spent together, the more infatuated he became with her.

Now, if only they could figure out who was after her. Egypt and Laz had found some interesting information on Elijah. A sealed juvie record and a couple of misdemeanors in his adult life. He owned a courier business, but still, there was nothing that led them to believe that he was a danger to Zenobia. Angelo had insisted they keep digging.

Glancing in his mirror periodically, Angelo had changed lanes three times, only to see the truck do the same thing. Now he was certain they had a tail. The driver probably hadn't done anything crazy because of traffic, but now there weren't as many cars on the street. Ten o'clock on a Wednesday night, and the traffic was thinning as they drove toward Highway 85.

"If somethin's wrong, tell me." Zenobia glanced over her left shoulder to look out the back window as Angelo activated his car's Bluetooth while he increased his speed. He wasn't sure who was on front desk duty at Supreme, but it didn't matter. He wanted to at least alert someone of the possible problem.

"What's up?" Kenton's voice boomed through the vehicle's speakers after one ring.

Instead of saying that he thought they had a tail, Angelo gave his friend their location, knowing Kenton would immediately get Wiz to tap into the vehicle's GPS. "We're heading southeast. Huge, dark four-door Ford truck with equally dark windows, three…no, two cars behind us and picking up speed."

Cameron "Wiz" Miller, one of the owners of Supreme

Security-Chicago, was a computer genius who could hack any network, including the city's street cameras. The guy had developed numerous systems and devices to keep all of their people safe. Even their cell phones and some of their personal vehicles had built-in mechanisms that could be tracked through Supreme's network.

Angelo didn't have to look at Zenobia to know that her gaze was burning into him. She remained quiet, but her breathing increased as she shifted in her seat to look behind them.

"An—Angelo," Zenobia stammered, panic in that one word as she gripped his right arm while looking out the back window.

His gaze shot to the rearview mirror, just as the truck cut off the car that was right behind Angelo. "Ken, we have a problem."

"Laz is in the area, and Wiz is taking care of the cameras. We got you. Stay safe."

They disconnected and Angelo pressed on the gas. He swerved into the left lane, cutting a car off, ignoring the blaring of their horn, and sped ahead. Weaving in and out of traffic, he managed to put some distance between them and the truck.

"Stay safe?" Zenobia screeched, her nails digging into Angelo's arm. "Shouldn't they, Laz, Kenton, and whoever else, be doing more?"

"They are. Don't worry. Just hold on." He swerved back into the right lane and sped through an intersection on a yellow light. A quick look in his mirror showed the truck running the red light and quickly gaining on them. Angelo's stomach muscles twisted, and his pulse pounded in his ear. He wanted to stay on the main drag so that Wiz could get them on camera. Yet, he also wanted to lose the asshole who was determined to run them down.

Though she looked tense, Zenobia said nothing as he darted in and out of traffic, then at the last possible second, Angelo took a sharp right. Tires squealing, he made the turn almost on two wheels and barreled down a side street. The driver who'd been following them had missed the turn, but Angelo had no doubt that they would show themselves again soon. He zigzagged around a few parked cars and made a couple of right turns, then a left that would take him back to the main street. He pulled back into traffic which was thankfully unusually light.

"I think you lost them," Zenobia said, splitting her attention between looking out the back window and out the front one.

He floored the gas pedal. "I need to get us out of—"

"Look out!" she screamed.

"Sonof…" Angelo's heart leaped into his throat as the Ford truck appeared from his right, barreling into the intersection toward them. "Hold on!"

Before they cleared the intersection, the crunching sound of the truck slamming into the side of his car, along with Zenobia's screams, was deafening.

The rear passenger window exploded. Tires squealed. Horns blared. Angelo's blood chilled as he gripped the steering wheel.

The car spun. Once. Twice. Clipped another vehicle. They went around and around until the driver's side of the automobile collided into a pole.

"Ohmigod! Omigod! Omigod!" Zenobia panicked cries clawed through Angelo as he shook his head, blinking several times trying to clear his vision.

He swallowed hard. Snubbing the churning in his stomach, he pushed down the bile that crawled up his throat. His chest heaved as his breaths came in short spurts. He had to pull himself together, but his mind was fuzzy as thoughts pinged around in his head.

Truck.

Crash.

Zenobia.

Danger.

Angelo twisted in his seat and bit out a curse when his

ribs screamed in agony. It was sheer determination that helped him undo his seat belt than Zenobia's. Still blinking away the dizziness and attempting to see her despite the darkness of the interior, he reached for her.

Zenobia's irregular breathing filled his ears when she leaned into him, and he cupped her face between his hands.

"Look at me," he searched her eyes. "Are you hurt?"

"I—I don't think so," she sputtered, her hands trembling as they covered his. "You. Ar—are you—you okay?"

"Yeah. Yeah, I'm—" His words lodged in his throat. A big, burly figure with a black scarf covering his lower face staggered toward the passenger side of the car.

Heart hammering double time, Angelo gently pushed Zenobia to the floor and reached for the pistol in his ankle holster. "Cover your head and stay down," he ground out just as the man lifted a crowbar and swung at the window.

Zenobia's terrifying shriek echoed through the air, and Angelo lifted his arm to block the sudden spikes of glass that blasted into the car. The man reached into the vehicle.

"No! No!" Zenobia shouted hysterically, clawing at the guy as he roughly tried pulling her up from the floor. "No! Help!"

Angelo lunged forward, gripped her arm and tugged her toward him, but the attacker held on. Her screams tore Angelo up inside. He couldn't fail her. He aimed his gun at the guy, but the man was too close to Zenobia. Shooting at him was too risky.

"Let her go!" Angelo roared, needing to distract the man enough for him to loosen his grip. When that didn't happen, Angelo leaned over the center console and slammed the butt of his gun into the side of the man's head.

The attacker cried out. His grip loosened enough for Zenobia to get free, and Angelo fired. The gunshot sounded like an explosion rattling his eardrums, but he hit his target. The attacker howled in pain, grabbing his shoulder and stumbled back.

Panting, Zenobia crawled over the center console. She

frantically climbed into Angelo's lap, practically knocking the gun from his hand in the process. He held her close, and she buried her face against his throat.

A second man, dressed similar to the first, in all black and a scarf covering the lower part of his face, came into view. Angelo lifted his arm to fire again, but the guy didn't approach. Instead, he roughly jerked the first attacker's shirt and pulled him toward the truck. Within seconds, they peeled away from the scene.

Sirens sounded in the distance.

Side throbbing. Ears ringing. Breaths coming in short spurts.

Angelo held Zenobia's trembling body. "We're okay," he mumbled, despite his body feeling like one big throb. Not as dizzy as before, but his mind was still a jumbled mess.

Footsteps on crunching glass snagged his attention.

Angelo tightened his hold around Zenobia with one arm, and raised the other, pointing his gun at the missing passenger side window.

"Lo, it's me. Lower your weapon." Laz's commanding voice punched through the thick fog of Angelo's mind like a fist through a paper bag. He slowly lowered his gun but maintained his hold on Zenobia, who was gripping the front of his shirt like a lifeline.

They were alive.

They were safe.

Acknowledging those facts seemed to zap the energy right out of him. Willing his heart rate to settle down, Angelo dropped his head back against the headrest and closed his eyes.

He didn't know who was behind this attack, but whoever it was would soon learn that he was not a man to take lightly. Everyone involved would pay.

Chapter Fifteen

Curled up on her family room sofa next to Angelo, Zenobia nibbled on her thumbnail. Tension lay lodged against her breastplate. Someone wanted to kill her. She could've died tonight. *They* could've died. She didn't even want to think about what would've happened had Angelo not been with her. His quick thinking and determination to keep her safe meant everything.

Once Laz had showed up, he took charge. As a former detective with Atlanta PD, he seemed to know all the cops on site. Some were glad to see him, almost to the point of hero worship, while others gave him a wide berth.

Laz was also able to deal with Angelo's stubbornness. Who knew her bodyguard boyfriend owned the trait? Apparently, his team.

Laz had threatened to strangle him if he didn't cooperate. He barely answered the cops' questions, adamant that they should be looking for their attackers instead of wasting time questioning him. Angelo had also refused to be transported to the hospital by ambulance, though he was clearly in pain. He really lost his shit when the cops tried to pull her away from him to question her. He made it clear that he didn't trust anyone but his team, and he had no intention of letting her out of his sight.

Kenton, Myles, and a few other guys Zenobia didn't know, showed up in big SUVs with dark, tinted windows. They escorted her and Angelo to the hospital. Kenton drove the SUV that she and Angelo rode in, while Laz led the way in another vehicle, and Myles was in yet another trailing them. There had only been one other time in Zenobia's life when she'd felt so protected. A time that was just as scary but had a different outcome.

With her head resting on Angelo's shoulder, and her arm looped through his, Zenobia leaned into him even harder. He'd saved her life…again…and had been her rock since returning to her home.

"Looks like the media is slowly starting to thin," Myles said as he peeked through the vertical blinds. The picture window gave a view of the front yard, long driveway, and the street beyond the front gate.

One of Zenobia's biggest concerns had been the media getting wind of the crash. They'd been escorted through a private entrance to get into the hospital. When it was time for them to leave, Kenton confirm that the paparazzi were outside both hospital entrances. Zenobia had no idea who had informed them that she was there, but it didn't matter. Atlanta's Finest had proven to be as good and resourceful as they'd vowed during her initial meeting at Supreme. The men were a protective wall around her and Angelo as they loaded them into the SUV.

Now, some were still milling about her house. Based on the savory scents floating to her nose, Sofia was cooking despite it being after midnight. Myles was the only one in the family room with her and Angelo, and the others were in the kitchen.

"Do we have any information yet about the men who attacked us?" Angelo asked.

Zenobia startled and lifted her head from his shoulder when he started to stand. She fisted the side of his T-shirt to keep him from moving. The anxiety that had been simmering inside of her since leaving the hospital suddenly grew into a boil.

He glanced at her. She'd been strong for much of the night, but fear that he was leaving tightened around her like a straitjacket. She couldn't let him go.

"Try to relax. I'm not going anywhere." He placed his arm around her and pulled her close until her cheek rested on his chest. He gave her a little squeeze. "I have no intention of leaving you. Okay?"

She gave a shaky nod and willed her fingers to release his T-shirt. She couldn't. Her anxiety climbed. Her childish behavior was embarrassing, but she couldn't help it. The terror that engulfed her when their attacker tried pulling her from the car consumed her again.

Her head spun. Her chest heaved. Her breathing increased. What was wrong with her?

"Hey, look at me." Angelo leaned back slightly, forcing Zenobia to lift her head. He cupped her cheek and tears pooled in her eyes. "You're safe. We won't let anyone hurt you. *I* won't let anyone hurt you. I promise."

She would not cry. Not in front of him. Not in front of anyone. Instead, she dug down deep within herself and drummed up as much courage as she could. Releasing a shaky breath, she loosened her hold on his shirt.

Her gaze followed every step Angelo took. Back and forth he paced in front of the coffee table. For the last few hours, she couldn't seem to get her body to move, and he couldn't keep still. Earlier, while the doctor was checking her out, Angelo paced. He claimed moving helped him think better. Now that he was moving again, his body was stiff, and his expression pinched as he walked up and down the length of the family room.

Zenobia half-listened as Myles told him that a witness got a partial license plate from the truck that crashed into them. Wiz, who she hadn't met yet, was doing something with city cameras. He had the ability to determine when they'd picked up the tail. They were also digging deeper into Octavia's life. Especially since Zenobia hadn't told anyone that she'd be at her manager's house during that time.

They were also in touch with local hospitals, staying abreast of the gunshot victim Angelo had shot, in hopes he'd seek medical attention. None of that seemed enough for Angelo. His voice grew louder and angrier with each question he asked.

"I want to know who those assholes are!" he growled.

Goosebumps raced over Zenobia's skin. He'd been kind and gentle with her since day one, but tonight she'd seen other facets of him. He'd been fearless, even shooting a man to protect her. He was possessive, not wanting her out of his sight. He was also a take-charge kind of guy. Laz might've stepped in at the crash site, but since then, Angelo had been giving orders and following up on the team's progress.

Zenobia glanced at the two men. Myles said something that she missed, but it must've been something that riled Angelo. He huffed out a breath, while combing his fingers through his hair.

"They weren't trying to kill her. They wanted her. They were trying to take her from me!" he choked out and pounded his chest.

Tears pricked the back of Zenobia's eyes as his anguish cut through to her heart. She'd have to be blind and unfeeling not to notice that she and he were getting closer. Not in a bodyguard/client kind of way. No, there was something special happening between them, had been since the first time they met. Only right now, she wasn't sure if he was pissed that she'd almost gotten snatched on his watch. Or if it was something more that he was feeling.

Suddenly exhausted, Zenobia brought her knees up to her chest and wrapped her arms around her legs. If only she could clear her mind. She rested her forehead on her knees.

The crash and everything that followed played on loop in her head. Especially when her attacker slammed something hard into the car window. His strong, beefy hand had grasped at her hair, neck, and shoulders. Then he gripped the shoulder of her shirt so hard, he'd ripped it. She'd fought with everything within her. Yet, he still managed to grab her upper arm and lift her from the floor of the car.

And then there was the gunshot.

And screams. Hers and the attacker.

Her ears were still ringing from it all.

Zenobia rocked a little. Strands of her hair flopped back and forth, hitting the side of her face and brushing her shoulders. Those guys could've done anything to her. The crash, the attack…it was all a little too, too…familiar.

She shook her head. *No. Don't go there.*

She wasn't allowing her mind to go down that road. A road that led back to her past and the worst time in her life. She survived, barely. Her attackers hadn't. They'd never be able to hurt her again.

She had survived then, and she survived tonight…thanks to Angelo. This was twice now that he had saved her. Each time he had put his life on the line for her. She didn't want there to be a third time.

But what if they came back? What if they were successful on the third attempt? What if they didn't stop coming for her?

Zenobia's breathing increased as one scenario after another festered inside her mind.

I'm okay. I'm okay.

She kept telling herself, desperately needing to believe the words. But the screeching of tires, the loud *boom* of the truck slamming into them, her screams…all of it bombarded her mind. What if Angelo and his team never found the guys? They would come back, and next time…

Zenobia's heart leaped into her throat and her head shot up when she felt something on her shoulder. It was as if an army of ants were sprinting across her skin. Heart racing. Pulse pounding. She flung her arms around, trying to shake them off, all the while scooting to the corner of the sofa.

"Whoa." Angelo reared back, his hands up and out in front of him. "It's just me, baby. It's just me."

Breathing hard and trembling, Zenobia's frantic gaze

bounced from Angelo to Myles. They both stood at attention. Neither said a word. They stared at her as if watching an alien come unhinged.

Laz strolled into the room, but slowed. He looked back and forth between them. "What's wrong? What happened?"

Feeling like a total idiot, Zenobia covered her face with shaking hands. She was losing her mind. The dam that she'd been holding off for hours finally broke. Tears spilled from her eyes.

"Zenobia," Angelo said quietly before she felt his hand on her back.

The gentleness of his touch should've been comforting, but instead it made her cry harder. She'd freaked out after the crash, but she hadn't cried. Even when she recounted what happened to the cops, she'd been able to hold it together. But now...

"Come on. You've had a long day. Let's go upstairs," Angelo said. When she didn't move, he lifted her into his arms.

Not wanting any of them to see her fall apart, she immediately buried her face against Angelo's neck. She found some comfort in his fresh scent and the steady beat of his pulse, but her heart ached.

Why was someone after her? What had she done to make someone want to hurt her?

Tears make you weak, and you're not weak. You have to stay strong.

The familiar words from her past seeped into her soul.

You have to stay strong.

Angelo hissed and his body stiffened when he climbed that first step. That's when Zenobia remembered he wasn't a hundred percent healthy. His left side was bruised. Thankfully, his ribs were okay, but on the way to the hospital to get checked out, she could tell he was in pain. Yet, here he was carrying her.

She sniffed, swiped her hand down her face and wiped feverishly at her tears. "You're hurt. Put me down."

"I'm fine," he huffed as he cleared the top step. Shifting her slightly in his hold, he walked the short distance down the hall until he reached her bedroom door. "All I care about right now is taking care of you."

"You don't have to take care of me. I'll be fine. I—I just had a moment, but I'll be okay," Zenobia insisted, though deep down inside she didn't know if she would ever be all right. Physically, her aching body would recover. Mentally, she wasn't so sure. The last thing she wanted was to begin seeing a therapist again, but she wasn't opposed to it.

Angelo strolled across the room to her sitting area and set her in her favorite seat, an overstuffed sack chair that could hold two people.

"Don't move," he said in a tone that left no room for argument.

Inhaling deeply, she slowly released the breath, and then repeated the act as she glanced around the cozy space. Besides the kitchen, the master suite had played a big factor in her putting an offer in on the house.

The space was split into two adjourning rooms. A sliding, frosted door separated them. Her sitting area was where she curled up when she wanted to relax, read, or just think. The plush furniture, pale yellow walls, floor-to-ceiling windows on one side of the space, and the fireplace made for a relaxing environment.

A knock on the bedroom door snagged her attention. Zenobia wasn't sure if Angelo was still in there, and she couldn't see the door from where she was sitting.

Wiping her hands down her face, she stood.

"Where you going?" Angelo asked, appearing in the entry way with a tray topped with a couple of covered dishes. On one of his arms hung a small picnic basket.

He entered and set the items on the storage chest made of reclaimed wood that served as a coffee table.

"Angelo," Zenobia started, touched by the sweet gesture. She hadn't been able to eat when Sofia insisted on feeding her earlier. Once she had arrived home, all she'd wanted to do was take a shower and hide under her bed covers. She made it through the shower, but anxiety got the best of her the moment she was alone in bed. Which was how she'd ended up curled up against Angelo in the family room.

"I'm not really hungry," she said as he settled in on the love seat, sitting within arms' reach of her.

"Good. Then there's more for me."

He uncovered the dishes, revealing tacos, rice, and vegetables. In the basket was a bottle of bourbon whiskey and two shot glasses.

"The food is for me. The bottle is for you."

He poured the dark liquid into one of the glasses and handed it to her. Muttering something about it not being good for her to drink alone, he poured himself a shot.

He tapped his glass against hers. "Drink up." He threw back the liquor.

Instead of drinking hers, Zenobia watched him pour himself another one.

"Drink. It'll knock the edge off and help you relax."

So, she did. Her eyes slammed shut and her body shivered from the alcohol's burn as it went down her throat. By the third shot, she felt no pain and could barely see straight.

She wasn't a drinker, especially of hard liquor, but Angelo was right about one thing. The alcohol did help her relax, and suddenly she was hungry.

They ate, mostly in a comfortable silence, except for when they discussed safe topics. Topics that didn't have them reliving the last few hours. After they finished eating, Angelo escorted Zenobia to her bed.

"Why don't you try to get some sleep," he said as he pulled back the covers. Tired, she climbed in between the cool, soft sheets. Then, like before, impending dread settled over her like a two-ton boulder. Her pulse amped up, and her heart pounded inside her chest as her body shivered.

"Ca-can you stay with me, at least…at least until I fall asleep?"

Angelo looked as if he was going to turn her down, but Zenobia wasn't sure what he saw on her face. Before she knew it, he had dimmed the lights and kicked off his shoes.

"Scoot over and don't try any funny stuff," he cracked.

She hadn't planned to, but now that he brought it up…

Chapter Sixteen

"Take off your clothes."

Angelo's brows shot up. "Excuse me?"

He sat on the edge of the bed. Maybe it hadn't been a good idea to supply her with so much alcohol. Even if he had learned a couple of things about her after she'd slammed back shots.

She cursed more after a drink, and alcohol made her brave. She'd been speaking her mind for the past thirty minutes, and saying things she wouldn't normally say to him. Such as, *"Drinking makes me horny. Maybe you can do something about that."* He'd store that info away for future use.

Zenobia didn't look as terrified as she had a moment ago when she thought he was leaving, but she was still trembling. He meant what he said to her. He had no intentions of leaving her alone. Like she seemed to need him, he needed her, too.

Her hand rested on her chest while she inhaled and released a breath slowly. He wasn't sure if it was the crash that still had her on edge or something else. She'd had moments of panic since they got her home, but a tightness in his gut told him that something else was going on.

A loud yawn escaped her and Zenobia rubbed her eyes as she snuggled deeper into her pillow. As if suddenly remembering that he was sitting there, her head popped up and she looked at him.

"Go ahead. Take 'em off. I want to see your fine ass."

Angelo chuckled and stretched out on top of the covers, clothes and all. He fluffed the king-size pillow behind him and leaned his back against the headboard. She didn't know what she was asking. He might've been tired, but being close to her and the tiny outfit she wore gave him life. If he got too close, he wouldn't be able to control himself from all that he wanted to do to her luscious body.

It was already hard keeping his distance. He had a love-hate thing going with the tank top and short shorts she preferred sleeping in. When she walked out of the bathroom in the outfit after her shower, his mind had immediately taken him back to the night they'd danced in the kitchen. She hadn't worn a bra that night, but tonight she had one on. Thank goodness. He would've had to poke some of his friends' eyes out downstairs if he'd caught them looking at her wrong.

"You can't be in my bed with clothes on," she said sleepily.

"Okay. I'll bring one of the chairs from your sitting area in here." It was probably better to put a little space between them anyway. He started to move off the bed, but she reached out with quickness and grabbed his arm.

"Please...don't leave." Her voice cracked, but then she hurried to clear her throat. "I don't want to be alone."

The vulnerability he saw in her eyes twisted his gut. The crash shook them up, but the deepening anxiety painted across her face confirmed his suspicions. The attempted kidnapping triggered a fear inside her—and this fear had nothing to do with tonight. This fear represented past demons.

Who had deserted her, Angelo wondered, because he knew someone had left her behind. He also knew that the remnants of that desertion forever marred Zenobia, leaving her scarred and broken.

"I already explained that I'm not leaving you."

"Then take off your clothes and get under the covers."

Angelo shook his head and grunted. She might be a little traumatized, but her special style of sass that showed up off and on over the past week was still there. Getting undressed and into bed with her was a bad idea. A very bad idea, but he'd be lying if he said that he didn't want to hold her close.

"Do you wear boxer or briefs?" She yawned again, watching him intently.

"Why don't I just show you. Put your mind at ease so that you can get to sleep."

Grabbing the T-shirt at the back of his neck, he pulled it over his head. He took his time unbuckling his belt and then went for the zipper on his jeans just as slowly. All the while her appreciative gaze took him in.

"Don't look at me like that." She already stirred something in him that kept him at a constant state of arousal. "Otherwise you're going to see more than you bargained for."

"I'll take my chances," she said sleepily, her gaze steady on him as if she was in Vegas watching the Chippendales perform. All he needed was a little music, and he'd be giving her a real show.

Angelo stripped down to his boxer briefs, leaving his clothes in a heap on the floor next to the bed.

"Wow." Her voice was light and loaded with awe. "I knew you had an incredible body, but man. Your muscles are stacked on top of each other. Not a lick of fat."

Angelo chuckled as he climbed in next to her. "Come here so you can get some sleep." He stretched out his arm and she scooted up to him, laying her head on his chest.

"And you smell so good," she murmured sleepily.

He held her close, grateful that they had survived the car crash. Now all he had to do was survive having her lush body molded against his. Angelo put his other arm behind his head and sigh.

It's going to be a long night, was his last thought before he drifted off to sleep.

Hours later, Angelo's eyes popped open. He glanced around the dimly lit room, illuminated by the lamp on the side table next to him. His coworkers' voices flowed up the stairs, and the night's events flashed through his mind. They were probably strategizing on next steps. It had been decided after leaving the hospital that his focus would be solely on Zenobia, while his team worked with authorities.

Angelo lifted his arm and glanced at his watch. *Five-fifteen.*

He hadn't planned to doze off. His intention was to wait until she was sound asleep, and then check in with Myles. He and Parker were now full-time on Zenobia's detail, and planned to stay at the house. If anything jumped off, he had no doubt they'd wake him.

Turning slightly, Angelo looked at Zenobia. She was no longer in his arms but still laying close to him. As he stared down at her, his heart swelled. Somehow this sweetheart of a woman had gotten under his skin. She had him thinking about changing their fake relationship to something real.

How crazy was that?

How was it possible that he had fallen for her so quickly? He couldn't explain it. All he knew was that she was important to him. In his mind, she was already his. Which was even crazier. There was just something about her that touched him deeper than any woman ever had. Angelo might not know everything about Zenobia, but he would one day. Until then, he would hang onto their powerful connection and see where it took them.

Reaching back, Angelo turned off the lamp and snuggled up with Zenobia. He threaded his fingers through her hair, pushing some of the strands away from her face. She was so beautiful and seemed so small and fragile.

He could've lost her tonight. Lost her to some unknown enemy for some unknown reason. It would've gutted him, not only to have lost her, but to have failed her.

Laying there with her felt like a new beginning. A second chance to get to know her on a different level. Not as a bodyguard boyfriend, as she often called him. Or as an assignment.

Angelo wanted Zenobia in his life. All of her. Even if he didn't know where their relationship would lead.

He snuggled closer as thoughts circled his mind.

Could he trust her with his heart?

*

When Angelo woke again, he lifted his head off the pillow, only to turn and find Zenobia staring at him. She was propped up on her elbow, looking deep in thought.

He rubbed the sleep from his eyes and blinked several times. "What's wrong?"

"Nothing. I was just wondering if you always woke up with an erection."

Well…dang. Wasn't expecting that.

Angelo dropped his head back onto the pillow and covered his eyes with his forearm. "Yeah, I do when I'm dreaming about the most beautiful woman in the world," he mumbled. He was too exhausted for conversation, and the last thing he wanted to discuss was his shaft unless he was putting it to good use.

Normally he slept in the nude, so his erection pressing firmly against his boxer briefs wasn't the most comfortable. Even worse, now that he knew she was staring at his junk, it was going to take some time to get his body under control.

"I'm not sure how I feel about you dreaming about other women while you're in my bed."

He lifted his arm slightly and turned his head to look at her, trying to determine if she was serious. "Sweetheart, you're the only woman who has occupied my mind and controlled my body since the day we met. Trust me. I don't have the capacity to think about anyone else. Only you."

She studied him for a moment. A slow smile crept across her tempting mouth until it blossomed into a full-blown grin. Was she really surprised by his response? Surely, she realized by now that he was totally wrapped up in her, but… Maybe she didn't know.

"If that's the case, maybe we should do something about

your um…predicament." Without another word, she straddled his body, shocking the hell out of him. "I'm up for a ride. If you're game."

Angelo gritted his teeth and gripped her hips when she started moving on top of him, only making him harder. "Babe," he said on a moan. Damn, she felt good and perfect on top of him. "Zenobia, I have used every bit of restraint I have to remain professional. If you keep moving like that, I won't be responsible for my actions."

She stopped and planted her hands firmly on his bare chest. "Aren't you tired of being responsible? We could've died last night. I don't know who's after me. If something happens, and I don't come out of this mess alive, I at least want to die with my sexual needs fulfilled."

With lightning speed, Angelo flipped her onto her back. Her eyes went wide and her mouth hung open as her nails dug into his forearm. He hadn't intended to frighten her, but he needed to get a couple of things straight.

"First of all, I'm going to keep you safe," Angelo said with more force than intended. He didn't know if she'd been kidding or not, but he couldn't have her thinking that she was going to die. "I'll give my life before I let anything happen to you. Do you hear me?" She gave a jerky nod. "Secondly, I want nothing more than to be buried balls deep inside of you. But, sweetheart, once we go down that road, there's no turning back. One time with you will never be enough for me."

Silence fell between them as they stared each other down. Propped up on his hands on either side of her head, Angelo was positioned between her legs. The only thing keeping him from sliding into her sweet heat was his underwear and the itty-bitty shorts she wore. All she had to do was give him the go-ahead and he'd make sure they were both sexually satisfied.

"What does that mean?"

"What does what mean?" he asked.

"There's no turning back. One time will never be

enough. What exactly are you saying?"

Yeah, what *was* he saying?

He was stepping into new territory here and had already broken a few of his professional rules. As a matter of fact, he was about to obliterate the *don't-get-involved-with-clients* rule.

"No more pretending to be your man. Not that I was doing much pretending, but I want to make this, whatever this is between us, official. I want to date you."

Last night, between the crash and their hospital visit, something shifted inside him. Every fiber in his body had been honed into her. He had already acknowledged to himself that she was more than just an assignment. But there was nothing like almost losing someone to make you wake up and realize how short life was.

Her brows rose to meet her hairline. "Are you serious? You want to date...me? I thought you weren't relationship material. That you weren't the long-term commitment type of guy. What changed?"

He wasn't sure. All he knew was that he couldn't stop thinking about her. There was no question that she was a beautiful woman, and he'd had his share of gorgeous women. With her, though, everything felt different. She was different. Sweet, edgy, and a little stubborn. She challenged him. Turned him on, and sometimes irritated the hell out of him. He liked her. More than he thought possible.

"You sang to me," he finally said. "I can't imagine my life without you."

"Be serious." She bumped his arm and knocked him off balance. He settled on the bed next to her.

Angelo could admit that his words sounded cheesy even to his own ears, but he meant them. Sometime between saving her from the attempted kidnapping well over a week ago until now, he'd fallen for her.

"Don't play me, Angelo. I've been used, abused, and betrayed too many times. Please don't play with my emotions."

Used? Abused? Betrayed?

What the hell? Each day she shared a little more about herself, but *abused*? He wanted to dig deeper into her painful past, but he also wanted her to open up to him in her own time.

Leaning on his elbow, Angelo stared down at her and brushed a strand of hair out of her face. His heart flipped inside his chest at the vulnerability in her hazel-brown eyes.

Now this was the woman he had fallen for. A fighter, but sweet. A thief, but kind. A celebrity, but real. The woman, who without trying, had gotten under his skin.

Angelo brushed a light kiss on her lips. "I would never intentionally hurt you, and I am very serious about us dating. I like you. A lot. I want to get to know you better on a personal level and see where this relationship takes us. So, what do you say?"

After a slight hesitation, her smile was back. "I say I think I'm going to like having you as my boyfriend, but what exactly does that entail? Any special perks?"

Now he was the one grinning. "Oh yeah. I can think of a few right off the top of my head, but I can show you those better than I can tell you about them. As for what it'll be like dating me, I can promise you weekly dates, home-cooked meals, and a whole lotta kissing. Only thing is, you have to promise to do something for me."

Her eyes narrowed. "And what's that?"

His first thought was to tell her she had to be honest with him, but after last night, he wanted to keep the moment light. He also knew in time she would learn to trust him with her deepest, darkest secret.

Instead of saying all of that, he said, "You have to promise to sing to me every day."

She nodded. "I can do that. If you also promise to serenade me daily." She ran the tip of her finger down his chest. A shiver scurried over his skin, and Angelo sucked in a breath. Her touch on his body wielded more power than she probably realized. He covered her hand with his, then brought the back of her fingers to his mouth.

"Deal."

"I think we're going to have a good time together. Especially when we figure out who's after me."

Angelo sighed, hating that this crap she was involved in was hanging over their head. He couldn't wait to get his hands on the person or people involved. It was only a matter of time before they zeroed in on them. Until then, he would do everything in his power to take Zenobia's mind off of the situation. At least for a while.

He lowered his head and covered her mouth with his, kissing her with a hunger that left no doubt to what he wanted them to do next. Their tongues tangled to a rhythm that was quickly becoming their own. She was his, and he planned to treasure every moment they had together.

When they finally came up for air, Zenobia ran her soft hand over the scruff on his cheek. "In case you hadn't figured it out, I like you, too. A lot."

"Good to know." Angelo recaptured her lips, devouring her sweetness as he slid his hand down the center of her body. Wanting to take his time, but also wanting like crazy to be buried inside of her.

Easing his mouth from Zenobia's, they worked together to relieve her of her shirt and shorts. The only thing left: a pair of red lace panties.

"Damn, baby." Those were the only words he could form to describe her shapely mouth-watering curves. The sexy underwear only enhanced the already perfect package.

He was a breast man, and that's where his gaze lingered the longest. She was more than a handful. Just the way he liked. His hand slid down the valley between her breasts and moved over her flat stomach until he reached the V between her thighs. Zenobia arched into his touch when he palmed her lace-covered center.

"Angelo," she breathed. Her eyes were closed and her arm was around his back. Her cold hand on his skin felt amazing and did nothing to snuff out the fire building within him. But he sucked in a breath when she bumped against the bruise on his side.

Zenobia froze and her eyes popped open. "Oh, my God. I'm sorry," she said in a rush and started to lift up.

He urged her back down when he covered her mouth with his. "Nothing to be sorry about," he mumbled against her lips. He'd had plenty of bumps, bruises, and broken bones over the years. In comparison, this one was only a scratch. He sure as hell wouldn't let it stop him from giving them both what they wanted and needed.

Releasing Zenobia's mouth, Angelo placed kisses along her jawline, her neck and continued his way down until his lips tasted her beautiful breasts. Unable to hold back, he cupped one of her mounds and lightly flicked his thumb back and forth across her pert nipple. Zenobia whimpered his name and squirmed beneath him, only making him want to experience more of her.

Squeezing her gently, Angelo pulled the dark nub into his mouth and sucked. Her lower body arched with each tug and lap of his tongue. He paid the same homage to the other nipple, loving the sounds he evoked from her.

Upon first meeting, never in a million years would he have believed that they would be at this point. He didn't do serious. He didn't do relationships. Yet, that's exactly what he wanted with her. Sometime during the night, he had stopped questioning why and decided to just go for it. Still, decisions had to be made about their professional relationship.

For now, though, he'd make sure they both enjoyed the here and now.

Chapter Seventeen

Moans filled the room. So intertwined, Zenobia couldn't tell if they were hers or Angelo's. He had kissed, sucked, and caressed her breasts like a hungry man devouring his last meal. That act alone had her quivering all over and brought Zenobia more pleasure than she had experienced in a long time.

In record time, he had rid them both of their underwear, and now she lay cradled against him. Their tongues tangled as his finger slid in and out of her heat. Zenobia's lower body arched to his touch, humping his hand as his digit moved in and out of her. She whimpered into his mouth with each stroke. Her heart beat harder and her body vibrated as she neared an orgasm.

"You like that?" Angelo murmured against her lips. With the pad of his thumb, he massaged her clit with enough pressure that practically had her crawling out of her skin. He slipped another finger into her.

Zenobia's breath caught, and electric currents shot through her body. Her hips moved up and down off the mattress, and she snatched her mouth from his, panting. "Oh yes. Please...don't stop." Her voice held a husky edge as she moved with each thrust of his fingers. He picked up the pace, going deeper and harder, getting her so close to the release she desired. "Please," she begged.

Just when she started to plead with him again, he touched a spot within her and a powerful orgasm was ripped from her body. Zenobia cried out and Angelo quickly covered her mouth with his, silencing her scream while her body convulsed against him. She struggled to catch her breath, feeling as if she was still free falling out of the sky.

Angelo continued his sweet torture. He placed feathery kisses on her cheeks, and down the column of her neck. Tingles scurried through her body. When he worked his way back up, he kissed her lips sweetly. If moments like this was one of the perks of dating him, she already loved the direction their relationship was going.

Zenobia reached between their bodies, wanting and needing to touch him. She wrapped her hand around his shaft, reveling in the feel of the veins brushing against her palm as she slid her hand up and down his long, thick, hardened length. Angelo hissed between his teeth when she squeezed him gently and ran her thumb across the tip.

"Aww, baby," he whispered close to her ear. His hardness pulsed within her hand. "We...I... Shit, I can't think straight with you doing that." He covered her hand with his and slowly eased out of her grip.

"Angelo," she whined, wanting to bring him as much pleasure as he'd just brought her.

"I know." He gave her a quick kiss on the lips, telling her not to move.

Still reeling from her release, she watched as he reached over the side of the bed for his jeans. Within seconds, Angelo had ripped open the foil packet and quickly sheathed himself.

"You ready for me?" he asked, moving between her legs and nudging them further apart.

"Definitely," she purred, marveling at the sheer size of his erection as he aligned their bodies. The man's physique was absolutely flawless, and now it was hers. He belonged to her.

She savored Angelo's passionate kisses as he took his

time inching into her. Inch by delicious inch, he stretched her while stroking her interior walls, and her eyes drifted close. It felt so good as he moved inside of her.

"Look at me," Angelo whispered, but the demand in his voice had her opening her eyes and meeting his gaze. "I want to see you, the look in your eyes, when I make you come."

His words and his dark, piercing gaze, as well as the way he moved inside of her, sent a sweet thrill shooting to the soles of her feet. The heightened passion had her hands fisting the sheet on either side of her as her head thrashed back and forth against the pillow. Her back arched, lifting her hips higher off the bed. Her moves were frantic as she bucked against him and neared her release. She was so close. So very...

Zenobia's eyes slammed shut. She cried Angelo's name as her powerful release attacked every nerve within her. Wave after wave of pleasure pulsed through her body, making her buck and jerk uncontrollably against him.

As she glided on a cloud of bliss, Angelo pumped in and out of her body, picking up speed with every stroke. After one hard thrust, he stiffened and trembled above her, groaning her name as his release charged through him. He collapsed but kept his weight from bearing down on her as his forehead dug into her pillow. Their heavy breathing mingled in the quietness of the bedroom.

Seconds ticked by before he eased out of her and rolled onto his back. "Man..." he huffed out, his chest rising and falling with each breath. They both laid next to each other in satisfied bliss until Angelo slowly sat up. "I'll be right back."

Zenobia watched as he crossed the room to the bathroom to dispose of the condom. His firm butt, rounded to perfection, made her want to reach out and grip both butt cheeks. She marveled at how good he looked going as he had coming. Once the bathroom door closed, Zenobia pulled the covers up over her breasts and stared up at the ceiling.

A smile tugged the corners of her mouth as she thought about what they'd just done. She knew they'd be good together, but the real act exceeded anything she could've imagined.

Angelo was a gentle lover. Just how she knew he'd be. More than that, he was hers. The night before, he gave a few hints that she meant something to him. However, he hadn't mentioned them exploring the attraction between them. Either way, Zenobia was on board. After so many bad choices, being with Angelo felt good. It felt right.

The smile dropped from Zenobia's lips as she thought about what dating a man like him would mean. At some point, her past would come up in conversation. Angelo was too curious of a person not to ask more questions. She was actually a little surprised he hadn't pressured her for some answers yet. She appreciated him taking his time with her, but how long would he wait? She wanted to share more of her history, and probably would as they got to know each other better. Her past was a time in her life that she never wanted to revisit, even if it was only in her thoughts. But with Angelo, she would. She felt safe with him and knew he wouldn't judge her.

After finishing in the bathroom, Angelo climbed back into bed and pulled Zenobia against his hard body. One of his large hands rested on her hip, and the other lifted her chin. When his lips touched hers, pleasure flowed through her like warm honey.

God, I can get used to this.

Having this man in her life, in her home, and in her bed was like a dream come true. Being there with him almost didn't feel real. But it was very real. He was very real as he sucked her top lip, then nipped at the bottom one.

"That was amazing," he murmured against her neck, and Zenobia shivered at his heated breath brushing over her damp skin.

"I agree, and I can't wait to do it again."

Angelo grinned, his eyes sparkling with mischief. "Oh, we will definitely do it again. Over and over again. Do you have any appointments today?"

"I thought I didn't, but I checked my voicemail this morning and Kevin, the guy producing my album, left a message. There's a scheduling conflict. If we want to use his friend's studio, the only opening is late tonight. I'm thinking I need to take it so we can finish laying the tracks for a couple of songs."

"You sure you're up for that? I thought you were still working on lyrics?"

"That's for a different song, and I might be done. I'll see what Kevin thinks of what I've come up with."

The producer had left the message during her meeting with Octavia. In light of the accident from the night before, he probably would consider rescheduling if she asked.

Zenobia leaned her head back farther, to look at him better, then touched his chin. He'd been clean-shaven for much of the week, but now he had a little scruff on his cheeks and chin. The rugged look added to his sexy, dangerous presence.

"What about you? Will your team need you to go over what happened last night?"

Zenobia had awakened before Angelo with the crash on her mind. Memories of it didn't freak her out like the night before. She was safe, and now sensationally sated.

"Yeah, at some point, I'll need to touch base with them. I'm sure Myles is on top of everything, and hopefully they have news to share."

It made her feel even more safe knowing that she and Sofia weren't in the huge house alone. There had been plenty of times Zenobia questioned why she'd purchased such a large place. The two of them would've been just as content and comfortable in a luxury condo. After last night, though, she was glad she had the extra space. There was plenty of room for them and the security team.

"How about we spend the next few hours in bed? Then, after we leave the studio, we can go out for a late dinner," Angelo suggested.

"I'd love that. Our first date."

He kissed her lips. "You're right. I'm going to have to put some thought into how to make it special."

"Just being with you will make it special, but I'm a little hungry right now. For food and a little more of what you just gave me." She glided her hand up his chest, his shoulder, and then down his arm. He shivered beneath her touch.

Angelo rolled onto his back and pulled her on top of his body, letting her feel how hungry a certain part of his body was as well. "I think I can help you with both," he said. "How about we start with this."

With an arm around her waist, and a hand at the back of her head, he pulled her close and kissed her with so much passion, Zenobia could've cried.

Maybe this was the man who could finally give her that happily ever after.

*

Angelo couldn't remember the last time he felt so relaxed. Clearly, he and Zenobia had needed the down time, lounging around and enjoying each other's company. Their last round of sex had wiped them both out. After sleeping for a couple of hours, Angelo had awakened before Zenobia and took that opportunity to get in a quick shower. He had also gotten caught up with Myles on the latest with the crash.

It was only a matter of time before the truck was found, and Angelo hoped Supreme's team found it first. That would give their people a chance to search the vehicle and possibly get answers before Atlanta PD gained access.

But right now, after eating a late lunch in bed, he and Zenobia were snuggled together, talking. Most of their conversation was around her singing career, and his family. But Angelo needed to get her to open up more about her past.

"Last night you were terrified that I was going to leave you. Why is that?"

For the first time in the past hour, silence fell between them. She was laying in the crook of his arm, her head partly on his chest, while his hand rested on her hip.

She tilted her head slightly and glanced at him. After a long hesitation, she started to speak, but Angelo stopped her.

"Don't say it had something to do with the crash, because I know it was more than that. I want the truth."

"My mother gave up on me," she said dryly. "I know, mentally, she wasn't always in her right mind, but she knew what she was doing the day she took her own life."

"What do you mean?" Angelo was a little surprised by the comment. "If she was suffering from bipolar disorder and schizophrenia, isn't it possible that she didn't know what she was doing?"

Zenobia released a long sigh. "It's possible, but… The weeks leading up to when she killed herself, my mother had been having what I thought were good days. For the most part, the medications helped even though she didn't like taking them since they depleted her energy."

Angelo's heart went out to Zenobia as she described how removed from reality her mother was at times, as if her mother's mind wouldn't tell her what to do. Some of the simplest things like putting on a pair of pants or picking matching shoes seemed impossible.

"She always seemed so unhappy. I don't know if she really was, but she looked unhappy which was so hard to deal with. As a teenager, I didn't know how to help her. Loving her wasn't enough."

Angelo remained quiet. He couldn't imagine what it was like to lose a parent like that or lose a parent period. All he could do right now was listen and be present in that moment for Zenobia.

"She left me. I came home one day after school, and she had taken all of her medications at once. She died of an overdose. It was ruled a suicide because she left a note. *I'm sorry.* That's what the note said."

"Ah, baby." Angelo held her tight, wishing he could wipe the bad memories away. He didn't know what to say and hoped she felt how much he cared about her.

"When I found her on the bathroom floor, she didn't

have a pulse." Zenobia's voice was muffled against his chest, and Angelo loosened his hold a bit. "Even though I knew my mother was dead, I remember begging her not to leave me. I can't remember how long I sat on the floor next to her body, pleading for her not to leave me."

"I am so sorry you had to go through that." Angelo felt helpless. There was nothing he could say or do that would change Zenobia's past or give her comfort at that moment. All he could do was be there for her going forward.

"Thanks. That experience made me stronger, but there are times when I can't stand being alone. I'm sorry if I made you uncomfortable last night."

"I wasn't uncomfortable, but I was worried about you."

She scooted closer to where their mouths were inches apart. "Thanks for being here for me. I don't usually have meltdowns like the one last night."

"We all have breaking points. What happened yesterday triggered something inside you. Anyone would have been affected." He was glad she told him more about what happened with her mother. Still, Angelo couldn't help but wonder what other buried memories the crash had shaken loose.

"Yeah, maybe," she said noncommittally, then gave him a quick kiss. Angelo didn't try to stop her when she sat up and moved to the side of the bed.

She swiped a scrunchy from the bedside table and pulled her hair into a messy ponytail on top of her head. "I'm going to do some writing for the next couple of hours."

Angelo's heart lurched inside his chest, and his breath caught. *What the hell?*

A scar. A skin-tone burn. Not just any burn. A capital letter C with a smaller C dangling from its end, peeked out from under Zenobia's arm. The branding, a bold two-inches-in-diameter circle, was familiar. He'd seen it on more than one occasion while with the DEA.

He had kissed, licked, sucked, and loved on her body for much of the day. How the hell had he missed the familiar skin branding? It might've been well hidden on her side and beneath her arm, but he was paid to be observant.

Angelo's heart beat double-time at the realization of what the branding signified. It only meant one thing.

Zenobia glanced at him over her shoulder. "What time are we plan…" She frowned and turned to him fully. "What is it? What's wrong?"

The shock that was simmering inside of him quickly turned to anger. If she kept something this serious from him and his team, what else hadn't she told them?

"Why didn't you tell me you were a part of the Cameeso Cartel?"

Chapter Eighteen

"Wh—what? H—how do you know about the cartel?" Zenobia stammered, tripping over the end of the bedsheet hanging on the floor. She hurried to cover her naked body, putting on the sweats that she had discarded earlier.

Angelo scrambled out of bed as if the mattress was on fire. Within seconds he was in his T-shirt and jeans. "Answer the damn question, Zenobia!"

She flinched at the tone of his voice, then swallowed hard, trying to gather her thoughts. The Cameeso name hadn't been spoken in her presence in over a decade. Of all the people to suddenly mention it, she never would have guessed it would be Angelo.

"I'm not answering any questions until you tell me what you know about them," she countered with more bravado than she felt.

"I was a DEA agent for almost fifteen years. I know more about drug cartels, the types of drugs they push, and their territories than I even want to think about. I also know the Cameesos were known for branding their women."

"I was not their woman!" she shouted, rage building inside of her at his assumption.

"Then tell me why the hell you have their symbol branded on your damn body!"

"They took me!" she screamed, then swiped everything off her nightstand with one swing of her arm. Fury roared through her veins as her chest heaved. Did he honestly think she would *let* someone brand her?

Zenobia startled when someone pounded on the door like the police. "Everything okay in there?" Laz's voice bellowed from the hallway.

"Yeah, we're fine. Get away from the door," Angelo said with less force than what he'd been using the last few minutes. He started toward Zenobia, but stopped suddenly at the foot of the bed, maintaining his distance. "Talk to me," he pleaded.

Zenobia shook her head and rubbed the back of her neck as she trudged across the room to the patio door. Thankfully, they had closed it earlier when it started raining harder. Otherwise, who knows who would've heard their yelling. It was bad enough that Angelo's team had probably heard them arguing.

And how the heck did she not know that he was former DEA?

Just my luck I'd fall for a former drug enforcement agent.

She would laugh if she could find any bit of humor in that statement. Instead, she searched her memory. Had they ever really discussed his past career? Atlanta's Finest all had either military backgrounds or law enforcement, but Zenobia had *assumed* Angelo was a former cop.

How could she possibly tell him about her involvement with the Cameeso Cartel without letting him know how ignorant she'd been back then?

Through the reflection in the patio door, she saw that he had sat on the edge of the bed. He was leaning forward, his elbows on his thighs and his gaze on the floor.

Zenobia wrapped her arm around her midsection as she stood looking out over the backyard. Normally, the view of the manicured lawn, beautiful flowers, and the waterfall connected to the pool brought an internal peace she couldn't get from anywhere else. Not today. Today, the dark clouds that hung low and the storm brewing outside resembled the chaos circling inside of her. She was being forced to relive a time she never thought she would survive.

Secrets destroy.

Sofia's words rattled around inside Zenobia's mind. No truer statement had ever been spoken.

Thing was, the secrets of her past weren't brought on by her. She'd been the victim countless times because of the secrets of others.

"Tell me about the cartel, Zenobia."

"I wasn't with them willingly, despite what you might think," she spat, bitterness dripping from each word.

She kept her back to him, not wanting to see judgment in his eyes. If a person could like and hate someone at the same time, that's how she currently felt about Angelo.

How dare he force me to remember…

Zenobia closed her eyes and lowered her head. Her shoulders dropped as she released a long, drawn-out sigh.

Since the day they met, all Angelo had ever tried to do was help her. In the process, he'd put his life on the line twice to keep her safe.

He had also captured her heart.

It wasn't his fault that her past was riddled with crap that nightmares were made of. He didn't deserve to have her back to him. If she was going to share a little of her story, the least she could do was do it face-to-face.

Zenobia turned to him. Her heart pounded so hard inside her chest, she was sure he and everyone else in the house could hear it.

"Tell me," Angelo said quietly, and she lifted her gaze to him. He was now standing near her dresser, his muscular arms folded across his chest. The distance between them was more than just spatial. The last eight hours of their sexual interlude was a distant memory, and in its place… Mistrust. Disappointment. Confusion. She could see all three in Angelo's eyes. At least he was no longer scowling at her.

"Twelve years ago, I lived in Miami," she said, her voice

cracking on the last word. She cleared her throat, determined to tell him what he wanted to know without breaking down. "While I was doing some waitressing at a small diner, a guy kept showing up. He came every day for at least three weeks, always sitting at one of my tables."

Zenobia stared up at the ceiling as her mind took her back to that time. There were days when her life in Miami seemed like yesterday. Other times, it seemed as if that horror happened a lifetime ago.

"At first, I was standoffish to his blatant flirting, but after a while I enjoyed our banter. He was extremely charming, super *fine*, and he was a big tipper. His tips alone in one week almost covered my rent for that month,"

Granted, she had lived in a crappy studio in one of the worst neighborhoods, but still. The money had come at a time when she needed it most.

"After about a week, he started asking me to go out with him. Each time, I said no. I was young, dumb, but smart enough to know that he was probably a drug dealer. He was flashy with his nice jewelry, his BMW, and wads of cash. So, I kept saying no, but appreciated the tips.

"Then one day, everything that could go wrong, did. Actually, it had started the night before, when I got home and someone had broken into my apartment."

Zenobia bit down on her bottom lip and blinked back the tears. Anger and grief warred within her, clogging her throat. She'd always wondered if there was some dark cloud following her around for a large chunk of her life.

Angelo started toward her, but she held up a hand. He stopped. If he said anything or touched her, she'd fall apart, and he wouldn't get his answers.

"I had a shit life," she continued, her voice thick with anguish until she cleared her throat. "The little I did own, someone either stole or destroyed that day."

Zenobia sniffed and swiped at a rogue tear. "The day after the break-in, I had to go into work. It took every bit of motivation I could muster to get there. I hadn't given up on life, but I'd been close. A person can only take so many knocks before saying *I quit.*

"When I got to the diner, there were a dozen roses with my name on them next to the time clock. I didn't have to guess who had sent them. All I knew was that they were right on time. A few minutes later, my admirer sat at my table and asked me out again. I said yes."

"What was his name?" Angelo asked.

"Leo Cameeso."

Angelo didn't speak. He glanced away but not before she saw something like fear in his eyes. Rubbing his chest, he took a step back and bumped into the side of the dresser.

"Angelo?"

His gaze shot to hers, and then his expression softened. "Go on," he prompted.

Zenobia told him about how she and Leo had dated a few months. He had wined and dined her, paid her bills, bought her a new wardrobe and showered her with attention. At eighteen, alone and broke, she mistook the material things and his attentiveness as love. When all along he'd been grooming her for a different type of life.

Leo introduced her to his father. At the time, Zenobia hadn't known much about the family. She had no idea his father, Lance Cameeso, was the most dangerous drug kingpin in Miami and Mexico.

She quickly learned that he was also the most heartless, and he'd been grooming Leo to be the same. The man she thought she loved, had lured her into her own personal hell. Leo's whole intent when it came to her was to *give* her to his father, a man who was into human trafficking.

Emotionally spent, Zenobia stopped talking. She had shared more with Angelo than she'd ever shared with anyone, even Kira. Her cousin knew about some of her past, but not everything. Zenobia and Kira hadn't known each other existed until Zenobia was put in foster care.

Who knew her mother had a sister? Not Zenobia. Just one of many secrets her mother had kept. Her newly-found aunt had become Zenobia's guardian, but after a few months, decided she couldn't care for her own child and Zenobia while working two jobs. Zenobia was returned to the state's custody.

It wasn't until she moved to Atlanta over five years ago that she and Kira reconnected. Monty 'Rock' Rockwell, of all people, had been responsible for reuniting them.

"How'd you get out?" Angelo asked.

Zenobia stared at him. She heard his question, but her mouth wouldn't open. It was as if her brain couldn't form the words bouncing around in her head. Or maybe it was that she didn't want to respond. She had already said too much.

She startled when Angelo grabbed both of her hands within his, as if knowing she couldn't tell the rest without support.

"How'd you get away from Cameeso?" he asked gently.

"Sofia."

"Sofia?" Angelo squeezed her hands as they stood face-to-face. "How did she get you out?"

"She..." Zenobia started, not knowing how to tell him about Sofia's role. Instead, she said, "The Cameesos had me under lock and key. There were guards always on duty with machine guns in their hands. It was like something right out of a mafia movie. Even though the elder Cameeso told me I was special and no one was to touch me, I was a prisoner. I could either cooperate with him, or..."

Tears sprang to Zenobia's eyes and she tried to pull away, but Angelo wouldn't let her go. She swallowed hard, struggling to keep her composure.

"He said he would...he would kill me if I tried to run."

"How long were you at their compound?"

He even knew they lived on a compound. There was no way she could tell him the whole story, not if she intended to keep the agreement she had with Rock. He'd done too much for her to betray him in any way.

"Months," Zenobia said, deciding to only answer questions related to the Camesso Cartel. "There were a couple of other girls, but after a while, it was just me he kept at the house. I found out by accident that he was involved in human trafficking."

Zenobia shook her head and tugged her hands free of Angelo's hold. "I can't do thi—"

"I need to know what happened. Baby, I need you to trust me."

The sincerity in his eyes was almost her undoing. She didn't understand why he needed to know all of this. How could she leave the past in the past if he was insisting on her reliving it?

"Trust me," he repeated.

"One night I was able to sneak into his office, and I called Sofia. I didn't know if she would help me, since the last time I'd seen her we'd had a big argument about me dating Leo. She knew of him and his family from when she lived in Mexico. All she'd said was, 'stay away from him'. I was so stupid. God, if only I had listened."

"What happened when you called her?"

"I told her I needed help. That the Cameesos had me. I didn't get to say more. A guard caught me in the office. I might've been considered *special* to Lance, but that night…" Zenobia shivered at the memory as tears blurred her vision. "Lance beat me so bad I only remember snippets of the days that followed."

This time Zenobia couldn't stop the tears that spilled from her eyes and choked her voice. When Angelo pulled her into his arms, she went willingly and cried harder, soaking up his warmth and strength. She shook violently as deep sobs racked her body. There were days she still couldn't believe that she had survived. So many people didn't live to tell about the wrath of Lance Cameeso.

Zenobia didn't know how much time had passed, but eventually her tears slowed, and she started to feel a little steadier on her feet.

"I'm sorry," she said, wiping her face with the sleeve of the sweatshirt.

"You don't have to apologize. I'm sorry you went through all of that. I had no idea."

"I know. After Lance beat me, I lost consciousness. It was the last time I saw him. I woke up at a clinic in Mexico with my head bandaged. Part of my face had to be reconstructed."

"Who—"

"Sofia was there," Zenobia quickly interrupted, afraid he would convince her to share more than she could. "All I can and will tell you is that her family got me away from the Cameeso cartel."

Angelo sucked in a long breath, then released it noisily as he ran his fingers through his hair. "Christ, Zenobia. Why didn't you tell us?" he asked with so much anguish in his tone. "This is the type of shit you should've told Mason and Hamilton during that initial meeting."

"Do you honestly think I want everyone to know how stupid I was back then? I allowed a slick-talking drug dealer to charm me, then lure me to his father, a misogynistic psycho who got off on hurting women. More importantly, I let fear keep me there. Do you know how many times I've beat myself up for not trying hard enough to get away?"

"Just stop, baby. Doing undercover work for the DEA, I've been up close and personal with some of the most merciless drug dealers. You wouldn't have stood a chance against them. I've seen firsthand how they mistreat women and the people they deem their enemies. Human life means *nothing* to them."

The misery in his tone made Zenobia wonder just how many dealings he had with drug cartels. The torment in his eyes made her want to reach out and hug him.

"One drug dealer in particular didn't think twice about blowing up some of my coworkers. I will never in my life forget that day. If that compound where you were held was as heavily guarded as some I've been to, you would've gotten yourself killed trying to escape."

Heavily guarded was an understatement. Lance had his

lackeys stationed at every inch of the place. They either worshiped the ground the man walked on, or they were too afraid for their families to go against anything he said.

Zenobia rubbed the back of her neck, so ready for this conversation to be over. "That was my past, Angelo. They're all dead now. Lance, Leo, the entire cartel no longer exists. So, there is no reason for me to relive that nightmare by discussing this further with you or anyone else."

She started to move away from him, but he gripped her shoulders, forcing her to look at him.

"Are you for real right now? You think just because a cartel has been disbanded that they can't reorganize?"

"Wh—what?" Her blood chilled at his words. "You...you think the Cameeso Cartel have rebuilt?"

Angelo pulled her into his arms, his chin resting on top of her head as he held her close. "Sweetheart, there's always a possibility. For our sake, I pray to God that's not the case."

Chapter Nineteen

An hour later, Angelo sat in the living room of the guest house, located behind the main house, numb from the story Zenobia had shared. He should've asked more questions. It was a horrifying tale, but he knew there was more. He had heard too many similar horror stories during his DEA days, but this one gutted him deeper than he could imagine. God only knew what else they did to her besides the branding.

The brand.

Knowing those assholes burned her gorgeous body made Angelo want to reach into their graves and kill them again. At least the symbol was well hidden. Most of the cartel women had been branded on their hip. Where Zenobia's mark was located, the side panel of her bra hid it well. But still...

Angelo leaned forward in the upholstered chair, his elbow on his thighs and his face in his hands. He growled into his palms. No matter how much work the DEA did to rid the streets of miscreants like the members of the Cameeso Cartel, it would never be enough.

He prayed his suspicions weren't right. That the group hadn't reassembled.

But he knew better.

He sat up, huffed out a breath and glanced around the cozy space. The two chairs and side table faced a wood-

Sharon C. Cooper

burning fireplace that looked like something straight out of a hunting lodge. There were no photos, paintings, or décor gracing the off-white walls. The original maple hardwood flooring was the best feature in the space. The one-bedroom, one-bathroom place was nothing fancy, but it suited his needs while he got his thoughts together.

He needed answers.

Pulling the cell phone from the front pocket of his jeans, he dialed Jared. It rang twice before his friend answered.

"I guess if you're calling me, you're no longer mad about me asking you to come back," Jared said without preamble.

"Nah, I'm still pissed." Angelo stood. He walked into the tiny kitchen and leaned against the butcher block countertop. Facing the window that gave him a view of the pool, he said, "I need some information."

"What do you need?"

Angelo had done a little research on his phone while Zenobia had been in the shower, but he needed information that couldn't be found on the internet. "What do you know about the Cameeso Cartel?"

"I know that you're the second person in a matter of weeks who has asked me that same question."

Angelo straightened. "What? Who else is asking?"

"One of our Miami agents heard chatter about some new *halcones* trying to take over a couple of territories," he said, using the Spanish word for what some groups called street soldiers. "A couple of their lieutenants used to be aligned with the Cameeso Cartel."

"That's not good."

"Tell me about it. We're still collecting intel, but it looks like one of the territories they're after is Rock's."

"So, the rumors about him trying to go legit aren't true?"

"Oh, no, they're true. I gotta hand it to the guy. He's cleaned up his shit and kept his head down. But we know that ain't gonna last. It's only a matter of time before we get his ass for a couple of murders we think he was behind."

Angelo shook his head, not wanting to hear anything

168

about Rock. Even if he looked good for those deaths, he wasn't in custody because there were too many layers between him and the little people. The man wasn't sloppy. He was smart, ruthless, and thorough. He also had enough power to get people to admit to crimes they never committed.

"That was one of the reasons I wanted you to go back undercover," Jared said, pulling Angelo's attention back to the conversation. "All we have to do is leak that Johnny Garza is alive. Reincar—"

"No," Angelo said simply.

As far as he was concerned, Johnny Garza was dead. Angelo had used that identity for years to go deep undercover in Rock's organization. Those days were gone and never to be revisited. Johnny died during his last op, where they'd lost several DEA agents in an explosion while trying to get to Rock. There was a death certificate to prove it.

"Tell me more about the Cameeso Cartel," Angelo said, steering Jared back on track.

"Like you, I don't know a whole lot about them. Just some basic shit. They were out of the picture by the time you and I joined the Miami office." Angelo heard Jared typing. "I do know that was around the time Rock scooped up some solid alliances. He—"

"Damn, Jared. Why do all of our conversations have to circle back to Rock?"

"Dude! If you'd shut the hell up for a minute and let me finish, you'd know why!"

Angelo huffed out a breath. "Fine. Continue."

"Rock was instrumental in wiping the Cameeso Cartel off the face of the map."

No surprise there. During the few years Angelo spent in the man's organization, Rock was serious about keeping other drug dealers and gangs out of his territory. If he was involved in getting rid of the Cameesos, then...

Angelo's mind skidded to a halt. What were the chances that Rock had anything to do with Zenobia getting away? Part of him was tempted to pose the question to Jared. But the last thing Angelo wanted to do was bring any more attention to Zenobia. Jared was like a dog with a bone. He'd want more details and might dig up more shit to harm her than help her.

Nah, Angelo would keep anything about her between him and Supreme Security. They'd get the answers he needed.

"All right, man. Thanks for the info," Angelo said. "If you run across anything useful about the cartel, let me know."

"Hold up. How you gon' ask me all these questions without telling me why? What are you working—"

"Later, man." Angelo hung up, knowing he would never hear the end of it for hanging up on his friend twice in a matter of weeks.

Angelo looked up just as Myles strolled to the front door. He gave a quick knock before pushing open the door.

Angelo set his phone on the counter. "Hey, what's up?"

"I could ask you the same thing. You stormed out of the house without a backward glance. Care to tell me what's going on with you and the angel?"

Myles referred to Zenobia as *the angel* since hearing her singing around the house. He leaned on the back of a rickety dining chair and gave Angelo a pointed look.

"I know you like her and all, but you're getting a little too serious. She's a client, remember?"

"Yeah, I know. Which is why I'm pulling myself off her detail."

Myles stared at him for a few minutes, then narrowed his eyes. "Really? You're that into her?"

Angelo nodded, and Myles released a long whistle. "Well, damn. So much for faking. I've never known you to fall for a client."

"Yeah, this is a first. I told you from that first encounter, there was something about Zenobia. We mesh. You know what I mean?"

"Hell, nah, I don't know what you mean. I try to stay as far away as possible from any romantic entanglements. You know, like you used to."

Myles had said on more than one occasion that he would

never marry, or even get seriously involved with a woman. Angelo had pretty much said the same thing but look at him now. He couldn't imagine being away from Zenobia for any length of time. That realization still boggled his mind.

"I know you're going to do whatever the hell you want, but be careful with this one. Zen seems like a real sweetheart, but I have a feeling she's more than what she seems. I'd hate for you to get in too deep."

Zenobia had a checkered past, but Angelo knew enough people, like Laz and Myles, whose pasts were just as shady. He had no intention of abandoning her just because of what she'd been through with the Cameesos.

"Too late. I'm all in," he said.

"Yeah, I figured." Myles stood up straight and folded his arms across his chest. "So, what's got you hiding out here? I assume it has something to do with why Laz was about ready to yank you out of Zen's room earlier. What happened and does it have anything to do with why she had to hire us?"

"Let's just say we might have a serious problem."

Not wanting to share every detail, Angelo gave his friend the highlights of his conversation with Zenobia. He wasn't surprised that Myles had knowledge about the cartel. As former CIA, he had associates all over the world and planned to make a few calls. That was one thing Angelo could say about Supreme Security. With all the contacts the bosses and security specialists had, the company was very well connected.

"Maybe you shouldn't have told Zen that the cartel might be back on the scene. She was skittish after the crash. How's she doing now?"

"Not too good when I left her upstairs. We were planning to go out to dinner, but she changed her mind, preferring to stay in until we know more."

"Actually, that's the other reason I came out here. One of Laz's contacts at Atlanta PD said they found the truck that slammed into you and Zen."

Angelo perked up. "When? Where?"

"A couple of hours ago on the Georgia/Florida border

about seventy-five miles north of Jacksonville. The truck was torched, along with a body inside that has two gunshot wounds."

Angelo growled in frustration. "Let me guess. One of those was a shoulder wound."

Myles nodded. "And the other, a close range shot to the guy's left temple. They're hoping to get an ID with the dental records, but the vehicle is toast."

"Of course it is," Angelo said dryly. At least the guy who attacked them didn't get away, assuming he indeed was the one in the torched truck. This news should've made Angelo feel better. Instead, it brought home the fact that the people they were dealing with were even more dangerous than he first believed. Realizing that the hit was professional sent his concern for Zenobia's well-being skyrocketing.

As if reading his mind, Myles clapped him on the shoulder. "Don't worry. We won't let anything happen to your woman," he assured as he headed to the door.

"I know, but considering all she's been through, it might take her time to believe it." Angelo grabbed his phone. It was time he called the office.

"Parker and Laz are on duty. I need to make a run. You need anything?"

"I'm good, but can you ask Sofia to check on Zenobia? I need to call Egypt."

"Yes, to Sofia, and good luck with trying to get off of Zenobia's security detail. If you walk, she might clam up, and I think she knows something that could help us. Something she probably doesn't even realize she knows."

"I'm not leaving her. I'm just going to be by her side in a different capacity...as her man."

Myles shook his head. "This has got to be a first." He chuckled as he left the house.

"Yep, definitely a first," Angelo mumbled and dialed Egypt.

"Hello."

"Well, if it isn't the future Mrs. Kenton Bailey. Got a

Egypt laughed. "*Mrs.* Kenton Bailey. It has a nice ring to it, doesn't it?"

"It really does, and I can't wait to witness the day you lock down my boy." Kenton was one of his best friends, and Angelo couldn't have picked a better woman for him.

"By the way, we're not having a long engagement. We're thinking Labor Day weekend. That gives us a few months to plan a small church wedding, and then maybe a cookout."

"Sounds good to me. I'll be there."

"So, what can I do for you?" Egypt asked. "How's it going with Zen?"

"It's...going. There have been a couple of developments that I need to fill you in on. First, though, what exactly did you find on her during your search?"

"I gave you what I found. Why? Did we miss something?"

"I need you to dig deeper. She never knew her father, but can you see what you can find on him and her mother? Also, can you get information on her cousin Kira's parents? And I need you to probe into Sofia's background, especially her family or any connections she has in Mexico City. No information is too small."

"Oookaay. Care to tell me what's happened?"

"Yeah. How much time you got?"

*

Hours later, Zenobia ventured down the back staircase that led into the kitchen, not surprised to see Laz standing at the bottom of the steps. That meant another security specialist was near the main stairs.

How had her life come to this? People watching her every move. Stuck in the house for fear of getting attacked if she stepped out into the real world. It was no better than being kept on the Cameeso's compound suffering under lock and key.

Guilt stabbed Zenobia in the chest at that last thought. Her current situation was nothing like her life in Miami. At least now, the people guarding her truly cared about her well-being, and she wasn't a prisoner in the house. It was on her that she was afraid to go anywhere. Angelo assured her that they'd keep her safe if she wanted to go out. But Zenobia wasn't in the right frame of mind to be out in public.

"Hey, Laz," she greeted. "You don't have to stand around. Make yourself comfortable. I promise I won't leave the property without letting one of you know." He nodded. The only visible sign that he considered her instructions was a slight loosening in his shoulders. Yet, he didn't move from the spot.

"I'm glad you came down, *mija*. I was about to check on you again," Sofia said when Zenobia walked into the kitchen and kissed her cheek. "You need to eat. I made a lasagna and a tossed salad for the boys and there's plenty left."

Zenobia smiled at her *boys* reference. The men of Supreme were huge and there was nothing boyish about any of them. Except for maybe how sweet they treated Sofia. It was going to be hard to see them leave once Zenobia didn't need round-the-clock protection.

"Angelo's not back yet?" Sofia asked.

Zenobia shook her head as she nibbled on the lasagna Sofia had set in front of her. "No, he'll be gone for a couple of hours."

After hanging out in the guest house, Angelo had returned to the house to let her know that he had to go into the office. He was no longer on her detail, and Zenobia wasn't sure how she felt about that. Would it mean she wouldn't see him as often? He said that wouldn't be the case. Yet, he wasn't there.

Then there was the fact that he had to share her story with his team. Even if she understood the reasoning, it still didn't make the situation less embarrassing. So far, no one treated her differently. Yet, it was like walking around with the scarlet letter C on her chest. They knew she'd been with Cameeso, even if it wasn't by choice. That had been one of those secrets she had planned to take to her grave.

Sofia pushed the plate closer to Zenobia. "Eat, *mija*. You no eat enough. You haven't eaten all day. Stop worrying."

Zenobia glanced toward the stairs, surprised that Laz wasn't standing there, but glad that she and Sofia were alone.

"I can't help but worry. What if Angelo is right? What if the Cartel is—"

"No," Sofia said forcefully, waving her index finger. "They will never hurt you again. *Lo entiendes?*"

"Yes, I understand," Zenobia said automatically, though she wasn't sure Sofia was right. Powerful drug dealers had their way of getting what they wanted. Zenobia didn't want to believe that the Cameeso Cartel had somehow rebuilt, but who else would be trying to get to her? Who else would be bold enough to try and snatch her right off the street? Who else would be reckless enough to try and yank her through a car window?

The ringing of her cell phone was a welcomed distraction. Otherwise, she would drive herself nuts thinking of the what-ifs. She glanced at the screen, hoping to see Angelo's number, but instead it was her cousin.

Zenobia pushed away from the counter. "I need to take this," she said to Sofia and started up the stairs. "Hello."

"Hey, girl. How are you?"

"I'm all right. How's things with you?"

"Oh no you don't. You've been held up in that big house with that gorgeous tall drink of water, and I want details. Is he as good in bed as I think he is? And don't even try and lie and say you haven't done anything with him."

As Zenobia entered her bedroom and closed the door, she couldn't stop the smile from spreading across her face. Now, Angelo, in that capacity was a subject she wouldn't mind talking about.

Feeling lighter than she'd felt all day, Zenobia giggled and fell back on the bed. "Girrrl, let me tell you. He's all that and then some." For the next hour, they talked and laughed about everything and nothing. She didn't give every detail of her rendezvous with Angelo but gave enough to let her cousin know that he knew how to please a woman. Girl talk was exactly what Zenobia needed to take her mind off her problems.

"Are you guys still attending Tremaine's release party this weekend?"

Zenobia stared up at the ceiling. Since she backed out of their *first-date* plans for the evening, they'd decided the party would be their official first date.

"We'll be there. What about you guys?"

"Please. You don't even have to ask. I've been thinking about that party for weeks, and I can't wait to rub shoulders with the rich and famous. Oh, and my dress came today. Elijah's eyes are going to fall out of his head when he sees me in this little number.

Zenobia laughed and scurried off the bed and went to her walk-in closet. It never got old to see the crystal chandelier sparkle to life when she flipped the light switch. As large as one of the spare bedrooms, the customized space was decked out. A center island with drawers on both ends held jewelry and accessories. Angled shelves accommodated over a hundred pairs of shoes. A remote-controlled lighting system illuminated the see-through cabinets easily displaying her clothes. Any feature Zenobia could have possibly wanted in a closet had been included.

As her cousin went on and on about her dress, Zenobia pulled out three outfits that she hadn't worn yet. A white strapless dress with a beaded bodice that stopped just above her knees. A red one-shoulder gown with a deep split that would showcase her left leg. And the last one was a little black dress that was conservative in the front, but the back had a deep V that stopped just above her butt.

"Well, let me get off this phone," Zenobia said. "I need to try these dresses on to make sure they fit."

"Oh please. Anything your little skinny ass wears looks amazing, but I'll let you go. Me and my boo are hitting the club tonight. I need to finish getting dressed."

After they said their goodbyes, Zenobia tried on all three

outfits. Twice. By the time she was done, she still hadn't decided which one to wear.

Wrapped in a short silk robe, she stood in front of the garments when the bedroom door opened, then closed. Seconds later, Angelo stood in the doorway of the closet.

Seeing him dressed in all black, like that first day they'd met at Supreme, stirred all of her girlie parts. He had left his suit jacket somewhere and only wore a black button-up shirt, tie and pants. Sexy and dangerous looking, the man had her nerve endings standing on edge and sizzling.

"You came back." Her voice was breathier then intended as she fiddled with the belt of the short robe.

"Of course I did." Angelo moved slowly toward her, undoing his tie with every slow step he took. "I told you, baby. We're in this together. That hasn't changed. *Nothing* has changed."

The ends of the black tie hung down Angelo's chest as he started unbuttoning his shirt, and a jolt of desire spread through Zenobia's body. She loved watching him undress.

"What were you doing?" he asked, dropping the shirt and tie onto the closet's center island. That left his muscular upper body completely bare, and her mind skidded to a halt.

"I um…I was um trying on outfits for the party Saturday night." She gave a jerky nod toward the three choices hanging on hooks in front of her. "Do you have a preference?"

"The white one," he said, barely glancing at either of the garments. His gaze was solely on her.

"The white one it is," she said absently, too caught up with watching him remove a condom from his wallet before he unfastened his belt. Aroused and ready for whatever he had in mind, Zenobia waited with bated breath as he undid his pants and let them drop, along with his underwear, to the floor. At some point he had already kicked off his shoes.

Backing her up to the island, Angelo caged her in with his hands on either side of her. "I've missed you," he said seconds before capturing her mouth in a hungry kiss.

No one had ever kissed her with such abandon, making

her feel like the most important and cherished person on the planet. There had been moments in the day when she wondered if he'd return. Questions bombarded her mind. Could they move forward as a couple? Would he think she was tainted? Would he look at her differently?

Now those questions didn't matter as his large hands slipped inside of her robe, and he caressed her bare skin. As a matter of fact, nothing mattered but the way he was worshiping her mouth and setting her body on fire.

We're in this together, his words from moments ago penetrated her muddled mind. *We're in this together.*

Zenobia gasped when he turned her suddenly and her back was to him. "Relax, baby," he crooned.

The ripping of foil caught her attention and while he sheathed himself, a sexual hunger she never knew existed filled her. Angelo nudged her legs apart and bent her forward slightly. When he started teasing her clit with the pad of his finger, Zenobia's knees went weak. Man, he knew how to get her juices flowing.

Angelo moaned near her ear. "I love that you're ready for me."

His shaft bumped against her moist opening, and Zenobia sucked in a breath, practically melted against him as he slid into her heat.

Holding her close, he moved in and out of her slowly at first but soon picked up speed like a man possessed. All thoughts flew from Zenobia's mind. With her hands splayed on the counter and her body vibrating with pleasure, she was barely hanging on.

"Yes, yes, yes," she panted with each thrust as they grew harder and more urgent, and Angelo's arm around her waist tightened. His fingers burned into her skin and Zenobia's breathing became more labored as waves of ecstasy throbbed through her body.

"Ze...nobia," Angelo growled against her ear and the gruffness of his voice along with another hard thrust sent them both barreling over the edge of control.

Zenobia's body exploded into a trillion little pieces, and she collapsed against the island. Angelo's weight bore into her as they both battled to catch their breaths. They stayed in that position for the longest time, neither mumbling a word. If this was what it was going to be like with him, she was all in.

We're in this together, the words continued to play through her mind. *We're in this together.*

Chapter Twenty

Angelo rubbed his hands together as he anxiously paced the family room. The guys had already been ribbing him about being nervous for a first date, but that wasn't what had him riled. Atlanta's Finest goal had always been to keep their clients safe, and normally Angelo didn't doubt their abilities. Until now. Now all he could think about was what if they failed Zenobia? What if this unknown enemy lurking in the shadows managed to get the jump on them?

He stopped and combed his fingers through his hair. He was tripping. He trusted these guys with his life, and hers, too. They were the best of the best and there wasn't a man on her security detail who wouldn't give his life to protect hers.

Angelo glanced at his watch. "What's taking her so long?"

"Man, chill," Kenton clapped him on the shoulder. "It's a celebrity party. Everyone will be fashionably late."

If anyone should know, it was Kenton. He usually got assigned to celebrity security details and was one of the few who didn't complain. It was the least favorite for many of the other security specialists, including Angelo. During his experience with some famous people, he found them to be too high-maintenance, fickle, and often disrespectful. At least that's what he thought until Zenobia fell into his life. Maybe he'd been a little too quick to judge the others because she was nothing like he would've imagined.

Angelo headed for the main stairs. "Let me go and see what's taking her..." His words died on his tongue when she appeared in the middle of the wide staircase.

Stunning wasn't a strong enough description to depict how gorgeous his woman looked. *My woman. My beautiful woman.* How was it possible that she could improve on perfection? She was breathtaking in the white strapless dress that showed off long, shapely legs that seemed to go on forever. The dangling diamonds hanging from her ears and around her neck accentuated the outfit. While her hairstyle, loose curls piled on top of her head with a few curly tendrils framing her perfectly made-up face, completed the lovely package.

Angelo's gaze went back to the dress and heat soared through his veins. "You can't wear that," he blurted.

Someone in the room laughed. It sounded like Parker, but Angelo couldn't be sure since the culprit covered the laughter up with a cough.

"Excuse me?" Zenobia walked the rest of the way down the stairs. She stopped in front of Angelo with one hand on her hip and the other clutching a small purse. "You're the one who picked this one. What do you mean I can't wear it?"

"I know but you look..." Angelo's words trailed off when he realized he wasn't sure what to say. What the heck could he say? She looked hella good, but he might have to break some chump's neck at the party if he looked too hard. "I mean, you look magnificent. I'm just concerned that it's too much...or not enough."

"What he means is that his ass will end up in jail if another man looks at you the wrong way," Laz said bluntly from the front door. "Now can we go?"

Zenobia burst out laughing and turned away from Angelo. "I'm ready, but I don't know about my uptight date."

Two hours into the party, and Angelo was finally starting to relax. One good thing about not being on Zenobia's security detail, he could have a drink. Unfortunately, not being on her detail also meant that he'd been stripped of communication with his team. He missed not being able to crack jokes through their invisible coms or discuss results of a basketball game. Tonight, according to Laz, Angelo's only role was to be eye candy.

Sipping on his scotch, Angelo glanced around the grand ballroom. Octavia was making her rounds. She had been the first person they saw when arriving. He was glad that she had several clients in attendance, meaning she didn't linger around him and Zenobia.

Angelo gave a nod at Parker who was several feet away, trying to blend in near the bar. Kenton and Laz were in reach of Angelo and Zenobia. Like Zen, a few other celebrities arrived with their own personal security, even though Supreme provided security for the whole event.

Zenobia slipped her arm through his. "Do you want something else to eat?" She had to practically scream over the loud music. Tremaine Dempsi spared no expense on food, drinks, and had the best entertainers present. Some, including Zenobia, had performed.

"Nah, I'm good, but I'll gladly get you something to eat or drink if you want," he said, slipping his arm around her shoulder and kissing the side of her head. He learned something else about her. She normally didn't drink alcohol. Which was why those shots of whiskey he had insisted she drink the other night had her so tipsy.

"I could go for a soda, but what I would really like is to sit down for a little while. These shoes aren't the most comfortable."

Angelo glanced down at the strappy sandals. How women stood heels for as long as they did was a mystery to him. "Your wish is my command."

A few minutes later, with drinks in hand, they sat at a table with Kira and Elijah. At the beginning of the party, it had been just Kira. Elijah just returned to town and was running late. It would've been okay with Angelo if the guy never showed up. He could have fallen off the face of the earth. Angelo couldn't pinpoint exactly why he couldn't stand the man, but his dislike grew even stronger since the first time they met.

"It's good to see Zenobia isn't sporting another black eye," Elijah said, a smirk on his face as he looked at Angelo. "I guess you took my warning to heart."

"Eli, don't start," Kira warned. "We're here to have a good time, not watch you two toss jabs at each other.

Angelo remained quiet, not bothering to justify either comment with a response. Apparently, his hate toward *Eli* was mutual.

Zenobia squeezed Angelo's hand under the table. He glanced at her, finding comfort in the small smile she gave him. He brought her fingers to his lips and kissed the back of them.

He leaned in close. "When you were singing earlier, I couldn't help but think you were singing to me."

"I was. It's part of our agreement, remember? Which reminds me: you haven't sung for me today."

Angelo laughed and shook his head. That's when he spotted Jared across the large space in deep conversation with a couple of women. Release parties weren't usually his scene, and Angelo wondered if his friend was there on business or pleasure.

"Once we get out of here, I promise to sing to you for the rest of the night. Right now, though, I need to go holler at a friend of mine. I'll be right back."

"Take your time. I'll be here."

Angelo kissed her and glanced at Kenton and Laz. They both nodded, acknowledging that they'd keep an eye on his woman. Then Angelo went in search of Jared.

*

Fifteen minutes later, Zenobia was glad to have the table to herself. Shortly after Angelo went to talk to his friend, Elijah excused himself to go to the men's room. And while Zenobia absolutely adored Kira, she was glad when her cousin left her alone to go and rub shoulders with the rich and famous.

Zenobia sipped her club soda and bobbed her head to Tremaine's latest release. At least until her gaze found Elijah far across the room, talking to a couple of men. It wouldn't have struck her as odd, except he had been watching Angelo the entire time. Even after he shook each man's hand before they walked away, Elijah's attention was back on Angelo.

Hmm…

Zenobia brought her glass up to her mouth, but stopped inches from her lips. She watched Elijah snap a picture of Angelo and his friend, then typed something into his phone.

"What the heck is that about?" she said to herself.

"You say something?"

Zenobia jumped in her seat at Kenton's voice close to her ear. There was always at least one of the security team nearby, but she had temporarily forgotten about them.

"Don't mind me. I'm just talking to myself."

He nodded, then stepped back. Zenobia's attention went back to Angelo who was deep in conversation. When she looked for Elijah, he was gone. Glancing around the room, she eventually found him weaving in and out of people, heading her way.

"Dance with me," he said reaching the table, his hand extended.

Kenton stood a couple of feet away, but Zenobia could've sworn she heard him curse. From her peripheral view, she saw Laz move in closer. Zenobia smiled. They might've been hired to guard her, but there was no doubt in her mind that their responses had just as much to do with her being their friend's woman.

Tremaine had left the stage and now a DJ was playing a slow song. Zenobia was tempted to say no to Elijah, but she wanted some answers. "Sure, I'll dance with you." She accepted his hand. Then she turned to Kenton who was now in arm's reach of her. "It's okay. I'll make sure we stay where you can see me."

"Damn, man. It's just a dance," Elijah said when Kenton didn't immediately back up. Again, Zenobia assured him that she'd be fine.

When she and Elijah reached the packed dance floor, he tried pulling her toward the middle of the throng of people.

"Right here is fine," she said. They weren't exactly on the edge of the dance floor, but pretty close. Close enough to where Angelo and his team could get to her quickly if needed. Besides, Laz stood on the dance floor with his arms folded across his chest, seeming oblivious to guests having to dance around him.

Elijah pulled her close and they swayed to the music. "What's going on, Zen? You've up security at your house and when you go out in public. Kira said you're just being more cautious because of some crazy fan, but I have a feeling it's more than that. What gives?"

Instead of answering, Zenobia asked a question of her own. "What do you have against Angelo? He's a great guy. Yet, throughout the night you've made snide remarks trying to provoke him. Why?"

"I don't like him. I know you and Kira think he's all that, but something's not right about the guy. Kira said you met him a couple of months ago when you were getting estimates for a new home security system. What do you really know about him, besides him working for a home security company? Did you do a background check on him? I don't think he's who he says he is."

Stunned into silence, Zenobia was slow to respond. "I've had him thoroughly checked out. I just don't understand why you care so much."

He leaned his head back and frowned at her. "You're like a sister to Kira, which makes you like a sister to me, but if you want me to back off, I will. I'm just concerned about you."

Zenobia slowed as the song neared its end. "I appreciate that, but I think I know what I'm doing with Angelo." She gave Elijah a hug before pulling out of his arms.

Elijah gently gripped her elbow. "How about another dance?"

"That's not a good idea. Angelo is the jealous type, and I don't want any trouble tonight. And that's exactly what will happen if I dance with you again. Besides, here comes my cousin. I'm sure you'd rather dance with her."

Zenobia turned and had barely taken a step before she found herself in Angelo's arms. He led her to the center of the dance floor and pulled her against his hard body. They hadn't danced together since that night in her kitchen, and she was glad the DJ was playing another slow song.

Zenobia's arms went easily around his neck and with a hand at the back of his head, her fingers sifted through his silky hair. He loved and hated when she played in his hair, which only made her want to do it all the time.

"I saw what you did," he whispered, his voice thick and his breath warm against her ear.

"What?"

"I know you just slipped Elijah's cell phone into my jacket pocket."

"Oh."

Of course, he had seen her. He was one of the most observant people she had ever met. Would she have followed through on her plan had she known he was watching? Probably. Elijah was up to something and they needed to know what.

"I thought we agreed that you were done with stealing."

"I agreed to never steal from you. I never said I wouldn't steal again. Besides, I didn't steal his phone. We're just borrowing it."

"Why?"

"Because he was watching you, and I think he took a picture of you and your friend. I'm not saying he's up to something or did anything wrong, but I thought it was odd. Especially when it looked like he had texted someone."

Angelo took so long to say anything, Zenobia thought that maybe she had gone too far. "Listen, I—"

"Supreme could use your special skills," he finally said, and kissed her so thoroughly, Zenobia hadn't realized the song had stopped and now a faster one was playing. "But no more *stealing*. It's too dangerous. Now, let's get out of here. I need to hand off this phone before that chump realizes it's missing."

Chapter Twenty-One

Late the next afternoon, Angelo strolled into Supreme Security, feeling good but exhausted thanks to his sexy songbird. In between lovemaking, dancing, and singing songs by some of their favorite artists the night before, he and Zenobia talked. Nothing too heavy. Just chatted about typical stuff one would discuss on a first date. Favorite color. Favorite food. The funniest thing that ever happened to them.

They kept the topics light. Each day Angelo learned more about her, only making him want to know everything. The more time he spent with Zenobia, the deeper his feelings for her were getting. Problem was, the situation with her unknown enemy was still hanging over their heads.

Angelo headed up the back staircase. Egypt had summoned him in for a meeting. He was cautiously optimistic that they had found something that could help Zenobia's situation.

When he reached the top landing, his phone chirped with a text message and he glanced at his phone.

Laz.

Hopefully his friend had some good news. Angelo had handed off Elijah's phone to Laz who knew people on both sides of the law. He claimed to have someone who could get into the locked phone. If they couldn't, Laz assured him that he could somehow get Elijah's phone records.

Angelo read the text.

No luck getting into the phone, but got someone going through the phone records. Looking for anything connected to you or Zen.

Angelo didn't know how he'd pull that off without a warrant and would never ask.

Thanks. Keep me posted, he texted back before returning his phone to his pants pocket.

When he made it to Egypt's office, she was standing next to her desk with a cell phone plastered to her ear. Angelo hovered near the door, wanting to give her some privacy, but she waved him in and pointed to one of the chairs at the small round table.

As usual, she was dressed to impress. The guys often referred to her as Queen. Not only because she played a major role in Supreme's operations, but because she came to work looking like a Nubian queen. Like now, she had on an African print button-up blouse that was yellow, red, green, and a host of other vibrant colors. It was paired with a straight navy-blue skinny skirt that stopped at her knees, along with sky-high navy-blue pumps. How she worked in shoes that tall all day was a mystery to him.

"Hey there," she said after finishing her call, then hugged him. "How was the party last night?"

"It was good. Saw a lot of entertainers, ate good, and of course, the music was on point. All in all, great evening."

"I'm glad to hear that." She moved her laptop from the desk and set it on the table. "Have a seat. Let's get right to it because Wiz is going to be calling in a few minutes. But first, I wanted to let you know that we heard back from our contact at Atlanta PD a few minutes ago. They have an ID on one of the guys who attacked you and Zenobia."

"Oookay. Who was he?" Angelo asked slowly. Jared had confirmed the night before that the Cameesos were rebuilding, but were in the early stages.

"His name was Reggie Sumpter and his last known

189

address was Miami, Florida. They still don't have any information on the other guy, but that truck was also spotted in Lake Geneva around the time Zenobia was there."

"What? Really? Did anyone—"

"That's all our contact knew. They're still waiting for more information."

"Do they know anything more about the dead guy, Reggie? Who'd he hang out with? Any cartel or gang affiliations?" Angelo asked, his pulse amping up as he pulled his cell phone from his pocket to call Myles. He and Kenton were on Zenobia's detail, and Angelo wanted them to be extra-attentive with her safety.

"If you're getting ready to call Kenton, you don't have to. I talked to him about ten minutes ago and gave him the same info. As for Reggie, he had a brother with ties to the Cameeso Cartel."

Angelo's heart thumped loudly in his chest. "Where is his brother now?"

"Dead. He was killed in a home invasion over ten years ago. So far, they don't know Reggie's affiliations, but said he'd been in and out of jail for much of his life."

Angelo eased out of his seat and paced around the room. "Well, at least he's off the streets. I want to know who Reggie was with that night he slammed into my car."

"I'm sure you'll have answers soon, but are you ready to hear what I found on Zenobia?"

Angelo rubbed the back of his neck, tension quickly building. "Not really, but I need to know." He preferred Zenobia told him anything she wanted him to know about her, but she had left them no choice. If the Cameesos or any cartel was after her, his team needed to know. Dealing with those types of criminals wouldn't be like dealing with some crazed fan. No, Atlanta's Finest would need to be extremely vigilant in keeping her safe.

"There are gaps in Zenobia's past. It looks like everything she told you about her mother is true, and there's no father listed on her birth certificate. But some of her background information is fake."

Angelo stopped moving and frowned. "What do you mean fake?"

"Like, she claims to have graduated with a two-year degree from a trade school in Miami. Actually, she never attended that school, but has her GED. There are also seven years unaccounted for. I'm thinking that might have something to do with the time she spent recovering in Mexico after the Cameeso ordeal.

"My limited tech skills and our connections could only get me just so far. So, I called Wiz. He's found something. He's going to call shortly."

Angelo shook his head and ran his hand down his mouth as his mind went in a hundred different directions. "Suddenly, I'm not sure I want to know more."

Egypt stood and laid her hand on his arm. "Whatever Wiz comes back with, just listen to him before making any judgments. Take it from a person who's lived a double life. Sometimes secrets are kept to protect. Maybe Zenobia hasn't shared her whole truth because of protecting herself or someone else."

Angelo nodded. Egypt had kept major secrets from all of them, but she'd had a good reason. It had been a matter of life or death, but in the end, everything had worked out.

But was that the case with Zenobia? Was she keeping secrets to protect herself?

Angelo shook the thought free. That couldn't be it. She had told him about the Cameeso Cartel. Granted, he had to force it out of her, but surely by now she knew she could trust him with anything. That meant she was protecting someone else.

"What did you find on Sofia Cardenas?" he asked.

"Nothing that I haven't already given you. Maybe when we hear back from—" Her office phone rang and she leaned over the desk. "It's him," she said before answering. "Hey, Wiz. I'm putting you on speaker. Angelo's here."

"Angelo, I'm glad you're there. I'm not sure how much

you already know about Zenobia, but we found some interesting information. Actually, you might want to sit down for this if you're not already sitting."

Dread seeped into Angelo's body. He dropped down in one of the guest chairs in front of Egypt's desk. "Let's hear it," he said, and Wiz started in on some of the information that Egypt had already told him.

"Egypt was right about Zenobia living off the grid for a few years. It looks like she and Sofia traveled around Europe during that time. Not sure how they managed to do most of it under the radar, but I'm working on that."

"Did Zenobia's mother have a life insurance policy?" Angelo asked, but then remember that Zenobia had been working in a café, barely making ends meet when she met Leo. If she'd had insurance money, she probably wouldn't have gotten caught up with Leo.

"I haven't found anything about an insurance policy, but I guess you're wondering how she could afford moving around."

"Yeah, she never mentioned how she'd managed to get from New York to Miami. Which is where she met her housekeeper, Sofia. How were they able to get to Europe?"

"If you're still referring to Sofia as the housekeeper, that means you don't know who she really is. Zenobia is a product of an affair."

"Wait. What? I'm not following you."

"Sofia's late husband cheated on her with Zenobia's mother. Technically, Sofia is Zenobia's stepmother."

Angelo's heart slammed against his chest and his mouth dropped open. He wouldn't have ever put that together. Why hadn't Zenobia just told him? She called Sofia *mamita*, but he thought she used it as a term of endearment.

"Sofia's late husband died from some type of lung disease. On his death bed, he confessed to the affair and told her that he had a daughter. It looks like that was around the same time Zenobia's mother died. Now here's where it gets a little interesting."

"Are you kidding me? How could it possibly get more interesting than that?"

"Are you familiar with Monty 'Rock' Rockwell?"

Hearing Rock's name had Angelo's blood boiling. He gritted his teeth and balled his fists at his sides. If that asshole had hurt Zenobia in any way, there wouldn't be anywhere the guy could hide. Angelo would hunt him down and deal with him once and for all.

"Yeah, I've heard of him. What's he got to do with Zenobia?"

*

Sitting in the back seat, Zenobia glanced out the window of the SUV as Myles expertly maneuvered through Atlanta's traffic. She was finally starting to get used to having security and being chauffeured around. Past experiences might've clouded her judgment about having a bodyguard, but Supreme had changed her frame of thinking. For the first time in a long time, she felt completely safe.

"Zen, did you need to go anyplace else before you head home?" Kenton asked from the passenger seat.

"Nope, that's it unless you guys need to make a stop."

They had taken her to the studio to finish her album, the salon to get her hair and nails done, and had even escorted her to Lenox Mall to pick up Kira's birthday gift. That wasn't a place Zenobia frequented because of being mobbed by fans. This trip hadn't been as bad. She gave plenty of autographs, but having Myles and Kenton guarding her made it more bearable.

The only thing—or person—missing from the day was Angelo. Since he was no longer on her security detail, he was working more at the office. Having him by her side all day for the past couple of weeks had spoiled her. Now she had to settle for seeing him whenever one of them wasn't working.

A smile played at the corners of her lips. It had been comical when she walked into the studio without him. The first thing Kevin had asked was "Where is Angelo?" Kevin had been concerned that she wouldn't be able to finish the album without her inspiration. Little had he known that Angelo had given her plenty of inspiration that morning before heading to work.

Twenty minutes later, they were pulling into her long driveway. She was a little surprised to see Kira and Elijah climbing out of his truck. Zenobia was throwing Kira a small, intimate dinner party to celebrate her birthday. But that wasn't for another few hours.

"I'll take care of the bags," Kenton said when he opened the back door for Zenobia and helped her out of the SUV.

"Thank you."

She walked the short distance to Elijah's truck, wondering at what point the night before did he realize he had *lost* his cell phone.

"Hey, you guys. I'm surprised you're here already. Happy birthday, cuz." Zenobia gave Kira a one-armed hug and said hello to Elijah, who was holding a birthday cake. They all headed to the front door. "What are you doing here so early? Your dinner party doesn't start for another couple of hours."

"I came a little early because Sofia's going to teach me how to make *mole poblano.*"

They chatted about other items on the menu as they strolled into the house. By the wonderful scents, it was safe to say Sofia had already started cooking for the dinner.

"Hey, *mamita.*" Zenobia walked over to Sofia at the stove and kissed her on the cheek. "You've been busy. I thought you were going to—"

"*Necesitamos hablar.* We need to talk," Sofia said, only loud enough for Zenobia to hear.

"Zen, did you finish the album today?" Kira washed her hands in the sink, then grabbed a beer from the refrigerator. She handed it to Elijah, who took a seat at the breakfast bar.

"I'm happy to say the album is done. At least my part is complete," Zenobia explained, glancing at Sofia. *Something must have happened.* Sofia's brows were furrowed and she was moving nervously around the kitchen.

"Where is she?" Angelo's voice suddenly boomed

through the house. "Zenobia! Where is she?" he yelled.

"What in the world…" She started toward the kitchen entrance, but pulled up short when Angelo came into view.

He always seemed larger than life when he entered a room, but right now, he looked like an imposing giant. His fair complexion was tinted with crimson as his eyes shot daggers at her. Only thing missing was smoke billowing from his ears.

She approached him. "What's wrong?"

"We need to talk," he growled. Before she could ask another question, he grabbed her hand and pulled her through the house and out the back door.

Zenobia jogged alongside of him in her three-inch heels, struggling to keep up as he tugged her across the lawn. They passed Parker and Connor, another security specialist, who were outside doing their scheduled walk around the property. Even they looked puzzled, seeing Angelo pulling her along like some misbehaving child.

"Can you please slow down?" she huffed as they skirted around the large swimming pool and headed toward the guest house. "Or at least tell me what's wrong. What happened?"

He didn't speak. He didn't slow down. If anything, he started walking faster. The moment they were inside the house, he slammed the door behind them and whirled on her.

"When were you going to tell me?" he roared.

"Tell you what? And stop yelling at me!" Zenobia jammed her fists on her hips. She had never seen him this angry, but she wasn't going to stand there and let him talk to her any kind of way. "What haven't I told you, Angelo? What has got you so riled up that you had to embarrass me in front of everyone?"

He narrowed his eyes and slowly approached her. With anyone else Zenobia would've feared for her life, but not with him. She knew in her heart that Angelo would never hurt her, no matter how angry he was.

"Why didn't you tell me that your birth name was Amanda Rockwell? You told me about the Cameeso Cartel and what you went through with them. Yet, you didn't trust me enough to tell me your real name. Or to tell me that Sofia is not just a housekeeper, but your stepmother."

Alarm bells blasted inside of Zenobia. How had he found out? No one was to ever know. She'd been careful. They'd been careful. That information was buried so deep, there was no way he could have found it.

Oh, God. If he knew about Sofia, then he probably knew...

"The other thing I just can*not* wrap my brain around..." Angelo said through gritted teeth, but stopped. He wiped his hands down his face and visibly trembled. "Why didn't you tell me you were related to one of the most ruthless drug dealers in the country? You didn't think it important that I know that Monty 'Rock' *Rockwell* was your brother?"

Chapter Twenty-Two

Zenobia was sure her heart had stopped beating. She didn't know how Angelo found out, but the hurt in his eyes and the anguish on his face was almost her undoing. She had fallen in love with him, and the last thing she wanted to do was hurt or cause him any pain. She hadn't lied. She just hadn't told him everything.

"How could you not tell me?" he roared, then punched the air with so much force it was a wonder he didn't throw his shoulder out. "That man killed my coworkers and could've killed me!"

"Angelo, I di—didn't say any—anything," she stammered, trying to get her words and thoughts to line up so that she could form a complete sentence. "You have to understand. It wasn't just about me. I promised to never tell anyone. I—"

"You know what?" He lifted his hands in surrender. "You want to keep secrets? Keep them. I'm done." He turned to leave, but Zenobia jumped in front of him and gripped his arms.

He snatched out of her hold. "Don't. Just don't touch me." He put several feet of distance between them.

"Then give me a chance to explain."

"You've had plenty of chances to explain. Why'd I have

197

to find out all of this from someone else? Why couldn't you tell me? Why couldn't you trust me enough—"

"It wasn't about trust! If I didn't trust you, I wouldn't have told you about Leo and Lance. Trusting you has nothing to do with this. I love you, Angelo, and I trust you."

"Then why?" he begged, the fight seeming to go out of him as he dropped into one of the upholstered chairs and scrubbed his hands down his face.

"Because I made a promise." Zenobia fell down on her knees in front of him. She had to make him understand. "Sofia was devastated by her husband's infidelity, but when she and Monty learned about me, and about my mother's death, they searched for me. They found out I was in foster care."

Zenobia took a breath as she sifted through the memories.

"Monty couldn't claim to be my next of kin because of being a drug dealer, so they helped me run away from the group home."

Sofia had shown up one day at Zenobia's high school and told her who she was and talked about Monty. At first Zenobia didn't know what to think or believe, but the next day Sofia returned with pictures. The resemblance between Zenobia, Monty and their father had been uncanny. Knowing she had a family gave her hope, even if she had to move to Miami to be with them.

It would take her forever to give Angelo every single detail, but she had to make him understand the reasons for the secrets. The reason why she and Monty had gone to great lengths to keep their family ties private.

"I was young and naïve when I moved to Miami. I had no idea at first that Monty was a drug dealer. All I knew was that he told me that no one could know that we were related. He said his enemies could use me to get to him." Zenobia took an unsteady breath. "When Sofia and I moved in with him, everyone thought she was the housekeeper, and that I was her adopted daughter. No one knew the truth."

Angelo sat back in the seat, rubbing his forehead. He looked worn out, but at least he was still listening.

Zenobia told him about her life that first year living with her brother. Monty had been strict those first few months. Zenobia hadn't understood why he insisted she never leave the house alone. He had told her that if she couldn't follow his rules, she could leave.

She did. A year later, she'd gotten caught up with Leo Cameeso.

"Monty killed for me, and after my ordeal with Lance, I went through a ton of surgeries, including reconstructive surgery on my face. Sofia nursed me back to health."

Zenobia had asked very few questions and barely talked after her ordeal with the Cameesos. She would only talk to Sofia, who had been a godsend. When Monty insisted she and Sofia live in Europe for a few years, Zenobia hadn't asked why. She hadn't known at the time that he was slowly taking out the Cameeso Cartel. It wasn't until he called and told them they could return to the States did she learn all of that. It was also then that Zenobia knew she wanted to be an entertainer, but she couldn't do that if people knew her connection with Monty.

"Why didn't you tell me who Sofia was to you?" Angelo asked.

Zenobia got off her knees and sat in the only other chair in the room. "Sofia is my everything. She sacrificed so much for me. If I told you how we came to be, you would've figured out the rest. I love you Angelo. I never thought I could feel this strong about anyone, but..."

"Sofia's your heart," he said quietly, repeating words that Zenobia often used when describing how much Sofia meant to her.

"Before I came along, she and Monty didn't talk. Sofia always said that she didn't raise him to be a drug dealer, and when he wouldn't give it up, she cut ties. Until his father...*my* father...died."

"She took you in even though you were the result of her

husband's affair."

Angelo's words were spoken more as a statement than a question. If someone had told Zenobia that her mother had been capable of having an affair with a married man, she never would've believed it.

Instead of saying that to Angelo, she said, "Sofia is the most selfless person I've ever known. She wanted me out of foster care, but could only get me out of New York with Monty's help. When I got to Miami, she refused to let me live in his house without her there. They both, in their own ways, have always protected me."

Silence fell between them. Zenobia wanted to know what Angelo was thinking, but was too afraid to ask. They hadn't known each other long, but in that short amount of time, he had become a part of her.

She couldn't lose him. Not like this. Not over this.

Angelo leaned forward, his elbows on his thighs and his eyes downcast. He wouldn't look at her. Even when she was on her knees in front of him, he avoided eye contact.

"So much makes sense now," he murmured, almost as if he was talking to himself. "The Cameeso Cartel, or whatever they're calling themselves now, are retaliating for what Rock did, and their downfall started with you."

Zenobia's eyes widened, and her heart tumbled down to her stomach like a boulder. "What are you saying? Do you know for sure that they're the ones after me?"

"I'm pretty sure. If they ever want to regain their position in the drug game, earn back some respect, they have to make a bold statement. They probably don't know your relationship to Rock, but someone knows who you are and that you're important to him."

Zenobia leaped out of her seat and couldn't stop shaking. "I look nothing like I used to look. Nobody knows. This...this can't be happening."

"And they're going to want you alive," Angelo said, still sounding as if he was talking to himself. He stood abruptly and headed to the door.

Zenobia's heart kicked inside her chest. "Wait." She hurried after him. "Don't leave." Supreme would be there to protect her, but she couldn't lose Angelo. "Please, don't give up on me. Don't give up on us. You said that we were in this together. That it was you and me. That—"

"I hate liars."

Startled by the venom in his tone, Zenobia took two steps back. His words were like a slap in the face.

"And your brother...your protector, as you call him...is a killer."

*

It took every bit of strength Angelo had to walk out that door without looking back. He needed air. He also needed time to process what he'd just learned. How could the woman who meant more to him than he ever thought possible, be related to the man who almost got him killed?

Brother and sister.

Now that Angelo thought about it, there was a small resemblance between them around the eyes, but he never would've made the connection. When he infiltrated Rock's organization all those years ago, it had been after the Cameeso situation. Not once did anyone say anything about Rock having a sister.

Angelo shook his head, feeling like someone had just ripped out his heart. Walking away from Zenobia felt like walking away from his future. In just a short amount of time, she had become a part of him. If he was honest with himself, he could admit that it happened the very first time their eyes connected. But that was before...

"You better not have hurt her," Kira ground through gritted teeth, glaring at him as she stomped past him and headed to the guest house.

Angelo barely spared her or a couple of the members from his team, who were standing on the other side of the large pool, a glance. He kept walking toward the main house and didn't stop until he was in the kitchen. Then he froze.

Rock.

"I said put those guns away!" Sofia spat, waving her wooden spoon around. Her other hand was on her hip as she glared at the four men in her kitchen.

It took Angelo a minute to make sense of what he was seeing—Myles, Kenton, Rock, and Rock's right-hand man, Gavin. They were all well over six feet tall and twice Sofia's size. They also had their guns drawn and pointed at each other, all except for Rock. He stood in the midst of the strange scene, but he was staring at Angelo.

"Put them away now," Sofia said again, still waving her spoon and looking as if she wasn't afraid to go upside any of their heads with it.

"Do it!" Rock said, still staring at Angelo, but talking to Gavin. When Gavin lowered his weapon, so did Myles and Kenton, but all eyes were on Angelo as if to say, *What the hell is going on?*

"Myles, Kenton, meet Sofia's son, Monty 'Rock' Rockwell." Angelo might've been pissed to learn that Rock and Zenobia were related, but he understood why she'd kept it a secret. If the media or any of Rock's enemies found out their real relationship, Zenobia's life would be in more danger than it was now. Myles and Kenton would know the truth soon enough. Just not yet.

Sofia walked up to him with her shoulders back and her chin lifted. "Is my *mija* okay?"

"Yes," Angelo said, though when he left Zenobia, she was pretty upset.

Angelo hated seeing her tears, but it had been best that he walk away before anything else was said that he couldn't take back. He had to get his head on straight before they could discuss where to go from there.

"You summoned him here?" he asked, nodding at Rock.

Sofia set the spoon on the counter and for the first time since Angelo walked into the kitchen, she looked a little nervous. "I did. He needs to fix this."

"I can't fix *this* or anything until I know what the hell is going on," Rock snapped, still staring at Angelo as if seeing a ghost.

Her son's tone didn't seem to faze Sofia. She patted Angelo's cheek in that loving way she'd done countless times. Some of the anger and shock that had consumed him eased through his pores.

"Zenobia's safety…and her happiness means everything to me," Sofia said. That was the first time she had used Zenobia's name around him. Normally, she referred to her as *mija*, my daughter.

"Talk to him, please." Sofia pointed at her son. "Tell him what needs to be fixed, and he'll do it."

*

The faster Zenobia wiped at her tears, the faster they fell. She finally found the man she could imagine spending the rest of her life with, and he hated her.

Secrets destroy.

Sofia's words from weeks ago bounced around inside Zenobia's head. Had she destroyed what she and Angelo were building? She understood why he was angry, but surely, he understood why she hadn't told him about her family. There wasn't a person alive who didn't have at least one secret that they planned to take to their grave.

Her ties to Rock was hers.

Kira walked back into the room with a box of tissues. "Come on, Zen. Talk to me. What happened?"

"Angelo and I had a fight." That was the understatement of the year. Within minutes, their relationship imploded and Zenobia wasn't sure how to fix it.

"That looked like more than a lover's spat. Angelo was livid when he dragged you out of the house. Nah, there's something you're not telling me. What gives?"

"It's nothing."

"It's something because that brotha was pissed. He didn't hit you, did he?"

"Of course not." Zenobia sniffed, dabbing her eyes. "He would never hurt me." At least not physically, she wanted to add, but kept that to herself. His parting words about hating liars was definitely hurtful though.

"Good because if Elijah found out Angelo put his hands on you, he—"

"He would what?" Zenobia stood and frowned at her cousin. "What would he do, Kira? Don't you think it strange that your man has been all up in my relationship with Angelo?"

"It's not strange at all. You're like a sister to me. Obviously, he's going to be looking out for you."

"Nah, something's up with Elijah. Ever since meeting Angelo, he's been trippin', acting like he's *my* man."

"Come on now, sis. Don't get it twisted. Elijah's not interested in you like that."

"I didn't say—"

"Then exactly what are you saying?" Kira pushed her micro-braids over her shoulder and jammed her hands on her hips. "I get that you're stressed because some lunatic is after you, and now Angelo has a bug up his butt about something. But you've been acting weird for weeks."

Zenobia threw up her hands. "How am I supposed to act? Someone is gunning for me and the man who I absolutely *adore* might've just broken up with me."

"Why?"

"Why what?"

"Why did he break up with you?"

"I said *might* have." Zenobia wasn't giving up on Angelo, and she wasn't telling anyone about their argument. She trusted Kira to a certain extent, but there was so much Kira didn't know.

When Zenobia and Monty made their agreement about keeping their family ties a secret, that included keeping it a secret from everyone. Kira only knew Monty as Rock. She was under the impression that he and Zenobia were once good friends, but that Zenobia had cut ties with him because of his line of work.

Maybe one day she could trust her cousin with the truth. This wasn't that day, but there was something she could share.

"Did I ever tell you that Angelo was former DEA and that he used to work in Miami?"

Kira's mouth dropped open. "What? Girl, no you didn't tell me. I knew he was a badass, but what does that have to…" Her words trailed off and her hand went to her mouth. "Oh no. Does he know Rock? Is that why he's pissed, because you used to kick it with a drug dealer?"

"Yes." It wasn't a complete lie, but at least she was giving her cousin something. If there was a chance of Angelo being in their lives, then there was a chance that his past career would come up in conversation anyway.

Kira waved her off. "Oh, girl. Considering how mad he was, I thought it was something serious—like you had cheated on him or something. He'll get over you and Rock once you assure him that there's nothing between you two."

"I hope you're right. I'm in love with Angelo, and I'm not giving up on us without a fight."

"Now, you're talking. Come on, Sofia's probably wondering where I am. I told her I'd be right back and that I was going to check on you."

Sofia. Zenobia had forgotten that Sofia had said they needed to talk. Maybe she had somehow found out that Angelo knew about their family ties.

"All right, let's get out of here." Zenobia looped her arm through her cousin's and headed for the door. "You need to finish your cooking lesson before dinner, and I need to find Angelo."

"Not so fast."

Zenobia and Kira whirled around to find Elijah standing in the short hallway that led to the back of the guest house.

"Dang, baby. You scared me to death." Kira pulled away from Zenobia and headed to him. "What are you doing here? Did Sofia—"

With a quickness Zenobia didn't see coming, Elijah snatched Kira by her braids and jerked her to him.

"Scream and I will kill you," he said with a gun to Kira's

temple then turned his attention to Zenobia.

Her heart skidded to a stop, and her mind raced trying to figure out what was happening. When he moved toward her, pulling Kira along with him, Zenobia backed up until she bumped into the wall.

"You wouldn't by chance have my cell phone, would you?" Elijah asked her, a scowl marring his face.

"N—no, I don't." Zenobia fought to control the anxiety that had her pulse pounding in her ears. She had to get her and Kira away from him. "Wh—what is this about? What are you doing?"

Kira gasped for air, her hand pulling down on Elijah's arm that was tight around her neck. "Please," she wheezed. "Eli, I can't brea—"

"Shut. Up," he growled at Kira, tightening his arm around her and holding the gun steady against her head. "I'm about to get paid and your cousin here has already cost me time and money!" He scowled.

"I don't know what this is about, but you're never going to get away with this," Zenobia said, looking around the small space for any type of weapon.

Elijah moved the gun to the hand that was around Kira, then pulled a cell phone from his pocket.

Zenobia looked around the space, hoping to find something—*anything* that could be used as a weapon. She hadn't done much in the form of decorating, but there had to be something.

A flashlight was on the end table and a half-empty water bottle sat on the old coffee table. She took tiny baby steps sideways toward the flashlight while keeping her eyes on Elijah.

"I have the package," he said to whoever he had just called. "We need to move quick. Meet me on the block behind the house in ten." He put the phone back in his pocket. "Zen, you'll be coming with me."

She froze. "I'm not going anywhere with you," she blurted without thinking. The last thing she wanted to do was piss him off.

"Oh, but you are. Someone's paying me and my cousin good money to have you delivered to them, and I intend to cash in. You were supposed to be an easy snatch. I even put listening devices around your house to keep track of you. Then you had to go and get security and a damn boyfriend."

"You're never going to get away with this," she said, trying to be inconspicuous as she moved closer to the table. "Security is right outside." At least she hoped Parker and Connor were nearby.

"Your security is out of commission at the moment. And I don't know what you did to piss that boyfriend of yours off. The way he burst out of this place, I'm sure he's long gone by now. So, let's go."

"No! I'm not going anywhere."

Chapter Twenty-Three

"Johnny Garza," Rock said, as he pulled a pack of smokes out of the front pocket of his pants. "I gotta hand it to you...you're good."

Like Rock was surprised to see him, Angelo couldn't believe they were standing in the same space. Sofia had insisted he and Rock talk in Zenobia's office. Angelo wasn't sure what their little meeting was supposed to accomplish. Then again, maybe he could find out what was being done about the cartel. He knew Rock well enough to know that he was on top of the situation.

"First you infiltrate my organization," Rock continued as he moved aimlessly around the office without lighting his cigarette. "Then you and your DEA roaches almost destroy everything I worked my ass off to build. And now I find out you're *fucking* around with my sister!"

Angelo didn't speak. Based on what Rock just said, at some point he must've found out that Angelo was with or had connections to the DEA. He didn't bother asking. Rock was resourceful if nothing else. Which was probably why it hadn't been easy to make the connection between him and Zenobia. There had been so many layers to keep their family connection hidden.

"My mother claims that you saved my sister's life—

208

twice—and that you're in love with her. Is that true?"

Angelo could no longer stand still and he, too, was moving around the large office, but keeping his eyes on Rock. "Does it matter?"

"Answer the damn question!" Rock snapped.

Angelo huffed out a breath as anger clawed through him. "Yeah, but it doesn't matter. Now that I know she's related to you, I'll be sure to stay as far away from her as possible." The words sounded hollow even to his own ears. No matter what he said, there was no way he could just walk away from Zenobia. It was too late. He had fallen in love with her.

Rock's lethal gaze on him would've made a weaker man crumble. Not Angelo. He didn't give a damn what the bastard thought of him, and he was prepared to take him out if it came down to it.

"Since we're putting our cards on the table, you should know that I didn't kill your people."

Angelo just stared at him, surprised by the shift in the conversation but keeping his guard up. He didn't trust Rock. The change of topic could be a way to distract him.

"It's true," his nemesis said as if reading his mind. "I had no idea that warehouse was going to explode. You think I would've been there if I intended to blow the damn thing up?"

Again, Angelo remained quiet. He'd thought about that years ago, but couldn't think of who else would've known they would be there.

"The DEA was responsible for that clusterfuck," Rock continued. "I was lured there. *We* were lured there."

That included Angelo. He had been undercover in Rock's organization when they showed up at that warehouse that night. "The only reason your ass is still alive is because I thought you, or should I say Johnny Garza, had died that night. Imagine my surprise when I found out you were very much alive and had played me...on my turf. Damn DEA," he snarled.

Angelo straightened. He had a couple of weapons on

him, but he hoped he didn't have to use them. He would if it meant his life or Rock's.

"Relax. I see you tensing up and can practically hear your thoughts. My mother would kill me if I did anything to you. She's a lot tougher than she looks," he cracked, shaking his head. "For some reason she likes you. I wonder what she would think of all the shit you did when you worked for me."

"I didn't work for you. I worked for the DEA."

"Yeah, don't remind me. Last week, I received a photo of you and my sister. I thought you looked familiar, but I couldn't figure out where I'd known you from. It wasn't until my mother called and told me what was going on that I realized who you were."

"Why are you here, Rock?" Angelo finally said.

"I'm here to take my sister and my mother back to Miami where I can keep them safe."

Panic sparked inside of Angelo. He might've been angry and told Zenobia they were through, but...

"Zenobia's not going anywhere with you," he heard himself say. He was pretty sure she wouldn't willingly go with Rock, but right now Angelo couldn't be too sure what she would do.

"She and my mother aren't safe. At least not until I finish with these Cameeso wannabes in Miami for once and for all. That's actually happening as we speak, but there's a loose end here in Atlanta that I need to tie up. I would give you the details, but I'm not sure where your loyalties lie."

"My loyalties lie with Zenobia."

Rock nodded, the unlit cigarette now dangling from his lips. "So, you *are* in love with her. Based on what I've been hearing, I figured as much, but here's the thing. I hate you. Yet, I have mad respect for how you were able to worm your way into my organization and live to tell about it. If Zenobia and my mother are cool with you, then I'm going to have to be, too. But hurt my sister and I *will* kill you."

"Rock, you have to know by now that you don't scare me. So, don't come on *my* turf and start slinging around threats. What happens between me and Zenobia is between her and I. And don't worry, your secrets are safe with me. You continue to stay away from her, and I'll stay away from you."

A charged silence fell between them until Angelo's cell phone rang. He dug it out of his pocket and glanced at the screen.

Laz.

"Yeah?" he answered, but kept his eyes on Rock.

"Where are you?"

"Zenobia's, why?"

"Elijah might be your guy. He's had multiple calls from a Miami number traced back to a relative who used to be with the Cameeso Cartel."

Angelo's stomach tightened and a numbness swept through his body. Elijah had been near Zenobia more times than Angelo could count.

"He was also a good friend of the guy you shot in the shoulder," Laz continued. "But get this, Elijah received a big sum of money recently. Twenty-five large was deposited the day before someone tried to kidnap Zen off the streets. What do you want to bet more is coming when the job is complete? He's not at his apartment or at Kira's."

"He was here earlier when I... *Shit*. He's gotta still be here." Angelo disconnected the call and bolted out of the room and into the kitchen with Rock hot on his heels.

"Elijah was in here earlier. Where is he?" Angelo asked in a rush. Myles and Kenton were still glaring at Gavin while Sofia busied herself around the kitchen.

Myles pulled out his cell phone, no doubt to check the house cameras. "He must have slipped out when these assholes...I mean Ms. Sofia's guest, showed up."

"Search everywhere. He might be our guy," Angelo said, pulling out his gun and running out of the kitchen. "I'm going to the guest house. Rock, you're with me."

Keep your enemies close, Angelo thought as he and Rock rushed out of the house and started across the back lawn. He saw a guy down near the edge of the pool and as he got closer, realized it was Parker. There was no blood. Angelo checked for a pulse.

"He's alive."

Angelo didn't see Conner but kept moving across the yard, knowing Myles or Kenton were nearby and would take care of their guys.

When he and Rock got close to the guest house, Angelo slowed and pointed at the bay window where he could see Zenobia. They couldn't see Elijah.

"I'll take the front. You go around back," Angelo instructed. "The backdoor squeaks so be quiet."

Rock nodded and took off around the house while Angelo tried to decide how he wanted to play this. He would never forgive himself if anything happened to Zenobia.

*

Elijah growled. "I don't have time for this."

He slammed Kira into a wall and Zenobia screamed when her cousin crumbled to the floor.

"*Kira!*"

"You think I'm playing with you?" Elijah turned his gun on Zenobia.

Angelo had mentioned that the cartel would want her alive in order to regain some respect in the drug world. Zenobia was banking on that as she picked up the flashlight, keeping it out of sight behind her back.

Elijah marched across the room, his arm stretched out and the gun aimed at her. Each step he took, Zenobia took one to her right. A little bit more and she could make a run for the back door.

Elijah lunged at her.

Zenobia screamed and swung the flashlight, catching him across his arm. His gun slid across the hardwood.

"Why you…"

Zenobia swung at him again, but he grabbed her around the waist and tackled her to the floor.

"Get off of me! Get off of me!" Adrenaline drove

Zenobia as she kicked and wiggled beneath him. She swung her arms, landing punch after punch until her fist connected with his eye.

Elijah howled and grabbed his face.

Run! Her mind screamed and she scrabbled, slipping and sliding across the hardwood floor to get away from him.

"Stop or I'll shoot!" Elijah yelled.

Zenobia tripped over her feet and crashed to the floor. Chest heaving, she glanced over her shoulder, shocked to see that he had the gun again. As he came toward her, she took off in a run.

The front door banged open and Zenobia dived to the floor as two gunshots rang out. Screaming, she curled up in a ball and covered her ears with her hands.

"Zenobia!" Large arms wrapped around her.

"No! No! Don't touch me!" she screamed.

"Zenobia, baby, it's me. You're okay," Angelo said, holding her so tight she could barely breathe.

"An—Angelo." She twisted and turned in his arms. *"Ohmigod! Ohmigod!* I'm so glad you're here. He was going to kill me."

"He'll never be able to hurt anyone else."

"What about, Kira?"

"She's going to be okay."

Zenobia buried her face into the crook of Angelo's neck. A host of footsteps and voices spilled into the small space, but she didn't bother looking around. All that matter at the moment was that Angelo was there and he had saved her life.

"You didn't leave," she sobbed. "You didn't leave me."

Angelo leaned back, forcing her to lift her head and look at him. "I will never leave you. I am so sorry about earlier." His voice was thick with emotion as unshed tears filled his eyes. "I love you. I swear I will *never* leave you." He planted kisses all over her face before capturing her lips in a heated kiss.

Zenobia didn't even want to think about what would've happened had he not showed up.

213

When the kiss ended, he pulled her back into his arms and squeezed her.

"Zenobia."

Her head jerked up and her heart thudded at the familiar sound of her name. Over Angelo's shoulder, she spotted her brother.

"Oh, my God. *Monty?*"

Angelo loosened his hold, and Zenobia ran to her brother and leaped into his arms. It had been years since she'd seen him. He might've been a ruthless drug dealer to some but to her, he was the man who gave her a new life.

He set her on her feet and a grin spread across his handsome face as she looked him over. His shoulders seem wider, but his spicy, woodsy fragrance still smelled amazing, and his dreadlocks were still well maintained. All in all, he hadn't changed a bit.

"I can't believe you're here."

He placed a lingering kiss on her forehead. "I had to come and make sure you and Momma were okay."

"Are we?" Zenobia asked in a shaky voice, the adrenaline from moments ago seeping from her body. "Is it over?"

"Yeah, it's over. You're safe."

Chapter Twenty-Four

Three weeks later...

"God, this hurts," Zenobia gritted out over the humming of the tattoo machine.

"He's almost done, baby," Angelo assured as he held her hand while Tito, the tattoo artist, put the finishing touches on the design.

Angelo hated seeing her in pain, but she had insisted it was time to do something about the Carmeeso brand. She'd been wanting to get it done for years, but hadn't been brave enough to go by herself.

As Angelo looked on, he had to agree that the small angel design she had chosen perfectly camouflaged the brand. It still blew his mind that those bastards had scarred her. Each time he thought about that ordeal and the one she'd gone through with Elijah, he got angry all over again. There hadn't been anything he could do about the Cameeso Cartel years ago, but he blamed himself for Elijah getting the chance to hurt her.

Angelo kissed the back of Zenobia's fingers, trying to distract her when she groaned in pain. If only he could distract himself from constant thoughts of that day at the guest house. Zenobia insisted it wasn't his fault. Angelo knew better. He was to blame that his team's attention had been pulled away from protecting her. Had Angelo not showed up at the house in a tirade, Elijah wouldn't have gotten the jump on them. It was also because of him that Zenobia had been left vulnerable in the guest house after their argument. Angelo would have never forgiven himself had he lost her.

"All right. All done," Tito said. "What do you think?"

Zenobia stood in front of the mirror and lifted her arm. She studied the tattoo, moving back and forth to see it at different angles.

"What do you think?" she asked, looking at Angelo through the mirror.

"I think it's amazing. Question is, what do you think?"

Zenobia looked at the artwork again then smiled. "I love it." She moved away from the mirror and faced Angelo. "Thank you for coming with me. I couldn't have done this without you."

His heart swelled as he cupped her face and stared into her beautiful eyes. "Sweetheart, you're the strongest woman I know. You could've done this on your own, but I'm glad you wanted me by your side."

"Always." She tugged on the front of his shirt and kissed him. "I'll always want you by my side."

God, he loved this woman. As Tito put ointment over the tattoo, Angelo thought about how resilient Zenobia was. It amazed him how she hadn't allowed her past to keep her from living. He meant it when he said she was the strongest woman he knew.

After settling up with Tito, Angelo escorted Zenobia to his new Land Rover. He'd been thinking about buying a new vehicle for months. Since his car had sustained a ton of damage in the accident, he took the plunge and purchased his dream truck.

"Are you still okay with us stopping by Kira's place before you drop me off at home?" Zenobia asked when Angelo climbed into the driver's seat.

"Of course."

Kira had been keeping her distance since she blamed herself for allowing Elijah into their lives. Zenobia refused to let her cousin pull away from her, insisting she was a victim, too.

The day at the guest house, Kira had been knocked unconscious and had suffered a concussion. Though they hated she got hurt, Zenobia was glad Kira hadn't seen Rock. Her brother and Gavin had left the house, not wanting to be around when the cops showed up. Angelo and his team had agreed. Later that night, Mason and Hamilton had arranged for Zenobia and Sofia to visit with Rock at Supreme Security before he headed back to Miami.

Angelo had mixed feelings about Rock. He appreciated how he took care of Zenobia over the years, but he didn't want her anywhere near the guy. At least no time soon. Not until all of Rock's businesses were legit, and his life no longer put her in danger.

"Hey," Zenobia said, pulling Angelo out of his thoughts when she touched his arm.

He reached for her hand, something he did often these days. She brought a peace to his life over the last few weeks that he couldn't get from anywhere else.

"Stop thinking," she said. "I can feel your tension all the way over here. It's over. Me and Sofia are safe. Kira's going to be okay. Rock's back in his world. More than all of that, I love you."

He squeezed her hand. "Not as much as I love you, and I'm going to spend the rest of my life proving how much I adore you."

"*And* you're going to sing to me every day. As a matter of fact, this happens to be one of my favorite songs."

Angelo laughed and turned up the volume on the radio. As Freddie Jackson's "Jam Tonight" blasted through the speakers, Angelo and Zenobia sang along.

If anyone had told him months ago that he'd meet a singing sensation and fall madly in love with her, he would've laughed in their face. Now, he couldn't imagine his world without this amazing woman, and he planned on singing with her for the rest of his life.

Epilogue

Three months later...

Zenobia and Angelo stood in the small pulpit of the church, singing to Kenton and Egypt's wedding guests about an endless love. When Angelo reached for her hand and stared into her eyes at the part of the song about hearts beating as one, Zenobia barely contained her tears. The words filled her soul, as she never imagined that she'd one day find her special someone.

When the song came to an end, Angelo curled his arm around her waist and pulled her close. "I love you," he whispered. Zenobia would never tire of hearing those three words from his mouth. "I'll be back." He gave her a quick kiss, then took his place next to the other groomsmen.

The wedding venue, a small church, was beautifully decorated with a purple and white theme. As the guest and wedding party of four bridesmaids and four groomsmen looked on, the unity candle ceremony started and Kenny G's "Forever in Love" played through the speakers.

Zenobia stepped back from the mic, feeling a calm settle around her. Her life had changed considerably in the last three months. Now she only sung for pleasure and not because she had to honor a contract. Those days were over. She would no longer be in the spotlight.

All ties with Octavia were cut, and instead of a manager, Zenobia had an agent, Wesley Bradford. Going forward she would only write songs, and already her new career was paying off. She'd signed four contracts in the last three months to write songs for some of her favorite singers.

"Family and friends. We are gathered here today to witness the…" The minister started after the candles were lit.

During the ceremony, each time Zenobia glanced at Angelo, he was looking at her. And when the minister asked Egypt if she took Kenton to be her husband, Zenobia couldn't help but wonder when she and Angelo would marry. She had no doubt that they would one day walk down the aisle. It was just a matter of when.

After he had found out about Rock, she thought she had lost her man for good. He once claimed he wasn't the forgiving type, but thankfully he had forgiven her for not being forthcoming with him. Since then, they'd been working on their relationship that was growing stronger every day, and she couldn't be happier.

Now, surrounded by his friends, who had quickly become her friends, Zenobia's life felt full. It was like they were all one big, happy family. If the Atlanta's Finest team wasn't enough, a couple of months ago, Angelo had taken her and Sofia to meet his large family. For Zenobia, it had been a little overwhelming being around his parents, siblings, nieces, and nephews. Yet, she already loved them, and Sofia adored them all.

Zenobia glanced at her *mamita,* who was sitting in the audience. When their gazes connected, Sofia blew her a kiss. God, Zenobia loved that woman. Sofia might not have given birth to her, but she was more of a mother than Zenobia could have ever hoped for.

"I now pronounce you husband and wife. You may kiss your bride," the minister said, cutting into her thoughts.

As the bride and groom kissed, Angelo rejoined Zenobia

and they sang the last song while the wedding party and guests exited the sanctuary.

"The wedding was beautiful," Zenobia said as Angelo escorted her down the aisle to join everyone in the hallway.

Angelo brought the back of her hand to his mouth. "I agree, and I'm thinking you and I will be next."

Zenobia's heart fluttered. "I'll be ready when you are."

Angelo grinned at her. "I'm counting on it."

*

Two hours later, Angelo was thinking that having a cookout instead of a formal reception was a brilliant idea. Everyone had changed clothes and were hanging out in Laz's back yard, eating, drinking, and dancing.

Angelo brought his beer bottle up to his lips as he glanced across the yard at Zenobia. They'd spent almost every day of the last three months together, and they'd been some of the best months of his life.

He smiled when Journey, Laz's wife, handed Arielle, their six-month-old baby girl, to Zenobia. Angelo immediately imagined her holding their baby one day. They both wanted at least two, which meant they'd need to get started soon.

"You know, if Zen keeps hanging out with Laz's daughter and Hamilton's baby boy, she's going to want a few babies of her own. You ready for that?" Myles asked, and sat at the picnic table with a plate of food.

"She can have anything she wants from me," Angelo said without missing a beat. There was nothing he wouldn't give or do for her, and he couldn't wait until they started a family. He had already purchased an engagement ring, but planned to wait until their Hawaii trip in two weeks to propose.

"Yeah, you say that now. We'll see." Myles ate a few bites of his food and wiped his mouth. "So, when you planning on…" He stopped talking when Geneva, Laz's sister-in-law, strolled over and started wiping down the table next to them. "Don't you think your shorts are a little too short? It's not that damn hot out here," Myles said to her.

Beer flew from Angelo's mouth and he coughed-laughed while trying to catch his breath. He laughed even harder when Geneva turned and scowled at Myles with her hands on her hips.

"If you got a problem with my shorts, don't look. *Asshole*."

She walked away and Angelo practically fell off the bench laughing. "I cannot believe you said that to her."

Myles shrugged and went back to eating as if he'd just had a normal conversation with the woman. Then he asked, "What do you know about her?"

"All I know is she's probably too much woman for you." Angelo tried to keep a straight face, but burst out laughing again when Myles glared at him.

As a former CIA agent, Myles was the most fearless man Angelo knew. He'd probably been a helluva spy back in his day. The guy moved in and out of rooms like a ghost, blending in to his surroundings and able to disappear without detection. If anyone could handle the prickliness of Geneva Ramsey, it was him.

Myles dug more into his food. "So, I'll take that as a— you don't know a damn thing about her."

Angelo pointed his beer bottle at Laz who was adding more meat to the grill. "That's the person you need to be asking." He waved their friend over.

Laz wiped his hands on a towel before taking the seat on the other side of Angelo. "What's up?"

"Myles wants the scoop on your sister-in-law."

Laz shook his head and chuckled. "I suggest you stay clear. She eats men up, chases them down with beer, and then spits them out without a second thought. Trust me. She is *way* too much woman for you."

"Man, screw y'all. I've never met a woman I couldn't handle," Myles said and left them sitting there cracking up as he stalked away.

"You've been warned," Laz called after him.

They watched as Myles tossed his plate in the trash and

walked across the yard to Geneva. He sidled up next to her and wrapped his arm around her waist.

"How much you want to bet she punches him?" Laz asked as Myles whispered something in Geneva's ear.

Angelo shook his head. "I don't know, man. Myles is pretty smooth. I wouldn't count him out."

"What are you two up to?" Zenobia sat next to Angelo and followed their line of sight.

"We're about to witness Myles make a fool of himself," Laz insisted and sat up straighter when Geneva grabbed hold of the front of Myles's shirt. "Okay, here it comes. She's going to...what the..."

Angelo and Zenobia roared when Geneva pulled Myles close and planted a lingering kiss on his lips.

"Damn, I should've took that bet." Angelo shook his head as Geneva led Myles into the house. He could only imagine what came next and had a feeling that if those two got together, the city of Atlanta would never be the same.

Hours later, Angelo and Zenobia said their goodbyes to the few people who were still at the cookout.

"I love your friends. I can't remember the last time I've had this much fun," Zenobia said as they left the house.

Angelo slipped his arm around her. "I love you so much. I'm going to make sure that the rest of your life is filled with fun experiences."

She smiled up at him, and his heart danced inside his chest.

"We're going to have an amazing life together, aren't we?" she asked.

"Baby, you have no idea."

*

*If you enjoyed this book by Sharon C. Cooper,
consider leaving a review on any online book site, review site or social
media outlet.*

Join Sharon's Mailing List

To get sneak peeks of upcoming stories and to hear about giveaways that Sharon is sponsoring, go to **https://bit.ly/1Sih6ol** to join her mailing list.

About the Author

Award-winning and bestselling author, Sharon C. Cooper, is a romance-a-holic - loving anything that involves romance with a happily-ever-after, whether in books, movies, or real life. Sharon writes contemporary romance, as well as romantic suspense and enjoys rainy days, carpet picnics, and peanut butter and jelly sandwiches. She's been nominated for numerous awards and is the recipient of Emma Awards (RSJ) for Author of the Year 2019, Favorite Hero 2019 (INDEBTED), Romantic Suspense of the Year 2015 (TRUTH OR CONSEQUENCES), Interracial Romance of the Year 2015 (ALL YOU'LL EVER NEED), and BRAB (book club) Award -Breakout Author of the Year 2014. When Sharon isn't writing, she's hanging out with her amazing husband, doing volunteer work or reading a good book (a romance of course). To read more about Sharon and her novels, visit www.sharoncooper.net

Connect with Sharon Online:

Website: https://sharoncooper.net

Join Sharon's mailing list: https://bit.ly/31Xsm36

Facebook fan page:

http://www.facebook.com/AuthorSharonCCooper21?ref=hl

Twitter: https://twitter.com/#!/Sharon_Cooper1

Subscribe to her blog:

http://sharonccooper.wordpress.com/

Goodreads:

http://www.goodreads.com/author/show/5823574.Sharon_
C_Cooper

Pinterest: https://www.pinterest.com/sharonccooper/

Instagram:

https://www.instagram.com/authorsharonccooper/

Other Titles

Atlanta's Finest Series

A Passionate Kiss (book 1- prequel)

Vindicated (book 2)

Indebted (book 3)

Accused (book 4)

Betrayed (book 5)

Hunted (book 6)

Jenkins & Sons Construction Series (Contemporary Romance)

Love Under Contract (book 1)

Proposal for Love (book 2)

A Lesson on Love (book 3)

Unplanned Love (book 4)

Jenkins Family Series (Contemporary Romance)

Best Woman for the Job (Short Story Prequel)

Still the Best Woman for the Job (book 1)

All You'll Ever Need (book 2)

Tempting the Artist (book 3)

Negotiating for Love (book 4)

Seducing the Boss Lady (book 5)

Love at Last (Holiday Novella)

When Love Calls (Novella)

Reunited Series (Romantic Suspense)

Blue Roses (book 1)

Secret Rendezvous (Prequel to Rendezvous with Danger)

Rendezvous with Danger (book 2)

Truth or Consequences (book 3)

Operation Midnight (book 4)

Stand Alones

Something New ("Edgy" Sweet Romance)

Legal Seduction (Harlequin Kimani – Contemporary Romance)

Sin City Temptation (Harlequin Kimani – Contemporary Romance)

A Dose of Passion (Harlequin Kimani – Contemporary Romance)

Model Attraction (Harlequin Kimani – Contemporary Romance)